BRYN JAHR

LEAP OF FATE

By

Gwen Lanigan-O'Keeffe

Copyright © Gwen Lanigan-O'Keeffe 2024
This book is sold subject to the condition that it shall not, by way of trade or otherwise, be lent, resold, hired out, or otherwise circulated without the publisher's prior consent in any form of binding or cover other than that in which it is published and without a similar condition including this condition being imposed on the subsequent publisher.
The moral right of Gwen Lanigan-O'Keeffe has been asserted.
ISBN: 9798321783399

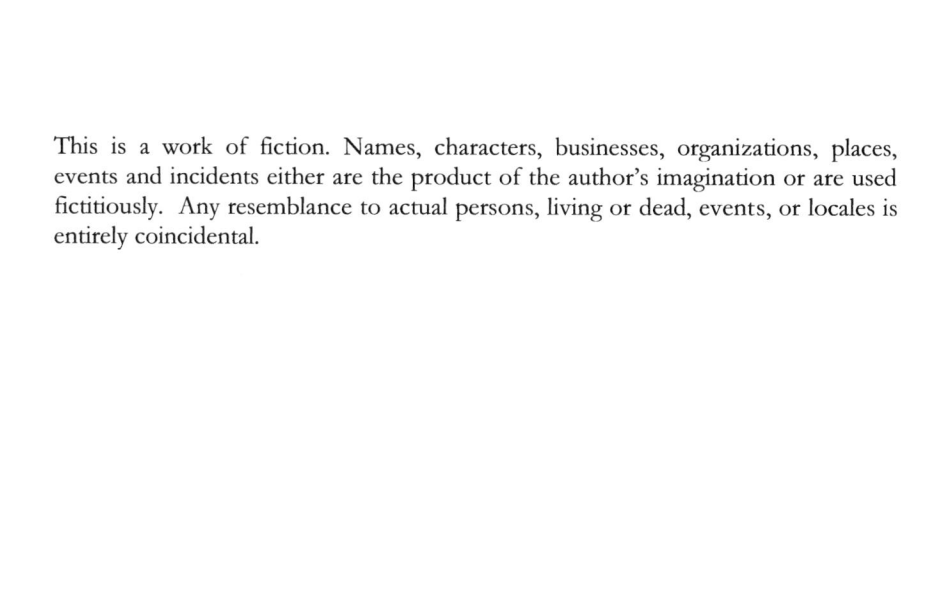

This is a work of fiction. Names, characters, businesses, organizations, places, events and incidents either are the product of the author's imagination or are used fictitiously. Any resemblance to actual persons, living or dead, events, or locales is entirely coincidental.

*To Monkey, Honey, Mum and Dad, Jeannie Bean,
Dots, Clarie Lou, Peds and Ní.
In loving memory of Snow.*

CONTENTS

PROLOGUE 1
CHAPTER 1 4
CHAPTER 2 8
CHAPTER 3 12
CHAPTER 4 15
CHAPTER 5 18
CHAPTER 6 22
CHAPTER 7 24
CHAPTER 8 28
CHAPTER 9 33
CHAPTER 10 36
CHAPTER 11 39
CHAPTER 12 44
CHAPTER 13 49
CHAPTER 14 52
CHAPTER 15 55
CHAPTER 16 58
CHAPTER 17 62
CHAPTER 18 64
CHAPTER 19 68
CHAPTER 20 70
CHAPTER 21 73
CHAPTER 22 76
CHAPTER 23 82
CHAPTER 24 86
CHAPTER 25 90
CHAPTER 26 93
CHAPTER 27 96
CHAPTER 28 100
CHAPTER 29 104
CHAPTER 30 109
CHAPTER 31 113
CHAPTER 32 117
CHAPTER 33 121
CHAPTER 34 124

CHAPTER 35 126
CHAPTER 36 128
CHAPTER 37 133
CHAPTER 38 134
CHAPTER 39 137
CHAPTER 40 138
CHAPTER 41 140
CHAPTER 42 143
CHAPTER 43 145
CHAPTER 44 148
CHAPTER 45 150
CHAPTER 46 155
CHAPTER 47 158
CHAPTER 48 161
CHAPTER 49 164
CHAPTER 50 166
CHAPTER 51 169
CHAPTER 52 171
CHAPTER 53 173
CHAPTER 54 177
CHAPTER 55 180
CHAPTER 56 185
CHAPTER 57 188
CHAPTER 58 191
CHAPTER 59 193
CHAPTER 60 196
CHAPTER 61 198
CHAPTER 62 201
CHAPTER 63 205
CHAPTER 64 208
CHAPTER 65 211
CHAPTER 66 216
CHAPTER 67 218
CHAPTER 68 221
CHAPTER 69 224
CHAPTER 70 228
CHAPTER 71 232

CHAPTER 72 236
CHAPTER 73 239
CHAPTER 74 243
CHAPTER 75 246
CHAPTER 76 249
CHAPTER 77 253
CHAPTER 78 254
CHAPTER 79 258
CHAPTER 80 262
CHAPTER 81 264
CHAPTER 82 268
CHAPTER 83 271
CHAPTER 84 274
CHAPTER 85 277
CHAPTER 86 279
CHAPTER 87 282
CHAPTER 88 284
CHAPTER 89 288
CHAPTER 90 289
CHAPTER 91 293
CHAPTER 92 297
CHAPTER 93 301
CHAPTER 94 304
CHAPTER 95 308
ABOUT THE AUTHOR 311

PROLOGUE

Thud! Bryn's head hit the ground hard as he fell from his bunk. Instinctively, he moved his hand to where it hurt. But before there was a chance to assess the damage, or to even open his eyes from the depth of sleep, he began to roll. The ground beneath him was moving, swaying from side to side. He needed to get up. He had to get to his feet despite the feeling of complete disorientation. Grasping at the bunk frame, he rose. Close to being fully upright, the floor beneath gave way and he was momentarily weightless. And then he wasn't. This caused him to crash to his knees, his hands' firm grip protecting him from the full impact of another fall.

The oilskins Bryn had been wearing, just before he lay down, were hanging off the end of the bed, still wet. He had put them within reaching distance so he could gear up when he woke. That was the plan. Edging towards them, he noticed that one of his boots was missing. Cursing under his breath, Bryn lay down to survey the cabin. His mother would not have been impressed with the use of foul language, but at that moment, he didn't care. What was he thinking, embarking on a journey such as this? He wasn't ready. The look on his mother's face as he left, told him as much.

The missing boot revealed itself from under the opposite bunk, on the next roll. It landed close to the other, so Bryn grabbed them both and sat on the edge of his bed. One hand for himself, one for the boat, the captain instructed when he came on board nearly a week before. And, that was what he did. It made the task of dressing slower and more cumbersome than he liked but there was no other option. His body was bent over to protect his head from the bunk above, the ache from the fall reminding him to be careful.

The stench of diesel from the engine smelled stronger than before.

The strain of heaving the weighty boat through the swollen seas was taking its toll. Bryn needed fresh air. He needed to be out of the stuffy cabin, to rid himself of the queasy feeling building in the centre of his stomach. Getting to the hatch was no easy task. The force of movement wasn't ebbing. There was no rhythm, no direction. It was like he was caught in an eddy, a swirling whirlpool. A rollercoaster ride that had lost control. He wanted to get off.

Grabbing at anything he could find fastened to a bulkhead, Bryn made his way through the dimly lit galley. The contents of each cupboard and drawer rattled with every wave. Luckily everything was safely and securely stowed away, he hoped. He raised a foot to climb the seven shallow steps that led through the hatch, to the wheelhouse. Violently, they jerked from side to side. A risk, Bryn thought, not worth taking. Securing both hands to the hatch opening, Bryn hoisted himself through. The steps seemed to be too much of a hindrance, and his desire to leave the cabin had become overwhelming.

In the wheelhouse, Captain Ruben was preoccupied watching the oncoming behaviour of the sea and studying the boat's compass. His wife, Gabriella, who also happened to be his first mate, took charge of the wheel.

Damio, Ado and Macario, the crew of three brothers from Portugal, were drenched. They had been out on deck checking that the lines were protected, and the remaining hatches were locked and firmly fixed. Together they watched the light from the masthead illuminate the crests of the dark, soaring waves as they loomed, as the weather worsened.

Bryn was in too much of a daze to care about anything except the need to get outside. His stomach was beginning to heave, like the sea. His mouth was dry. Everything was becoming blurry and out of focus.

No one had noticed his presence as he made his way to the opening of the cabin. No one was watching as he grabbed at the latch to escape. The door flew open and a gust of fresh, cool air hit Bryn's lungs. He felt grateful. Just for a moment. Then, he had a sudden urge to throw up, which he did. Over the side. And, as he emptied his guts of the toxins that had been building, a giant swell gushed over the bow and hit him with the full force of its weight. Ruben, Gabriella and the crew of the *Carla-Marie* watched in absolute disbelief as their passenger disappeared along with the surge.

CHAPTER 1

One cold, dark evening, in the spring of 854AD, a lone man trekked through a mountain range in desolate terrain, on unfamiliar soil. He was cold and tired. Hadn't eaten for two days. The grounds were treacherous. His path often blocked by fallen rocks and icy stretches. Einar had been sent by fellow Norwegian pilgrims, not long after landing, to find suitable territory they could inhabit, and thus far it had been a fruitless quest, the landscape becoming more barren as he went on. Reaching the coastline, he realised his journey was most likely a waste but decided to rest before he turned back. He slept under a blanket of bearskin, waking early the following morning. Instead of returning the way he came, he decided to travel along the shore, still hoping he might find greener pastures.

As he continued his journey, a strong odour began to fill the air. He could see steam ejecting from pores in the earth, making a slight hissing sound as it broke through. Einar had heard of this occurrence but had yet to witness it. If what he had heard was true, there could be a pool of warm water ahead where he could bathe. Excited, he quickened his pace, searching every crevice and ravine until he saw a rather large body of water with steam on the surface. His desire was so great to experience this phenomenon that he was careless where he trod and tripped over a rock, falling into a geyser large enough to swallow him whole. The warm water sucked him in, pulled him down into a dark, bottomless grave. Seeing nothing but blackness, the light fading from above, he knew impending death would follow in a matter of moments.

Fellow pilgrims eventually gave up on Einar returning. They settled on a hillside that gave little shelter and provided land that barely produced enough food to feed their families.

Two hard and perilous winters later, the community suffered tragic losses from freezing temperatures and starvation. The vessel they arrived on was long gone, pilfered in the dead of night by the few who were determined to go back home, soon after they arrived. As a result, they were stranded on desolate lands, with no means of escape.

Huddled around a campfire one evening, a fight broke out over food rations. It was a regular occurrence as they grappled over portions sizes. Amidst the furore, they took no notice as a figure approached from the darkness, wielding a flaming torch.

He called from afar, quickening his pace as he neared.

The tribal pilgrims were jolted from their hostilities, distracted by the light and the shouting from the stranger as he approached. They swiftly became protective, their leader and stronger members grabbing what they could find close by, to use as weapons.

As this outsider crossed the verge of the campsite, one woman struggled to get to her feet and slowly moved towards him, as others backed away. He was wrapped from head to foot in warm clothing, unlike anything they had seen before. But she knew. He looked different. Healthier. Stronger. When he removed the scarf from his face, he briefly smiled. There was no doubt. Her husband, who had been missing for nearly two years, had returned.

Einar was overcome with sadness seeing his wife, Astrid, so frail and in such poor health. As she touched his face in utter disbelief, he embraced her gently, aware of how fragile she had become.

One by one, the others dropped their makeshift weapons. As he brought his wife closer to the fire, the light revealed Einar to all who stood nearby. He had indeed returned. In the haze of confusion and shock, he declared that the following morning they would leave for finer pastures. The tribe had no energy to argue, no strength to ask questions. The next day they did as they were told, until the journey led to the geyser Einar had fallen into. As they gathered around it, he instructed them to jump in.

Not only were they revolted by the notion, some openly stated that Einar had lost his mind. Unconvinced, Einar had no other option. He announced that he would make the leap and return by nightfall. There was a cave not too far away, where they could shelter. That was where they would meet.

Astrid, fearing she would lose him again, decided to join her husband. If it was to lead her death, it would be better than the slow death she would face alone. Holding his hand, she pulled him to the edge of the steaming water pool. Amidst the voices of rage and disbelief, Astrid tugged on her husband's hand, not wanting to delay for fear of changing her mind. Being protective, Einar wrapped his arms around her waist, and they jumped. They were quickly pulled under. Barely a ripple on the surface. They were gone in an instant. After a few minutes, with no sign of life, the majority decided that it was a tragic occurrence. A waste of life.

A debate ensued, whether the tribe should go back. Their ageing leader declared that they had nothing to go back to. Only death and despair. Even if they wanted to make the trek, it would be dark, and they could lose their way. The cave was dry enough to stay the night and a decision would be made in the morning. Not one person entertained the thought of Einar and his wife returning. Questions were asked, and no answers were found, about where Einar could have possibly spent the previous two years.

As darkness fell, a fire was lit by the cave entrance to keep warm. Children slept by its side, huddled together with their parents protecting them from the cold wind. No one had the energy or inclination to speak. The only sound came from the sea as it hit the shoreline, and the occasional call of a wolf in the distance.

Meagre rations were passed amongst the group. Nobody argued this time. Their minds were elsewhere. And as the light from the fire began to fade, just as they settled down for the night, voices could be heard calling their names.

It wasn't possible. No one could believe what they were witnessing.

From the far end of the cave, too deep to explore, Einar appeared, followed by Astrid. She was dressed in similar, snug attire. This time there was no torch. They just appeared, as if from nowhere.

The leader of the tribe decided it was time to listen, encouraged and astonished by their miraculous re-emergence. But Einar didn't say much. Astrid just repeated how unbelievable it was and that they had to see it for themselves. And they did. At dawn, each person was given an option of jumping into the water or staying behind. Without speaking a word, people began to gather by Einar and Astrid. No one waited for approval. Not one person could fathom, or begin to discuss, the miracle they had witnessed the night before.

Families leapt in together. Some people made the journey alone. Others were frightened so waited. Einar and Astrid were there to encourage, the last to leave. Einar knew he needed to be, for fear someone might have a change of heart. One of the most difficult conditions Einar was given, before he made the journey back to his tribe, was that once the opening to the geyser was disclosed, along with the power it held, not one soul was permitted to stay behind. No one left to tell the tale. This was non-negotiable.

As he clasped his wife's hand, preparing himself for his final leap, he wondered if he should have told them that they were never coming back. As he took one last look at the world he once knew, his wife pulled him forward, eager to get back to a world she'd barely discovered. A world that they would inhabit for many generations to come.

Apart from the intermittent gushing and natural flow of the geyser, it was left undisturbed for many years. While the landscape changed with centuries of volcanic activity and coastal erosion, the size and tempo of the foundation remained unchanged. The same could be said for the cave Einar emerged from. Both existing as if protected by a higher power so that someday they could be used again.

CHAPTER 2

Bryn was only seven years old when he was expelled from the local village primary school in North Yorkshire, England. The headmaster had witnessed him lift and propel a fellow student a distance of over twelve feet, with more than the strength of a fully grown man. He stated that he wouldn't have believed it if he hadn't seen for himself. It was both shocking and nauseating to watch. The poor victim suffered a broken arm and his mother wanted to press charges, he told Bryn's parents, Lars and Sanne Jahr.

Bryn sat in silence as the headmaster explained, in very simple terms, that such violence would not be tolerated. In all his years he had never seen such a deplorable act displayed by a child. He had no alternative but to expel him and could not, with good conscience, recommend he attend an alternative educational institute, until Bryn was deemed fit to be there.

Lars and Sanne neither argued against the accuser nor sided with, or provided excuses for their son. With a resigned acceptance, they led Bryn from the school acutely aware that they were being observed, and most probably scrutinised, by the faces peering behind children's posters, from the windows of the classrooms they passed.

In the car, on the drive back to the family farm, Sanne turned to Bryn and calmly asked him to explain what had happened. One solitary tear travelled down Bryn's reddening cheek and it seemed to be taking all his emotional strength to stay composed. He didn't say a word. He couldn't because he didn't really understand what had happened. That boy was hurting his friend. Picking on him for no reason. Just because he could. All Bryn wanted to do was get him to stop, push him way. He didn't mean to break his arm.

Crack! He couldn't get the sound out of his head. Or the scream that followed.

Both Lars and Sanne decided it would be best for Bryn to be home-schooled from that day forward.

In the years that followed, Bryn grew up in relative solitude. Rumours of what had transpired at the school had spread through the village, the family greeted by strange looks and hushed voices anytime they ventured from the farm.

Lars and Sanne were not unfamiliar with this behaviour as it was similar to when they first arrived, before Bryn was born, from their native country, Norway. They were strangers moving to a townland of natives who had inhabited the area for generations. It had the beautiful, lush-green landscape associated with the Yorkshire countryside. There was no large city close by. It was quiet, secluded, disconnected from the realm of conventional civilisation. Possibly the most isolated hamlet in the dales. Perfect for their needs and lifestyle.

The local community were certainly bemused by the arrival of outsiders. However, Bryn's parents were no ordinary newcomers. Lars towered above any man he met, his shoulders wide and burly, his fair hair plaited down his back. His demeanour solemn and subdued. A man of very few words.

Soon after they moved into their newly acquired old farmhouse, he began labouring at a local building site, gaining funds to buy a tractor, to start working on the fields. His employer, Mr Jones, told the lads down in the pub that he was the best worker he had ever taken on. Strong as an ox. Did the work of four men. Quiet. Kept to himself. He wouldn't have a bad word said about the man. He was only sorry to see him go.

Sanne was also tall and athletically built. Her features were striking. The locals thought she didn't look Scandinavian. Dark skin, large electric-blue eyes, chestnut-coloured hair. Exotic, the women claimed. She didn't mind the attention, at first. Kids would point, men would stare. Mothers at the school would ask the inappropriate question of where she was from… originally. Sanne knew this behaviour was born from genuine curiosity. No malice intended. But she had to concede that she was quite glad not to have to wait, or converse, by the school gates anymore. She felt a pang of guilt admitting it, but she also realised that the solitude was best for the family, although she knew it would take time before Bryn would understand.

Life at the farm was simple. With no electronic gadgets, television or mobile devices, the Jahr family spent their days working hard. Allowing time for Bryn's allocated schooling curriculum and the physical training Lars insisted he completed daily, there wasn't time to miss out on the idea of modern conveniences.

Though Lars and Sanne were content, Bryn knew by the age of sixteen that the isolation he felt was stifling. He continued with chores, and the life that was created for him, but he was not happy. Academically, he knew he was strong enough to attend college. It didn't have to be the most prestigious institute. Just one that would give him a chance to leave home.

On the eve of Bryn's eighteenth birthday, Lars was due back from a trip to his hometown, near the coastal city of Bergen. Bryn was in his room, rereading the application form for Brighton University. It was a warm, early March evening. He was nervous. There was no way of knowing how his parents were going to react to his plans to leave. There was no point discussing it before then. They might have tried to change his mind, insist he stayed to look after the farm. Fully grown, he could make his own decisions. He was going to break the news the following day and wasn't sure how he felt about it. Part of him would be relieved that his plans were out in the open. The rest of him felt as though he was betraying them, in a way. He would be letting them down. Disappointing them. That was never his intention.

It was close to midnight when Bryn heard the car approach, the lights beaming through his bedroom window. His father was gone for only a few days this time, on a trip he took every couple of years. One that Bryn was never invited on. Usually, he was away for a month or two. This time, he must have cut it short.

He always missed his father when he left. However, the greatest sentiment he felt was envy. Being told that farmyard chores were more important, was no consolation. His mother also always stayed behind. Bryn thought she preferred it that way. She was an only child; her parents had died many years before. She had no one to go back to in Norway. Her life was on the farm. Bryn couldn't imagine his life being so unfulfilled. Though there still was ample time before he was planning to leave, he needed that time to let his parents get used to the idea, with the hope of them supporting it.

The heavy front door creaked as it opened. A sound Bryn was familiar with. When he was young, no matter how late Lars returned, Bryn would hear the groan of the hinges, jump out of bed and scurry down the stairs to greet him. Not tonight. He was hesitating. He heard his mother approach the door as he entered. They truly missed each other when they were apart. Generally, they didn't display their affection, but every time Lars came home after being away for several weeks, or in this case just a few days, they embraced as though he had been away for years.

Bryn was used to the routine. He sat on the edge of his bed, ready to go downstairs. Just as he was hiding his acceptance letter in the pages of a book he was reading, he heard something new. An occurrence he was completely unfamiliar with. The voice of a stranger. It was booming through the rafters. As Bryn approached his door, he realised the visitor was speaking German and greeted his mother as an old friend. His nervous demeanour was suddenly replaced by genuine curiosity.

CHAPTER 3

Bryn descended the stairs slowly. All the while, his gaze never left the figure standing at the bottom. He could only see the back of his pony-tailed, golden braid, which reached below the base of his tanned, suede coat. He was speaking to his father like they were the closest of friends. Brothers.

His mother eventually caught sight of him. She exchanged glances with Lars, who turned to greet his son with open arms.

'Bryn, you are here! I was beginning to think you had snuck out,' he teased. 'Come! There is someone here you must meet.'

The stranger turned. It was hard to believe that there was someone who could appear larger and fiercer than his father. A man possibly in his fifties, though he could have been many years younger or older. His face was rugged, unshaven, with wisps of grey in his stubble. Bryn believed that each line and wrinkle on his face told a story. His nose, broken more than once. It was as though he belonged to another era. A Viking, perhaps. He offered Bryn his large, calloused hand once he was released from his father's embrace. Bryn, who was unaccustomed to social etiquette, took a moment before he offered his in return. When he did, the stranger pulled him forward. Mere inches from his face, he spoke.

'I hope you're ready for this. I haven't given up on your father yet. So, don't mess this up,' he said in a broad German accent.

Bryn could do nothing but glance at his parents, before his father interrupted.

'We haven't told him yet, Gregor. I only just made the decision. It'll be fine.' He shrugged.

Gregor turned to Lars.

'What do you mean, you haven't told him yet!' he bellowed.

'Forget it. We can do this some other time. Lars, pack your things. We'll leave early. Where am I sleeping?'

Lars looked at his wife, then pointed to the room at the end of the hallway. Gregor left without saying another word, stomping his way to the guest room, which had never been used before that night.

'He's not ready,' Sanne told Lars. 'He's still a boy. Just give him a couple of years. He'll be ready then.'

'He'll be gone then,' Lars responded. 'This lifestyle isn't healthy for a young person.'

Lars turned to Bryn, who was stumped into silence. 'You have plans, don't you, boy? You're turning eighteen tomorrow. An adult. You were not thinking of staying on this farm with us forever, were you?'

Bryn knew better than to lie to his father. 'College,' he said. It was the only word he could muster.

Sanne looked visibly disappointed.

'I knew you might leave someday but I wasn't expecting it to be so soon, Bryn,' she said.

'I think you were hoping it wasn't going to be so soon. If he goes, we will lose him, Sanne.' Lars spoke softly now, holding his wife's shoulders with both hands. 'This way, we can make up for all the years we stole. A consolation, if you like.'

Sanne suddenly understood. Grasping Bryn by the hand, like she had when he was a young boy, she led him to the kitchen. Lars followed.

'Sit down, Bryn,' she instructed. 'Your father has a something to tell you. Then, you need to make a decision. You do not have the privilege of time. As you heard, Gregor will be leaving in the morning. You can choose to go with him, or your father can go. Either way, the outcome must be determined tonight.'

Bryn did what he was told, sat down and stayed silent. He didn't know what he should say. The truth about college was out in the open. It wasn't how he wanted the conversation to go but he was relieved. That relief was slight, however, compared to the sense of marvel and nervous energy he was now feeling. He wanted to ask questions, make sense of what had transpired only moments ago. It wasn't the time for that. Looking into his father's eyes, he knew he was going to discover whatever he had been hiding – possibly learn why they lived the life they led – and understand if he was ready for what his father was proposing.

Lars stole one last glance at Sanne, knowing that once he began talking, he could never take those words back. With all three sitting at the table in the dimly lit kitchen, Lars began.

'I should probably have told you this years ago, Bryn. I held back because of our family tradition. It is thought best not to discuss this until you are old enough to appreciate its importance and fathom the responsibility. It can be tough to keep secrets when you are young. I know. I have been where you are now. It feels a bit daunting and that's okay.' He paused.

'Great strength needs to be nourished,' Lars continued. 'We are stronger than most, faster than most, and I am not sure if you fully realise that. Every day we have been training. Fitness, endurance and discipline. I have taught you what I can. I think you're ready. And I think your mother might think so too.'

Lars reached for Sanne's hand and she grasped it tightly.

'Now, Bryn. I am going to tell you a story. You have heard it many times when you were young boy, just before you went to sleep. It's a story of warriors and creatures you can only imagine to be true. The story of Zhivrah. Do you remember it?'

Those words evoked memories from Bryn's past that seemed like a lifetime ago. Images of his father sitting by his beside narrating a tale, a legend that he had never read of in a book. One that stemmed from his father's imagination, so he thought. It was told with such fervency and spirit that Bryn often imagined himself there as a child, living amongst its people, having adventures of his own.

CHAPTER 4

Long before the civilised world developed, possibly as the world itself was created, an anomaly was hidden beneath its surface. This was not a tangible, physical presence. It could only be described as transcendent. Almost divine.

When Einar had accidentally fallen into the geyser in Iceland, he was absorbed by its power. Swallowed by the energy it produced. He assumed his life was over and feeling death draw near, he closed his eyes and accepted his fate. Drifting into unconsciousness, his only thoughts were of his wife and how much he would miss her. When he awoke unexpectedly, he felt he had slept for months. His body was sluggish. He was barely able to move. His eyes were slow to focus. Head aching and ears pulsating, he gradually realised he was not alone.

The voice that spoke to him was foreign, speaking in a language he had never heard before. As Einar's eyes adjusted to the bright light overhead, a figure emerged from the darkness. A form that felt unfamiliar. Taller and more slender than the average person, Einar sensed that he was in the presence of the unknown. As a face drew closer, all Einar could make out was a large forehead on honey-coloured skin, with black markings on each side leading to each temple, which encased two unnaturally large eyes. From behind, more shapes began to emerge. It was all too much. Einar was weak and unable to cope with what his mind was trying to process. Drifting back into an unconscious state, the only hope he held was that this was all a dream.

Einar's experience was the first ever human contact with the Hazuru tribe. Unbeknownst to him at the time, it was also the first time a human set foot on the land he would learn was called Zhivrah, loosely translated as The Golden Bridge. He would also discover that he travelled through a portal from his world, as the Hazuru tribe had through a portal from theirs, many generations before.

Although he couldn't speak their language, it didn't take long to understand that they were not so different. He knew the Hazurus were far more advanced than he was. He could tell from their use of artificial lighting, the utensils they used and the clothes they were dressed in. When he was eventually permitted to leave the building he was quarantined in, he was truly astounded by the sights, the landscape and most of all, the people, that greeted him.

Time passed by. Einar stayed in the complex that housed him. He was assigned a tutor to learn the language of the Hazuru tribe. In return, he taught the tutor his own. They traded lessons on cultural and historical events, customs and etiquette.

Every week, Einar approached the tribal council begging them to let him be reunited with his wife. He missed her, often dreaming of them being together in this wonderful world he imagined them growing old in. As time passed, he offered to leave and not come back, promising that he would never betray them by telling anyone of his experience. It would be like it never happened. Still, they refused.

It was only through his friendship with his tutor, Ru, that he finally succeeded. One year, ten months and seventeen days after being separated from Astrid, Ru convinced the council to let Einar return. Einar was given the stipulation that no one was allowed to leave the geyser, with knowledge of its power. The consequences of such actions would inevitably lead to vulnerabilities, jeopardising their home, their way of life and could ultimately destroy the world they considered a haven.

What Einar did not know was that Ru was ordered to follow him, under strict instructions to dispose of anyone left behind. If Einar decided to remain, or any directive was not met, he was also to be executed.

Ru hid discreetly amongst the trees when Einar first approached his wife and kinfolk at the campsite. He followed as they walked to the shoreline. He overheard how Einar's proposal was received with disbelief and outrage. That night, hiding near the opening of the cave, Ru listened to comments about Einar's obvious loss of sanity, how he had probably killed his wife and how naïve they were to follow him. He also heard the desperation in their voices, saw nothing but despair and sadness in their eyes. Ru hoped, for everyone's sake, that Einar's plan would work. If it didn't, he would not hesitate to kill each and every one of them.

CHAPTER 5

Life in Zhivrah evolved over time. Both tribes expanded and thrived. There was ample food and shelter for everyone. It was a scene of contentment and mutual respect between the races. Laws and legislation were enacted to prevent disruption and minor offences. People led a simple and fruitful existence, grateful for what they had, feeling blessed to live in such harmony.

Biologically, the tribes weren't so different. The Hazurus were stronger, more agile. The Earthians tended to physically develop at a slower rate but lived, on average, twenty years longer. Their close genetic disposition meant they were almost fated to interbreed. Over the centuries, some did, generating a new species of people called Panak. It was a union that wasn't encouraged, some finding the coupling almost repulsive. Though it was accepted, in general terms, it didn't stop people scrutinising, staring or judging. Eventually, most Panak families spread out across the land creating townships, developing cultures of their own.

As the years and generations passed, species from two other worlds entered through similar portals and joined the two tribes. One, from a realm far more advanced than the others, brought with them technology beyond imagination. They were known as the Goyteks, small in stature with undersized facial features and large foreheads, which was considered appropriate for they were thought of as highly intelligent but lacking spirit and sensitivity. The other migrants, known as the Shiakanas, were initially regarded as rather strange creatures. They were rather large, with arms stretching to their knees, and when they ran their bodies bounced from side to side, as if one leg was longer than the other. Their skin tone was a greyish green. Some had patches of darker green visible on their arms and legs. Most had a hairline that began close to the back of the head, stretching down past the neckline, though it was hardly noticeable, as it was thin and sparse.

When they first arrived, the Shiakanas were enraged that they were not permitted to leave. Infuriated by the notion that they had to answer to a higher authority, it took many years before they began to engage with and trust other tribes, and finally get involved with communal affairs.

A council, with equal representatives of each of the four tribes – the Hazurus, Earthians, Goyteks and Shiakanas – was established to discuss and enact government affairs. After a lengthy and heated debate, it was eventually agreed that trusted scouts were to return to their respective worlds to track change and gather data on scientific or industrial advancements. The group also collected information on policy and new ideas, sharing this new intelligence with the council and adapting it to their needs, improving their way of life.

On the return of one such trip, the council met as usual to discuss the discoveries of each expedition group. The Earthians spoke about developments in governments, religion and current affairs, the Hazuru spoke of the introduction of aviation and the dictatorship that governed their world, the Goyteks told stories of technology so advanced that the others had trouble comprehending such information, and the Shiakanas had nothing much to share but demeaning comments about the others' exploits.

When one of the chief Goyteks took offence to this ridicule, the Shiakanas expressed themselves in the only way they knew how. They challenged the council to compete in a battle of strength and stamina. This rhetoric was their usual retaliation, but instead of being ignored, the Earthians chose to consider their offer. They told the other members of the council of an event, which was created by citizens of their world, where people competed for glory alone. Throughout that afternoon the council was told of the story of the Olympic Cup, the history, the events, the pride and the patriotism. The council listened and unanimously decided to host their own such event, a contest of strength, stamina, agility and skill.

It started with a competition between members of the tribes within Zhivrah. Until they realised there was a lack of adequate participants, as it was a mediocre affair, with contenders giving a relatively average display of strength and agility. Not really the performance spectators were hoping for. But the concept was there, and it was an event the council wanted to expand and promote.

After an intense debate, the most incredible decision was made to recruit from the tribes' worlds of origin. It was a project that took years of planning, formulating and cultivating; finding only the most ideal candidates to partake. It was a mission like no other. For the first time in the history of Zhivrah, a ruling was made to recruit foreign representatives, who would also have the freedom to come and go. There were security risks and challenges far greater than any they would have ever experienced. People protested. Fears grew. A charter was enacted so that measures were fashioned to protect the citizens from any possible threat to their safety and way of life. The motion had to be put to the public, who voted in their masses. And, when it passed, it was only under guarantee that every precaution was in place. Concern was abated and cautiously replaced with excitement and anticipation.

Scouts were deployed, spending months travelling, researching and befriending suitable candidates. There was one stipulation that was proving immensely problematic. Not only would a contender have to believe and accept this farfetched and inconceivable challenge, they would also have to name an heir to their succession. A son and daughter of their own or a younger member of the bloodline. If they were unable to pass on the mantle, their entire experience would be scrubbed from memory. The consequences would be more severe if the existence of their world became public, even if it was just a rumour. So, vetted hopefuls were not given the location of the portal and were escorted on their first journey, right up as far as the council chambers where further interrogation would take place. Even then, the Goyteks had technology so advanced that any candidate could be returned to where they were found without the slightest inclination that their lives had taken a sudden dramatic change, even if it was just for a moment.

And so, in the summer of 1749 AD, training began for the first ever Warrior Games. From that day forward, life in Zhivrah was never quite the same.

CHAPTER 6

Sanne replenished the pot of tea, as Bryn and his father sat at the kitchen table in a moment of relative silence. Lars' summarised version of Bryn's childhood stories had reached the part where he had explained how potential warriors were recruited. He felt he needed to give his son a moment to digest what he had just told him. Then, he continued.

'Our ancestral bloodline has been participating in the games from the time it began, more generations than any other. Our inherited strength and conditioning have led us to be stronger than most. We are considered exceptional among the human race. Only a handful share our abilities. We are, in fact, bred to compete,' he finally explained. 'Now it's your time to take part. I feel you are ready.'

Bryn couldn't speak. He couldn't find the words to ask a question or acknowledge an inkling of understanding.

'There are options,' Sanne offered, sensing her son's angst. 'You can delay until the next competition. Or, your father has a cousin, whose daughter would be a very good contender. She's a little young but with time and training…'

'Bryn, you can do this,' Lars interjected. 'I have trained you since you could stand on your own two feet. I have seen what you can do. You just need to believe it too.'

Through the window, Bryn could see the horizon lightening. On a typical day, he would be getting up around now, having breakfast before he began his chores. But this was to be no normal day. In that moment, he knew he didn't need to fully grasp what he was being asked to do. There would be plenty of time for questions and concerns. He had spent half his life waiting for an opportunity to achieve something on his own, and no matter how farfetched the prospect seemed, he wasn't going to waste it. With that realisation, and as he turned his attention back to his father, he muttered one word. 'Okay.'

'Sorry, Bryn. Did you say something?' Lars asked, curiously.

'Okay,' Bryn repeated with clarity. 'I'll do it.'

He didn't truly understand why he was so quick to accept his father's strange and unexpected request. If he had been asked on another day, he may not have had the same response. If he had been asked by anyone else, he might have considered them ridiculous. The stories his father had told were conveyed with such passion and detail that it wasn't difficult to imagine he may have lived through some of them. Though he wasn't thoroughly convinced, it was enough to begin a journey.

His mother smiled but appeared a little sceptical, or sad. Bryn couldn't tell. Lars' reaction was somewhat the contrary.

'My boy!' he roared, louder than Bryn had expected. The chair piercingly scratched the floor as he prepared to stand. 'My boy, I am so proud of you. I thought this would have been difficult, didn't I?' Sanne nodded quietly. 'You are going to love it, Bryn,' he continued. 'I remember my first time…'

The sound of heavy footsteps approaching interrupted Lars.

'Old man, you could wake the dead with all that shouting.'

Gregor entered the kitchen, hair dishevelled. His flannel shirt was only half tucked in. He carried his shoes.

'You are obviously excited about something.' Gregor's eyes never left Lars. 'Either you finally realised that you're definitely not too old to compete again, or you've actually managed to convince your young man that you are not actually crazy.'

Bryn's calm expression gave away the answer.

'You know, you have the same look as your father when he's unnerved or unsure of something. It confuses me. How can you look so calm when you're obviously terrified? It's not natural.' Gregor was now addressing Bryn. 'Now, go pack. We're leaving in an hour,' he added without letting Bryn answer.

CHAPTER 7

Gregor and Lars sat in the family's old Land Rover as Bryn said goodbye to his mother. It was a long affair and Gregor was getting restless, so he rolled his window down and told them to get a move on.

Bryn watched his mother wave, through the back window. He wasn't sure how long it would be before he saw her again. He swallowed hard and took a deep breath, then turned his head forward to the road ahead.

As they drove, Bryn watched for any sign or indication of where they were going, and within two hours he had a fair idea. It never occurred to him to even ask. The ferry port. He was becoming very excited but didn't express it, as he wanted to appear more mature to Gregor, whom he supposed would be his travelling companion for the foreseeable future. There was not much said in the car since they left, and Bryn already understood that this very large man wasn't one to practice meaningless conversation. Gregor sat in comfortable silence albeit a little too large for the seat he was firmly planted on. He was a man to be revered with one glance alone, similar to the way people regarded Bryn's father. He portrayed an undertone of confidence and prudence through a modest persona. His sheer build, matched with his aged features, exhibited a person who may have fought many battles, seen many changes and lived to tell the tale. Every word spoken was thought through and Bryn couldn't imagine anything unnerving him, but reckoned woe betide anyone brave enough to cross him.

The Land Rover stopped in a large car park, in an area with very few cars close by. Gregor climbed out, seemingly grateful to be able to stretch his arms. He went straight to the boot and emptied the contents of Bryn's luggage, scrutinising every item until he emerged with one rucksack, half-full.

'Now, we are ready! Say your goodbyes to your father. I must get our tickets.' Gregor addressed Bryn and then turned to Lars. 'See you soon, old man.' He shook his hand and as he headed to the ticket office, he shouted, 'You know, he may not make it a week.' He didn't seem to care that Bryn could hear his remark. It was so blatantly meant to be heard.

Lars now faced his son. 'Gregor does not hold back, Bryn. You're going to have to get used to it,' he said, making no apologies.

'Why does he call you "old man"? You look younger than him,' Bryn asked.

Lars smiled. 'Because I have retired, Bryn. It's our family tradition to hand down the right to compete to a son or daughter when they reach eighteen. It's not a stipulation and sometimes people choose to continue to a ripe old age. I hope you will do the same as I have, with your children. Anyway, Gregor thought I had retired too young and decided to call me "old man" ever since.'

'Any advice, Dad?' Bryn asked, knowing this was his last opportunity for a little fatherly wisdom.

Lars thought for a moment. 'Gregor is a great man. Trust him. Do everything he asks of you and you'll be fine. Oh… I almost forgot!' Lars went to the car and retrieved a long narrow object, wound in canvas. 'This is for you. Keep it hidden and you can unwrap it when you're safely on board. Goodbye, son. Gregor will be waiting. Do me proud!'

Lars hugged Bryn, a little awkwardly, and looked at him one last time before he got back into the car.

'Goodbye, Dad. I won't let you down,' Bryn said to his father and he meant every word.

As the car started to drive away, Bryn followed it with his eyes and felt a glint of loneliness for the first time in his life. He had ached for so long to leave the farm and he had not expected to feel this way.

His parents had always been there for him. This was going to be tougher than he expected.

Gregor's booming voice broke his stupor.

'Bryn, come on. We're running late!'

Bryn jumped to attention and headed after him, his walk breaking into a run as he saw that Gregor wasn't waiting, his excitement starting to build up again as he saw the large P&O North Sea Ferry. He met Gregor at the end of the gangway waiting to take them aboard, where they both stopped for a moment. Gregor sensed that Bryn needed a minute or so to realise they were at the very start of something that would be life-changing, and that he was leaving everything and everyone he knew behind. Bryn appreciated this and took the opportunity to watch the Land Rover, as it left the car park.

Gregor had booked them a small cabin with bunk beds, which neither of them could fit into comfortably. He informed Bryn that the cabin was more a means for private conversation than opulence, and that they had plenty of work to do so had little time for sleep anyway. Before they had a chance to talk, Gregor retrieved a flask from Bryn's bag and a couple of sandwiches he insisted they eat, as sustenance would help them focus on the task ahead. Bryn didn't argue but was becoming curious about the conversation that lay before them. They sat on two small chairs beside a little table near the window, and emptied the contents of the flask, which happened to be vegetable soup, into two plastic cups Gregor had picked up in the canteen en route to their cabin.

As he ate, Bryn watched land creep farther into the distance and observed seagulls flying alongside, with hopes of being fed scraps off the decks, he presumed.

It started to rain, and the wind picked up. Within moments, Bryn was aware of the gentle sway of this large vessel, cutting through the swelling sea, confident to brave any stormy conditions that might head their way.

Gregor didn't seem to notice the change of weather, being more interested in devouring the last of his ham sandwich and slurping what remained in his plastic cup. Bryn chose not to worry, as Gregor had probably made voyages like this all the time and he hadn't even flinched. Therefore, he decided to clear the table of crumbs and wrappings and as he did, he remembered the puzzling gift from his father he stowed on board. He reached over and picked it up from the bottom bunk bed. Gregor watched as Bryn laid it on his lap, looking unsure of what to do next.

'You might as well unwrap it,' he offered.

Bryn looked at him for a moment and then did as he was told, having no idea what to expect. As each layer came off, the object became thinner, and as he peeled the last piece of canvas, he felt a little confused.

His father had given him what appeared to be a rod made of wood. It was about three feet in length, cylindrical; portraying intricate etchings of hunters and animals, symbols and representations. None of which made any sense to Bryn, but he hadn't expected them to.

'What is this?' he asked Gregor, offering it to him for inspection.

Gregor stood and held the piece of wood away from him. He clutched it at its centre and clenched his fists. Out from each end popped a blade just over a foot long. This made the seemingly inanimate object appear fierce and powerful. Then Gregor twisted his hands in opposite directions. The piece of wood separated between his hands and now he held two short swords. Bryn was enthralled. He now understood the competition may not be all he imagined. Gregor retracted the blades, reattached the handles, and placed the weapon in Bryn's hands.

'It's called Scheda, has been in your family for generations. It's yours now. Take care of it. There isn't another,' Gregor warned.

CHAPTER 8

Gregor was very familiar with Lars' family heirloom and had seen it many times held by Bryn's father. He and Lars had known each other for many years, and he was heavy-hearted when he heard of his retirement. When Lars started competing, Gregor, being slightly older, took him under his wing. For someone so young, he was incredibly disciplined and focused. Rising to every challenge, no obstacle too large, it didn't take Lars long before he qualified for the team. Some years he seemed to take a step back, letting others have a chance to qualify – but Gregor knew he did it purposefully. Lars, to this day, would never admit it.

Bryn was one of the last trainees to be recruited that year, as his birthday was on the cusp of achieving a qualification. Gregor had made an exception, for Lars, though he could have insisted he wait another two years. He had witnessed, and celebrated, many parents pass the mantle to their children. It was a natural progression. A proud moment. But this felt different. Maybe Lars was too young to give up his legacy. He was still in his prime. Stronger, faster and keener than most. Or, maybe, Lars' retirement made Gregor feel old. He didn't really want to dwell on it. Gregor led a very different life. He had no family or friends outside the arena. No plans to settle down.

As he looked at Bryn, refocusing his attention. He was yet to see the potential, though he was possibly being subjective. He knew that most parents could be short sighted when it came to their children. The real test would be in the weeks to come. Gregor was hoping Bryn might display some of Lars' discipline and determination. Only time would tell. He could see Sanne's free spirit and impulsive nature reflected in Bryn's eyes. He hadn't seen her in years, but he could tell that her disposition hadn't changed much and felt unexpectedly relieved. He just hoped that one day they would decide to leave that godforsaken farm. It was not healthy for anybody to be locked away for so long.

Gregor broke the silence by explaining to Bryn that, the night before, he had contacted a friend of his in Rotterdam who would give him passage to Reykjavik in his trawler. They were due to arrive at midnight and would have no time to waste as he had intended to leave port straight away.

'Give me passage?' exclaimed Bryn, somewhat alarmed. 'Are you not coming?'

'Bryn, I need to travel to France. Apparently, there is a very promising young woman who might be joining you. It's the last of the recruitment drive and I'm under time pressure. You are going to have to trust me. I have written instructions down for your final journey to Strokkur and directions to the geyser.' Gregor handed Bryn an envelope and instructed him to put it safely away in his bag. 'Get some rest, young man. You look like you need it.'

Bryn didn't realise he was yawning. The gentle movement of the boat was prompting him to sleep. There was no point resisting. He clambered up onto the top bunk as Gregor announced he was going to get some air. It didn't seem to matter that the bed was too short or narrow to get comfortable. Bryn was asleep as his head hit the pillow.

'You sleep like the dead.' Gregor woke Bryn, who was disorientated, almost forgetting where he was. Through the porthole, it had become dark. There was no visible line between the sea and sky. At least the rain had stopped.

'What time is it?' Bryn inquired, sensing that he had slept for some time.

'Almost ten. We'll be landing in a couple of hours. Time to eat before the cafeteria closes.'

*

Gregor spotted Ruben at the entrance gate, where he was standing under a lamppost, which gave him an oddly orange complexion. He was small in stature, dwarfed by the two men he approached to greet. Just like Gregor, it was difficult to determine his age. Wearing oil overalls and rather oversized rubber boots, his fringe seemed to be matted to his forehead. He wore a woollen hat to cover the rest of his hair.

Gregor shook his hand with great vigour and introduced Bryn. Ruben acknowledged Bryn with a nod, subtly shaking his hand after enduring Gregor's beefy grip. Although Ruben proclaimed their need to get moving, Gregor took a moment to take Bryn to one side and offer a last piece of advice.

'Ruben's a good friend. Whatever you do, don't get in his way. Keep the instructions I gave you safe in your rucksack. I also wrote down how the geyser erupts every eight minutes. Get your timing right and leave it about two minutes before you jump in. The perimeter can be a little hot. This will probably be the biggest proverbial leap of faith you'll ever make. Just go for it. Don't spend too long at the edge milling things over in your mind. You won't regret it. I promise you that.'

Gregor shook Bryn's hand. 'I'll see you very soon, young man.' Clasping his other hand on Bryn's shoulder, he continued, 'You'll do fine, you'll do fine,' and walked away.

'Thank you, Gregor!' was all Bryn could manage to shout after him. He felt strangely alone as he stood beside the fisherman who urged him onwards without saying a word.

*

The port of Rotterdam was vast, hosting hundreds of ships and trawlers, most of which were enormous. It took over forty-five minutes for them to arrive at the *Carla-Marie's* dock. The trawler stood over twenty metres long, Bryn estimated. White with a red hull. Through the relative darkness, he could tell it was in need of a fresh coat of paint, traces of a previous darker colour and rust visible where the red was peeling near the back. Bryn wasn't worried about the aesthetics but did wonder for a moment if he should be concerned about its durability. They were about to embark on an ocean journey and, considering this was his first time venturing from home, he felt a little unnerved. Dim lights ebbed from the cabin. The call of a seagull could be heard in the distance. Another trawler's engine fired up, disturbing the late-night calm.

*

The crew of the *Carla-Marie* was made up of the skipper, Ruben, his warm and convivial wife Gabriella, and three Portuguese brothers – Ado, Damio and Macario – who barely spoke a word of English; between the three of them they were just about able to string a sentence together, which Bryn quickly realised was all they needed to get by. Their voyage would take six days, all the while searching for cod and other white fish.

He slept well the first night despite his long sleep on the ferry. The bucking motion of the sea and the constant whir of the engines brought a certain comfort, he came to realise. It was after two in the morning when he went to bed and was grateful he had the small, cramped cabin to himself. He was up early the following morning and noticed that two of the crew had retired to their bunks, sleeping on top of their blankets, Ado still with his shoes on.

Bryn chose, on his first full day on the trawler, to keep out of the way of the deck for fear of being a nuisance. He joined the crew for mealtimes in the galley and volunteered his services to Gabriella, who was rostered on to cook. She was rather impressed by his willingness to help out and very grateful that he was able to clean up after himself.

Before dawn on the second morning Bryn finally ventured onto the deck. The air was bitterly cold, and the sun was far from showing its face. However, it was calm, for which Bryn was thankful. Ruben spotted him from the wheelhouse and beckoned at Bryn to join him. Inside, Bryn could smell freshly brewed coffee and it felt surprisingly warm.

'Good morning, young man. Did you sleep well?' Ruben asked in a jovial manner, surprising for this hour of the morning.

'Well, sir. How about you?'

'Haven't slept yet, but we're right on course and I hear that the herring season is off to a good start. We might be steering straight into a huge haul, up ahead. I may need you to help out. I'm due to pick up an extra crew member when we reach port, but until then, I'm a man down.' Ruben wasn't waiting for an answer. 'And, Bryn, don't call me sir. We are no navy ship.'

Just then, Gabriella appeared with a large mug of steaming black coffee and gave it to Bryn. 'Get this in you, young man. It's going to be a long day.' She smiled and gave him a wink before turning her attention to her husband. 'Time for you to get a little shut-eye, Zoetie.' Gabriella didn't wait for a reply. She simply took the wheel, almost pushing her husband to one side.

'If you insist,' Ruben responded, knowing better than to argue.

'So, what would you like me to do first, Captain?' Bryn asked Gabrielle.

'I am the first mate, Bryn. The captain is the boss,' Gabriella informed him.

'I know, Gabriella,' he jested. She laughed loudly at his response.

'I need you to get the boys out of bed. Breakfast first. We'll need our strength. We've a long day ahead of us.'

Bryn turned to go.

'You'll need a set of oilskins. The boys will fetch some for you. Don't forget your life jacket. We wouldn't want you falling overboard in these temperatures,' she added, visibly encouraged with Bryn's readiness to get to work.

'And, get the kettle on. Keep the coffee pot full. We are going to need it.'

CHAPTER 9

With everyone fed, a meeting followed in the galley. As they waited for Ruben to get up, navigation charts were spread across the table, the Portuguese brothers studying them as though they had done it many times before. The air was filled with excitement, though partly contained by a sense of professional realisation. When Ruben appeared and as he finished off leftover scraps from breakfast, Bryn watched in admiration as he communicated the plan to his Portuguese crew with patience and calmness. The crew understood perfectly and conducted themselves in such a manner that it was almost routine. It was obvious that they were very experienced fishermen and had worked with Ruben for some time.

With everyone in the wheelhouse, they were waiting for the go-ahead from the captain to reel out the nets. Bryn was instructed to stay put for the first few hours, to watch what the boys were doing so he'd have some idea what to expect.

When the go-ahead was given, Ado, Damio and Macario got into their positions on the deck, expertly deploying the net from its reel, with the winch. They were back at the wheelhouse in no time, rubbing their hands together and smiling from ear to ear with anticipation of what was to come. It took a lot longer than expected for the alarm to sound, indicating the net was full. Although they were disappointed, they were not disheartened, as the day was young. Bryn was told to stay near the hatch to ensure fish didn't escape the drop. Damio was sent below to start the process of gutting, sorting and putting the fish on ice. About a third of the load was thrown back to sea, as they hadn't met the haul's requirements. They repeated this exercise at several locations before they all retired for an early dinner. Ruben went to bed for a couple of hours while Gabrielle and Macario took turns at the wheel. Bryn helped Damio clean up and Ado continued studying the charts, plotting the next course.

Before dawn, they were ready for the next run. All men were harnessed to the side of the boat, as the wind picked up, and the captain wanted to ensure their safety. When the first load came in, Bryn was sent below to help gut fish. The process wasn't difficult, but with the smell and the motion of the boat, it wasn't long before he had to clamber back to deck, where he lost the contents of his stomach over the railings. He learned quickly that a fishing trawler wasn't the place for due consideration and compassion for moments like these, as it was a common occurrence, a part of the job.

As it took less time for each full net to be raised from the water, moods were lifting to the point where the boys sang an old Portuguese folk song as they worked, and Gabriella joined her husband in the wheelhouse to watch their unyielding cargo.

Bryn was so caught up in the excitement he barely felt the cold and enjoyed the job he was given, although he felt he really wasn't making too much of a contribution.

Later that night and into the early hours of the morning, the crew of the *Carla-Marie* drank wine and rum. Damio and Macario cooked a fine feast. They sang and even danced a little, celebrating their catch and congratulated each other for their achievement. Bryn felt appreciated and blushed slightly with all the drunken hugs and kisses he received from the brothers, not understanding a word said to him. All he knew was they were near their quota and that meant each crew member was in for a hefty bonus when they reached Iceland.

The next morning, he helped mend the nets and even got the job of operating the winch to drop them. The haul wasn't as large, but the men were far from disappointed. As the week progressed, Bryn learned a lot about fishing and even a few words of Portuguese, which he found easy enough, as he was quite adept at picking up languages.

The trawler was laden with fish, which slowed their journey. Ruben was planning to auction it on in Reykjavik at a port he knew well. Their journey took a day longer than planned due to the load, but Bryn didn't mind at all. He was lavishing his voyage, gaining insight and knowledge along the way.

With only one night left on the *Carla-Marie,* Bryn packed the remainder of his belongings and rummaged through the front pocket of his rucksack for the instructions Gregor had left him, for the final leg of his journey. He read through the list of bus routes and timetables, and also found a small cache of local currency to help him get by. Gregor had thought of everything. Why was he surprised?

Back in the galley, it was Ado's turn to make supper and Bryn found Damio sitting on his own reading *The Count of Monte Cristo,* in his native tongue. He had been poring over it since they left port but hadn't made much of an impression on such a verbose hardback edition. He stopped for a moment, catching Bryn's attention, and produced from a shelf behind a little bottle, full to the brim with what Bryn could only assume was rum. Passing him the bottle, Damio managed to express his thanks for helping on board. Bryn did not know what to say so thanked him for his gratitude and for the bottle, which he was not sure what to do with, so stuck it in his bag along with everything else.

Ado appeared from behind him with bowls of hot vegetable soup, which he wasn't too proud to admit came straight from a can. Gabriella, who was nearby, told Bryn that she would fill his flask, if there was any left over, and throw in some rations in case he got hungry. She had become quite fond of Bryn and felt a little sad to see him go. She reached over and gave him a huge hug, all the while reminding him to make sure he had packed everything, including his socks, which were hanging by his bunk.

After supper, most of the crew went to bed, including Bryn – who was more exhausted than he realised. Ruben had the wheel and joked that they mightn't get a lot of sleep as there were warnings of bad weather up ahead. He seemed not overly concerned, so Bryn wasn't worried.

CHAPTER 10

Ruben was the first to react. He had spotted Bryn's reflection, from the windscreen, as he passed behind him. He didn't pay it any attention until he felt a gust of wind and rain come through the wheelhouse. Ruben watched, as they all did, when Bryn disappeared into the dark, wild abyss. And, for a short moment, mourned his loss. But something told Ruben there was hope. He got up and fastened his harness. Gabrielle almost protested but stopped herself. The crew followed their captain's precedent and readied themselves. Each harness was attached to the bulkhead and to each man to increase leverage. Ruben was the first to approach the hatch, securing the banging door open. He looked at his wife briefly before edging his way through the opening.

Damio followed suit and then his two brothers. Gabrielle felt helpless but someone had to man the wheel, or they could lose control of the trawler. All she could do was point the searchlight to starboard, knowing it might prove useful, and steer the boat around, hoping it wouldn't cause it to roll.

Outside, Ruben held tightly to the railing, losing his footing every time the boat hit a wave. No one spoke as they manoeuvred along the side deck. The wind tore the hoods from their heads, though they had been fastened tightly. Their squinted eyes scanned the seas. Ruben reached for the lifebuoy, readying it to throw but knowing that they needed to get to stern. Chances were that if Bryn survived, they had already left him behind.

Ado lost his footing but luckily one of his brothers stopped him from falling. They were making slow progress, but Gabrielle had managed to turn the trawler around, giving it a wide berth. Ruben's hope was fading as he suddenly realised that Bryn could be anywhere.

The brothers started shouting their frustrations at each other, which was deafened by the clamour of the engine, the howling wind and torrential rain. Ruben raised his hand to signal calm. They were at the back of the cabin and Ruben spotted something. Sliding downhill as the stern sank into the sea, it took the energy of all four men to hold steady, but Ruben's eyes were transfixed to the stern railing. As the bow dipped, gravity shifted. And, as the stern lifted into the dark night's sky, a flash of lightning illuminated the outline of two hands, one above the other on the outer railing. The movement of someone trying to pull themselves in. Ruben wanted to go to him but all he could do, at that moment, was point. The crew watched as the boat violently thrashed the seas. They couldn't move. There was nowhere to hold on, nothing they could do.

Bryn didn't feel ill. The terror diminished the effect. When he was thrown from the wheelhouse, he was lifted by the motion of the brutal waves. Crashing onto the deck, he slid headfirst before being lifted again, this time landing in the sea, metres away from the trawler. As the draw of the ocean tried to pull him away, Bryn somehow summoned the courage to fight back. Instead of wrestling with the surface current, he decided to dive below, hoping it might be a more effective endeavour. Bryn was a strong swimmer but within minutes he was beginning to struggle. Only when he saw the *Carla-Marie* start to come about, did he feel a slight relief, even though the searchlight was pointing the wrong direction. He needed to try to swim with the current. It meant that he would have to venture a bit farther away but there was no choice, he felt. The only way to get back was to work with the motion of the sea, no matter how angry it was.

Bryn could see the face of his father, urging him on. He had trained with him every day, as far back as he could remember. The one lesson repeated daily was to never give up. Even when he felt defeated, flat on his back, with his father standing over him, he would repeat those words. As Bryn grew, he learned to get back on his feet and try again. It was a hard lesson, but it was essential to him now. He was slowly gaining ground. The trawler was getting closer. On he swam. He could see Ruben and his crew clinging to the cabin. There was no point shouting. They wouldn't hear him. There was no point waving. The searchlight was still facing the other direction. He needed to muster on alone.

The trawler viciously tossed in every direction. Bryn realised the most dangerous effort was yet to come. How was he going to get back aboard? The most accessible side was the stern but seeing the propellors spinning in full motion, and the rudder flapping above water was nerve wracking. He didn't have time to think. He just kept his eyes on the railing that was fixed just above. It took five attempts to grasp it; each time Bryn was moments away from being sliced by metal blades. Each time, he had to swim away, for fear of going below the hull.

The rail was difficult to grip, only accessible when the stern dipped, but he finally managed to hold on before it lifted. His entire body was hoisted out of the water with the elevation. Bryn used the opportunity to climb, before the back of the hull was submerged under water, once again. He paused at the top, just for a moment, to gather his breath. With one last effort, he pulled his body over the top, the heft of his wet gear adding encumbrance. Water blasted the deck, but he held on, waiting for a moment to make his way to safety. That's where he saw Ruben and the crew, Ruben staring at him as though he had risen for the dead.

'I am okay!' he roared. Ruben raised his hand to his ear. Bryn knew he couldn't hear him. It didn't matter. He was okay. When the swell ebbed, he got up and pulled himself along the railing to where the crew were still holding on. Ruben hitched him onto the harness and they headed slowly back to the wheelhouse.

CHAPTER 11

Gabrielle put the steering on autopilot when she heard the men approach. The storm was dissipating, but the wind was still up. She embraced her husband when he entered, not minding the drenched oilskins. They had been out there for so long that she was unsure if any of them would return. The last person to come through the hatch was Bryn. Gabrielle couldn't believe it. She didn't know whether to hug him or shout at him. Instead, she told him to get out of the wet clothes, get to bunk and that they'd bring him some hot tea, not knowing how else to react.

The entire crew were speechless. An event like this was difficult to put into words. It was like a myth from an urban fishing legend. Bryn should not have survived what he did. No normal person could ever have survived that. Ruben had never questioned Gregor's intentions when he offered transit for his companions. He never asked what or why. Never even asked where in Iceland they were heading to. He was always glad of the extra hand, and occasionally a few surprises along the way.

*

Waking up rested, Bryn looked out of the porthole. It was a dark morning, and he noticed the lights of what he could only presume was land in the distance. With mixed emotions, he climbed to the wheelhouse hoping to get distracted by conversation with whoever happened to be at the helm.

'You're up and about early, young man,' Ruben remarked, looking more tired than he had the night before. Bryn could only presume he was at the end of a very long shift at the helm.

'Good morning, Captain. Am I right in saying that's land up ahead?' Bryn queried, pointing to a barely visible stretch of rock, on the horizon.

'You would be. Not long to go,' Ruben responded.

'I just wanted to say thanks again for risking your lives for me last night. It was a stupid and reckless thing to do. I really don't understand it myself.'

'You looked like you didn't really need our help, after all. Don't worry, Bryn. All forgotten.'

Bryn got them both a coffee and when he returned Ruben was waiting to address him.

'I realise you still have a bit of a trek when you leave us today, so I'd like to help. You've worked hard while you've been on board, and I think you deserve something that may lighten your burden when you disembark.'

Bryn's curiosity was twofold. What he was about to suggest and more importantly, did he know more than he was letting on?

'Bryn, I'm booking you a taxi as soon as we land. You'll get where you're going faster and in a bit of comfort. I'll pay with your share of the haul. If you need a passage back or fancy a bit of fishing, get Gregor to contact me. You'll be always welcome on board the *Carla-Marie*.'

Bryn thanked him for his generosity, feeling somewhat overwhelmed by his kind words. They both sat in silence for a while until Gabriella appeared, insisting Ruben went to bunk for at least an hour.

At the dock in Reykjavik, a taxi appeared in no time and after some fond farewells, Bryn was ready for the next stage of his journey. They drove through beating, icy rain, across the city and onto the rugged terrain of the countryside. His driver, Ari, turned out to be a pretty experienced tour guide. He filled Bryn in on the Viking history, its initial discovery in the ninth century and its eventual colonisation. He told him of its volcanic activity, causing geyser eruptions around the great island. Bryn found his deep insight fascinating but could not ignore the growing tension building at the pit of his stomach, realising what lay ahead.

As they travelled along the south-east coastline, Bryn noticed the terrain becoming more desolate and barren. The treacherous driving conditions didn't seem to bother Ari, who hadn't stopped talking since they left dock.

Bryn read through the instructions again, following landmarks guiding them on the right route. When he felt they were at their destination, he asked Ari to pull over. Stepping out of the car, he verified the location with a small map Gregor had drawn on the back of the page.

'This seems to be the place, alright,' he said to Ari while checking the lay of the land. The rain had slowed to a light shower, the sun beginning to peek through the clouds in the west.

'There's not much here apart from a couple of old geysers over on your right. Would you like me to wait?' Ari offered, demonstrating that he was slightly concerned.

'No thanks. I should be fine.'

'Well, there's a small town about a mile up ahead, if you run into trouble. Here's my card. Ring, if you need a ride.' Ari looked slightly baffled as to why someone would want to be dropped off in a place like this but knew better than to ask any questions. He had driven this fare before.

'Thanks, Ari, you've been a great help.'

With that, Bryn took off over a small ditch at the side of the road and across a dirt plain, which was mottled with hail stones. He turned and waved at Ari, ensuring he left before he continued any farther. When he was sure he was out of sight, Bryn fished deep into the pocket of his heavy winter coat and pulled his instructions from within.

He had to keep walking as a cold wind was already biting at his gloveless hands and his nose was beginning to numb.

When you reach the stretch of coast road with a steep incline on your left and flat land on your right, and a lighthouse at the far end, you need to walk toward the sea until you see a lone standing tree up ahead. Stand by that tree and wait until you can see an eruption (about ten feet) of steam nearby. Watch where you walk. Remember, it erupts every 8 minutes. Good luck Bryn.

Bryn reread the note several times as he walked, nearly tripping on some muddy, loose gravel. *Watch where you walk,* he told himself. He needed to be a bit more cautious. When he spotted the lighthouse from the car, he knew he was on the right track. Flurries of wet snow started to fall, and what little light shone from the west was already beginning to disperse. He had to hurry.

He suddenly saw the tree. It had to be the tree as there was only the one. He walked with a bit more care and attention, as he did not want to fall down this geyser before he was ready, especially if it was about to spew. Just then, he heard a slight rumbling in his otherwise silent surroundings.

A jet of what he presumed was steam ejected from somewhere up ahead. He could not believe his eyes. It seemed to have come from nowhere. Lasting only a few seconds, the geyser left a faint stench of sulphur in its wake.

So, there it is, he thought. He approached a hollow pit with a little basin of heated water alongside. Small stones circled the geyser. Bryn did not go too close as he was feeling slightly nervous, not believing what he was about to do. This was crazy and a bit too dangerous for his liking. He was not brave enough – or possibly stupid enough.

Less than a hundred yards away stood the tree. It was large enough to shelter a little from the wind, which had started to pick up. He felt he needed time to gather his thoughts, and the idea of Gabriella's tinned soup had become a most appetising distraction.

Standing under cover, sipping from the flask, he watched the geyser erupt three more times before he decided to approach again. This time he examined it more closely. He certainly couldn't see the bottom, but that was not surprising considering the time of day. He lowered his rucksack to the ground and from within he withdrew the small bottle of rum Dario had gifted him earlier. One large mouthful was all that was needed to heat his body from within, packing a punch the soup couldn't possibly compete with. Bryn winced from the sheer strength of alcohol his sip contained, but it was a welcome sensation. He returned the bottle to the bag and felt a new resolve, a mildly confident determination.

He had decided to jump after the next burst. He paid close attention to his watch so he could time it perfectly. It erupted. Two minutes, he had been told. He could do this. He had to do this. What choice did he have? It was way too late to change his mind. He had to remind himself that his father, the man who raised him and who he trusted implicitly, sent him on this journey.

One minute down, one to go. He held on tightly to his rucksack over his shoulder and prepared himself for the jump. He couldn't quite describe what was going on his mind at that specific time. It seemed to have gone blank. He checked his watch, one final time. Eight seconds. He counted backwards in his mind.

Taking a deep breath, he ran and leapt into the geyser.

CHAPTER 12

Falling into an abyss of darkness, panic gripped Bryn's body and he could not move a muscle. His eyes were closed tightly for the first few seconds, which felt like the longest time. All he knew was that he had not yet hit the ground and that seemed to some extent promising, however disturbing the outcome may become. He felt his legs kick, his arms flay. His eyes opened to reveal nothing. He was surrounded by a pure pitch-black, which concealed any hint or sign of the walls of the enclosure he entered. Looking up, he could only to see a pinprick of light from above and it was fading fast.

Panic seized him again, only this time he yelled with a voice he hardly recognised as his own. And yet, he was still falling.

Visions of his parents' faces came to him. He could see them at the farm going about their business. Then he saw Gregor's face, strong and wise, smiling, letting him know that everything would be okay. Flashes of images he barely could make sense of entered his mind, full of colour and vibrancy, masking the darkness that enveloped him. It was a bit bizarre but the fear was abating, being replaced with a sense of calm.

Suddenly from nowhere, he could see the flash of lightning strips in the distance. They were accompanied by a faint rumbling of what Bryn presumed to be thunder. *How odd,* was the only thought he could muster. Within moments, the lightning bolts seemed brighter and the rumbling more blatant. Whatever this phenomenon was, it was approaching rapidly, until the shards of light became so bright, and the thunder became so deafening that all he could do was close his eyes tightly and block his ears as much as the palms of his hands would allow. And then, he passed out.

When he came to, he returned to darkness but was aware that he was lying down with ground beneath him. He felt a thick, wet, viscous layer covering his extremities and spat several times to alleviate his mouth of this sticky substance. A dim light appeared overhead, and then another and another until he could identify one of his hands beneath a film of gel. Without a moment to gather his thoughts, jets of water hit him hard and a female voice came from an intercom system on his left, instructing him to remove his clothing. He didn't have the energy to even think at this stage, so just did as he was told, piling his garments on top of his saturated rucksack.

When the water abated, warm air blasted every drop of moisture from him and a voice again came over the intercom, this time telling him that he needed to look for a cubbyhole nearby, where he would find a fresh set of clothing. Bryn dressed in a beige kaftan, brown trousers and leather sandals, and awaited further instructions.

One of the side walls slid open and glaring light blinded Bryn for a moment. As his eyes adjusted, he could just about make out a small form standing at the doorway.

'Name, please!' it requested, in a matter-of-fact tone, with a voice that sounded more high-pitched than he had expected.

Through squinting eyes, Bryn could see that this form was that of a man, quite small, with a clipboard. There was nothing too unusual about his general appearance per se, apart from being slight in stature. However, his eyes, nose and mouth were slightly small, in proportion to his face. From where Bryn stood, it looked like the only hair on his rather large head, was a little tuft behind each ear. He wore grey overalls with a belt around his small waist.

'Name, please!' he repeated, as though Bryn may not have heard him the first time.

'Bryn... Bryn Jahr,' he replied in a quiet voice. Bryn still couldn't believe he had made it. His mind was so muddled that he was glad to have someone here – whatever he was – to prove, if anything, he was still alive. He emerged from the scant, dark room, happy that he was still in one piece and although he was a little stiff and sore, Bryn had no injuries to speak of.

'Ah, yes...' The little man referred to his clipboard. 'A new trainee. I must take you to section A.'

Without raising his head, he motioned at Bryn to follow him. Bryn hesitated for a moment, turning towards the door he came from.

'Your things will be sent over later,' he persisted, becoming impatient. 'Come on. We haven't a moment to lose.'

Bryn was adamant.

'I'll just be a second,' he said. He returned to the cubicle and retrieved the canvas-wrapped bundle sticking out of the top of his rucksack. It was a little slimy, but nothing he couldn't clean off with a bit of warm water. He could not leave that behind. Bryn followed his guide down a brightly lit tunnel, the walls of which were made of clay and garnished with metal fixtures. The little man walked a lot faster than Bryn thought his legs would have allowed. He had trouble keeping up.

Eventually, after a long trek down what seemed to be an endless corridor, they reached a door, similar to the one he came through, embedded into one side of the tunnel. His guide stopped and entered a code into a small panel alongside. They waited.

So far, not one word had been spoken since they started their journey, and Bryn was struggling to think of something to say to break the silence. But instead, he took a moment to study this creature in front of him, trying to recall what his father had said about the different tribes, and how to distinguish one from the other. In that instant, he could barely remember anything his father had spoken about. This whole experience had been too overwhelming to think straight.

A light on the panel turned green and the door slid open. Bryn was ushered forward. To his amazement, they entered through a secondary door and onto some kind of transporter. Bryn only assumed it was a transporter because there were several built-in seats, in rows of two, a control panel and concave windows at the front and back. He sat to the left of his guide who, when he occasionally lifted his head from his clipboard, had such an indifferent expression on his face. Bryn assumed that this routine was an everyday occurrence for him, and probably met new trainees regularly.

The guide looked up at Bryn, and realising how uncomfortable his neck felt in that position, pressed a button on the control panel. This action raised his seat so that he could look at him, face to face.

'That's better,' he said. 'Now,' he continued, 'before we leave, how much do you know about why you're here?'

The question took Bryn by surprise mainly because he hadn't expected this foreign-looking character to speak English so distinctly.

'I was told I'm here to try out for some sort of athletics competition called the Zhavia Shield,' he said.

'That seems accurate, according to your file.' His guide, being very official, referred again to his clipboard. 'It says here, your parents are Lars and Sanne. Is that correct?'

'Yes,' Bryn replied.

'Okay, that's interesting!'

Bryn wasn't quite sure how to react to that comment, but he was starting to feel tired so refrained from saying too much. The guide read over what he had written on his clipboard before finally putting it to one side. He now gave Bryn his full attention.

'First and foremost, my name is Tolk. I am one of the chief gatekeepers at this station. It is my role to ensure that everyone who passes through from your world does so with intention. That means that they were summoned here for a reason. The security of Zhivrah is my top priority. As you've probably been told, you are not at liberty to discuss any of your findings with anyone outside of Zhivrah. That would lead to unimaginable consequences. There is a lot here that you might not be fully accustomed to and may confuse you. Take your time getting used to your new environment. I am taking you to meet with the council and then you will go on to the training camp. Understood?'

He paused for a moment and studied Bryn's face to ascertain his comprehension. Bryn nodded.

Satisfied, he continued. 'We will be travelling in this capsule,' he said, swivelling his seat, gesturing at Bryn to survey this unusual piece of machinery closer.

Looking around, Bryn understood why it was named a capsule. It was as though someone had split a glass cylinder, affixed a piece of metal tubing through the centre, rooted a few seats to its base, polished it up and stuck a fancy control panel at either end. He was very impressed and smiled accordingly.

Tolk powered up by flicking a few switches and hitting a few buttons, one of which lit up strip-lighting in the dark tunnel that stretched out before them. Bryn suddenly became alert, forgetting how tired he was, completely focused on what might lay ahead. He was reminded of an instance in a Star Wars comic when fighter jets took off from a space station and wondered, with a little apprehension, if they were about to do something similar. Following directions from Tolk, Bryn managed to buckle up his safety belt and they started down the passageway, a lot slower than he had been expecting.

CHAPTER 13

As the journey progressed, they gathered speed but not much. Bryn could finally make out an opening at the end of the tunnel, and as they came closer, he could tell that instead of the space depiction he anticipated, they were approaching light. Not only that, Bryn became aware for the first time that instead of being propelled by some gravity-defying vehicle, they were travelling along on tracks, similar to ones used for trains back home.

Exiting the tunnel Bryn took in his surroundings, arching his neck to take in a better view. What struck him first was the sky. It was blue but had a yellow hue, slightly streaked and mildly tinted with red, pink and orange.

They had emerged onto the periphery, near the crest of the highest mountain Bryn had ever seen, the magnitude of which would have been extremely daunting if it wasn't for the most incredible landscape down below. The scene was a lush forest of green, as far as the eye could see, and spanning up the mountain range to its apex. Bryn had never witnessed so many trees and not a house in sight; just a twisted outline of a river veering off into the distance.

As the capsule trundled along, an exceptionally large bird glided past, a species Bryn had never come across before. Its head and neck were similar to a stork's and its body resembled an eagle's, but much larger. It seemed to travel with such ease. It did not take long for it to overtake them and soar on into the horizon.

'What was that?' Bryn asked in amazement.

Tolk saw what he was referring to.

'That is what we call a bird, Bryn!' he said, sniggering under his breath. Bryn realised he was making fun of him and couldn't help but laugh. He was starting to relax a bit, the first time in over a week, and probably laughed a bit more than Tolk's little joke justified, but he didn't care.

'Tolk.' Bryn wanted to tread carefully. 'Where are you from? Are you a Goytek?'

He didn't want to get too personal, but thought it was time for a few answers. Tolk looked at him for a moment, examining the baffled expression on his face.

'I was born and raised here, but my ancestors are Goyteks. I really don't know what that makes me.'

Bryn wasn't finished. 'You seem pretty familiar with our world and the language. How did that come about?'

'We were taught every custom from each world at the academy. They make up our heritage, you see. I needed to learn several languages to work at a landing station. Each landing station is made up of ten personnel and we take it in turns to act as a guide to any new visitors. We don't want to frighten anyone away with coming across too alien…' Tolk sniggered again. Bryn understood the pun and giggled along.

'Bryn,' he continued, 'you have nothing to fear here. We're a peaceful nation. Give it a few days and you'll feel right at home.'

Bryn appreciated the sentiment.

'So, what kind of bird what that?' Bryn asked, inquisitively.

'A tulcar,' Tolk replied. 'Impressive creatures, with a gentle nature. They nest along the mountain range. Is the inquisition over or can you think of any other questions you need answering before we part company?' He had been asked hundreds of questions over the years. Ordinarily, he didn't mind too much. But it was coming to the end of his shift and he was becoming tired, his patience waning.

Tolk looked at Bryn again, this time with a softer demeanour. He could see that through all of Bryn's innocence and naivety, he had a certain prudence, which could help him evolve into a wise man, someday.

Bryn was deep in thought. Finally, he asked, 'Tolk, if we're whizzing along in this capsule on the only track visible, what happens if another capsule is coming from the other direction?'

Odd question, Tolk thought, one he hadn't been asked before.

'That answer is simple. There is another track on the other side of this range. Most of our transport system is on a rail. You will see as we get closer that there is a network line, which is controlled by a satellite from the mountain above us. It operates each capsule on the track, ensuring they don't crash or come off the rail. There is a rail control hub that monitors the lines. It's been proven to be most dependable.'

'How interesting,' Bryn said. 'I have one other question I'm hoping you might be able to answer for me, Tolk.'

'Go ahead, Bryn.'

'Where are we?'

CHAPTER 14

'I can see that you have been given very little information before you travelled here, Bryn,' Tolk said, quite dismayed. 'Zhivrah,' he continued, 'is what you could call a space anomaly. It is very small and can only be travelled to through vortexes, via various portals in several galaxies. Nobody really knows why or how it exists and many have debated possibilities for centuries. It essentially comes down to belief. Many cultures have brought their faith into the equation – gods, magic, science and so on. You will have to decide for yourself. Does that answer your question?'

'I guess so,' replied Bryn, still uncertain.

He was suddenly distracted, when they rounded the final bend of the mountain, and became captivated by the sight of buildings poking out from the trees up ahead. He spotted another capsule, bigger than the one they were travelling in, crossing their distant path and soon lost in the foliage. As they approached, tracks appeared from every direction, crisscrossing and zigzagging off to some other part of this wondrous land. As they came closer, he noticed the buildings formed a sort of township, almost hidden in the dense forest. Structures stood in various sizes and shapes and from a distance they appeared to be made from clay.

As the capsule slowly came to a halt at a platform at the edge of the town, Bryn took a minute to absorb his new surroundings. There were four platforms, with tracks veering left and right, none seemingly entering the town itself. A few assorted-sized capsules were at a standstill up ahead, waiting to gather potential passengers.

Above him, he could see several half-moon bridges for pedestrians crossing the tracks and that was about it. He had trouble catching sight of anything else as trees stood in every direction, hindering his view. Tolk watched Bryn's apparent fascination with gleeful appreciation, knowing full well that this would be the start of the most extraordinary and inspiring experience he supposed Bryn would ever be exposed to.

When the capsule finally stopped, the doors hissed open and Bryn climbed out before Tolk had even time to unfasten his safety belt. The first thing he noticed was the quietude. Even the capsules came and went in silence. He had to get used to the fact that this was indeed another world and although he could assume that there may be similarities, nothing could be taken for granted and he would have to embrace this new existence entirely.

So, with fresh eyes, he took a long look at his new surroundings. Tolk joined him and followed his gaze, trying to visualise his first reaction.

'Where is everyone?' Bryn asked, spotting only a few figures afar.

'Bryn, you must remember, we are a small civilisation. This is our largest and principal town, with a residential population of just over four thousand people. As we make our way in, take a good look around but don't stare. You'll find many curious and unfamiliar sights, but you do not want the natives to misconstrue your inquisitiveness for judgement or your perceptions as critiques. Do you understand?' Tolk asked in a fatherly tone.

'Yes, Tolk,' Bryn replied, realising he had forgotten Tolk was by far the most unusual creature he had ever encountered. He had regarded his appearance with indifference as soon as they began their conversation in the mountains. He felt hopeful that he could appreciate others with the same regard.

Tolk gestured to Bryn to follow and led him toward the bridge up ahead. Bryn, feeling slightly naked without his rucksack over his shoulder, tightened his grip on his canvas package and followed his guide, subtly trying to spot a Hazuru, a Shiakana or even a Panak, hoping they wouldn't resemble anything he had seen in one of his 'Alien Invasion' magazines.

Before long, a figure approached the bridge they were crossing, from behind a row of trees. Bryn didn't want to appear obvious so directed his attention straight ahead. Only when the figure came into full view did he realise that the man he glanced at was no different from any other from his village back home. He wanted to go over to him and let him know that he was from Earth too and that he had also travelled through the portal, and wanted to ask him how he found the whole experience. However, the moment passed as the man did, completely oblivious to Bryn's presence.

Somewhat dejected, Bryn had almost forgotten that Earthians had populated this world for centuries. This man may have never set foot on his planet.

Fortunately, Tolk hadn't noticed this incident, as his eyes had barely left his clipboard since they departed the platform. He was crosschecking details he had filled in on Bryn's arrival, and rendered his business-like manner he portrayed before they engaged in conversation.

Once they crossed the bridge, a landscape opened in front of Bryn, one he could hardly begin to take in.

CHAPTER 15

At either side of them, a forest spanned into the far-reaching distance, but right in the centre, at the foot of the bridge, trees had intermingled with branches twisted and curved around each other, forming a deep tunnel-like archway, which appeared to have been masterfully pruned into shape.

The archway opened into a rectangular, cobblestoned courtyard. It had a simple but elegant water feature at its centre, which flowed into a circular stone basin underneath. Buildings edged along its perimeter. Four large, square ones at the corners – each with intricately sculpted figures embedded in their stone facades – and smaller, but equally impressive dwellings skirted the borders between them. From a distance, Bryn had mistaken these concrete buildings to be clay as the sky's reflection had given them a red tinge.

Bryn was taken aback by the masonry of each structure and felt that he could have easily stumbled into a village on the outskirts of ancient Rome. He also noticed passageways that led from the courtyard, through the centre of each row of houses and on elsewhere to the rear.

It struck Bryn how symmetrical everything in this town was. Each structure must have been perfectly planned and constructed. At the far end, he noticed stalls laden with produce. A vendor was selling fruit to a woman with a young child. An old man sat on a bench reading by the fountain and another hurried across the courtyard as if he was late for an important engagement. It was strangely quiet, even for a population of its size, and Bryn was curious to know where everyone was. He hadn't bothered to ask Tolk, as he had a more pressing question.

'Where are we going now?' Bryn asked. Tolk had barely lifted his head from the clipboard since they left the station.

'We need to go to the Embassy, where you will be registered by the Games Committee. From there, you'll be taken to the training camp. Don't worry. It's all formalities. Shouldn't take too long. It's the building at the far corner, on the right. Just give me a minute to finish up writing in your details.'

Bryn didn't mind waiting. It gave him more time to soak up his new environment. He was secretly hoping to catch sight of a Hazuru or even a Shiakana. His initial apprehension of his potential reaction had now been replaced by blatant curiosity.

However, he was out of time as Tolk had finally put away his clipboard, crossed the square, and practically been in the door of the appointed building before Bryn realised that he had left his side. He broke into a run to keep up, as he didn't want to be left behind, on his own, in a land where nothing had yet made sense.

Through the excessively large double doors of the Embassy was a small, relatively unfurnished room, except for of a row of crimson cushions, placed side by side on a vibrant, mosaic-tiled floor. The walls were a shade between white and cream. One picture hung on the wall, which faced the window, but Bryn was more fascinated that the window had actual panes of glass than what or who was depicted in the painting. It was such an ordinary entity in an otherwise extraordinary world. Another large door made of solid wood stood alongside the picture. Bryn imagined whoever they were meeting would enter through there at any moment.

Tolk told Bryn to sit on one of the cushions, which he did, awkwardly. Tolk sat on another beside him and they waited. Before Bryn could achieve a comfortable position, the door creaked slowly open and a figure beckoned them to follow before disappearing again. The figure in question was what Bryn guessed could only have been a Hazuru. From the brief glimpse, he could already tell that this character was fairly tall, but what struck him more were the large oval-shaped eyes he had shared contact with, for what must have been all of a millisecond. The whites of the eyes were the whitest of white and the pupils were huge, with a thin blue rim on the circumference. He had a slight orange tinge to his skin, with black markings down the side of his face and the back of his neck. Bryn wasn't sure if they were tattoos or part of his complexion. He nearly fell over as he was getting up, due to being completely overwhelmed, yet again. Tolk gave him a slight disapproving look before they both headed for the door. He instructed Bryn to remove his shoes before he knocked to gain entrance.

CHAPTER 16

Nothing could have prepared Bryn for what he set eyes on once he entered the room. It was a substantial space. From what he could see, there were two windows at the back and the décor, for the most part, reflected the room they had just left.

A large group of people were standing before him, at least twenty. Most were human, like him. However, several other individuals mingled among them and he was trying hard not to stare. There were Goyteks, who Bryn hardly noticed as everyone else dwarfed them, and as he had spent most of the day with Tolk, he was hardly alarmed by their presence.

The two Hazurus were a sight to behold. They stood about seven feet in height and were slender in build. Their skin had a darker complexion than the figure that greeted him at the door and both had long, pitch-black hair, tied neatly at the back. Each had similar black, patterned markings on their faces, down their necks and presumably elsewhere on their bodies. They were dressed in long green robes that fell to the ground. Their presence in the room brought an element of the majestic and an air of mysticism.

At the other end of the room, two robust figures stood, muttering away to each other in whispered voices so that no one else could hear. They must be the Shiakanas, supposed Bryn, as they resembled a cross between very large Sumo wrestlers and hairless apes. Their arms did indeed reach the floor and from what Bryn could see through their somewhat revealing attire, their hefty bodies were planted on short, stumpy legs. Unlike everyone else in the room, they seemed to be more interested in their own company than greeting the stranger who had just been delivered. They looked unkempt, though it appeared they had made a bit of an uncomfortable effort to dress for their peers.

They donned cloaks, which pretty much covered their almost naked bodies apart from a piece of loincloth hiding their nether regions. Their noses were bulbous, their eyes small and squinted and their mouths wide, virtually toothless. One was slightly taller than the other and his face appeared longer, which lengthened his features.

Bryn was surprised to see that although they were mighty creatures, their stature was smaller than he had expected. They were certainly shorter than the Hazurus and not much taller than he was.

An older gentleman stepped forward. He must have been in his late sixties, wearing a white linen robe and matching trousers, with a wine-coloured scarf tied around his waist. His hair was silver, and he was clean-shaven.

'Tolk! You can leave us now. I'll take your report,' he said, with a voice of authority.

'Yes, sir!' Tolk gave Bryn an encouraging look followed by a farewell gesture before disappearing through the door from which they came.

'So, I see you're here for the trials!'

The silver-haired man was addressing Bryn, stating a fact rather than asking a question. Everyone else in the room took a step back and one by one, sat cross-legged on the floor, waiting for his response. Bryn felt as though he was expected to perform in front of this abated assembly and was fearful they might judge him as weak if he addressed them submissively.

Putting on a brave face Bryn stood with his head held high and maintaining eye contact with the only man left standing in the room, he addressed him.

'I am here to compete in the Warrior Games for The Zhavia Shield.'

The silver-haired man was not moved by his confidence but some of the others exchanged glances at his tone. Bryn thought he might have been slightly overzealous but sustained his poise to show that he was determined.

'Sit down then,' the silver-haired man said, consulting the notes Tolk had left.

He paced the room for a moment before joining Bryn on the floor and putting the notes on his lap. They were face to face, no more than two feet apart, with everyone else behind eager to see what was to happen next.

'You are here to register for the trials, as a trainee. You merely hope to compete in the Games. We are the Games Committee, and my name is Samuel.'

Bryn felt Samuel was snidely putting his point across and chose to ignore the comment.

'We will just ask you a few questions before someone will take you to the camp where you can retire for the evening. We appreciate that you have travelled quite a distance to reach us and you must be tired.'

Samuel picked up the clipboard and ran a finger down the first page.

'I see here that both your parents have competed in the tournament in the past.'

'My father has, but my mother has never participated,' Bryn said, slightly puzzled as to why Tolk had gotten that piece of information incorrect. He seemed so proficient.

'Bryn, I don't know what your parents have told you, but I can assure you that both have competed. And may I add, one of them did rather well.'

'You must be mistaken. The information on your notes is inaccurate.' Bryn was bewildered.

'No, I can state categorically that I am not mistaken! I know your father well and I distinctly remember your mother's attendance!' Samuel said.

Murmuring and muffled voices came from the gathering behind. Samuel silenced it by raising his arm just above his head.

Bryn could not fathom what he had just heard and shook his head in disbelief.

Samuel suddenly turned from Bryn and addressed the assembly.

'We are going to suspend registration proceedings until tomorrow. It is getting late.' He then turned to Bryn and said, 'I will call in on you in the morning when we can discuss this further.' Standing up, he spoke again to the congregation. 'Meeting adjourned!'

CHAPTER 17

Everyone shuffled out of the room leaving Bryn alone with his thoughts. He had more or less come to terms with his father competing in such an elaborate contest, but it was ludicrous to think that his mother had contended as well. It must be a mistake or maybe it could be an elaborate test of some kind. Bryn just couldn't get his head around such a notion. Finally, he pulled himself together and headed through the door. He smacked right into the chest of a Hazuru.

'I'm really sorry,' he said, noticing how the Hazuru barely budged from the impact. Bryn excused himself and sidestepped to his right to manoeuvre out of the way. The Hazuru turned and faced him.

'I am your escort,' the Hazuru remarked. His voice was slow and monotone.

Bryn didn't say a word as he followed him out of the Embassy and across the courtyard. They continued through one of the alleys between the tall, solid buildings and on to the woodland behind. Bryn had hardly shifted his gaze from the ground below, lost in Samuel's words. When he finally raised his head, he couldn't help but arch his neck to look at the trees above. They were colossal, reaching far into the clouds. Not only that, but there seemed to be small lodgings scattered amongst the large, hefty branches.

He stopped for a moment to take in his view and through the corner of one eye, he spotted something, which was certainly far from ordinary. A small, glass escalator scaled up one of the trees, ascending to one of the many dwellings at its crown.

Suddenly realising the Hazuru was almost out of view, he chased after him, wondering how many more surprises lay ahead and whether he would ever get used to such a strange, yet inviting world.

The woodland seemed to carry on for miles, although as far as Bryn could make out none of the trees outside the periphery of the town were inhabited. The Hazuru had not uttered one word since they left the Embassy and that suited Bryn fine as he wasn't in the humour for conversation.

They had been trekking for over twenty minutes when Bryn noticed a clearing up ahead. He advanced on the Hazuru, not wanting to appear to be trailing behind.

Bryn had to readjust his eyes to the bright surroundings, devoid of trees, as they left the forest. He hadn't noticed how dark the woodland had been until then. The vivid sky lit up a landscape of luscious grassland, which glimmered several colourful shades reflected from above. A terracotta pathway led to an exceptionally long wooden border fence that rose over twelve feet high. Right at its centre stood a gate, also made of wood. It stretched the height of the fence and the width of a small house.

At the gate, the Hazuru waved his hand at a small scanner positioned at its centre. Bryn later found out it had a motion-sensitive detector, which photographed, recorded and identified each visitor entering the camp. It was useful as a security tool and as a logbook, recording people's comings and goings, alerting guardians if their pupils hadn't returned when they were supposed to.

As Bryn waited for the large gates to open, he was slightly surprised that instead of having the flamboyant entrance he was expecting, a door, not much taller than him, slid open. The Hazuru, who went in first, had to stoop to get through. Bryn followed suit, bracing himself for what lay beyond.

CHAPTER 18

The first sight Bryn witnessed as he entered the camp was small gatherings of Earthians, Hazurus and Goyteks chatting amongst each other, most with a certain air of familiarity. Everyone wore similar attire with only slight variations.

At the far end, a small contingent of Shiakanas congregated, occasionally glancing at the others, probably sizing up the competition.

It would take Bryn a few days to realise that the training camp consisted of four two-tiered, stone-faced dormitories, which were situated along one side of the cobblestoned courtyard, housing hopeful contenders, separated according to their tribal allegiance. There were four restricted meeting rooms, all segregated so that teams could discuss tactics without fear of being overheard. Behind each dormitory, there were divided training grounds, surrounded by large walls, so that practice wouldn't be interrupted or spied on. At the other side of the courtyard was one large canteen, where people could relax and mingle with competing contestants. There was also a small housing unit for instructors. There was another large gate, similar to the one they entered, at the back. Only instructors and guardians were allowed through there. It was deemed highly restrictive, which generated plenty of curiosity amongst the trainees.

The Hazuru guiding Bryn headed straight for the second dormitory, rapped on the door and walked straight through. Another door stood at the end of a short hallway, which opened as they approached. A fairly tubby, middle-aged lady introduced herself as Tilly, the guardian of the house. She greeted them in a large white apron with her hair tied up in a scarf.

'You must be young Bryn! Been expecting you. That'll be all,

Sutat!' she boomed as she dismissed the Hazuru.

Bryn realised she was American, probably from the south. She had a compassionate face and a smile that lit up her eyes. Bryn instantly liked her.

'That guy has barely a word of English. You were probably wonderin' why he seemed so withdrawn,' she said, as she scanned Bryn from head to toe. 'You've got a fine build and your father's eyes. I couldn't mistake those,' she said, returning through the door she had come through, beckoning Bryn to follow.

'You knew my father?' he queried, as he followed.

'Your father? Oh, yes! I knew your father. Mothered him as if he was my own. He will be missed. How is he and how's your mother? I haven't seen her in the longest time.'

Bryn, sensing an opportunity, wondered if he could ask Tilly the question that had been preying on his mind since he left the Embassy. They entered a small room, furnished with a small bed, an armchair and a desk with all of Tilly's trinkets. A large rug covered a polished wooden floor. A small cross was attached to a wall over her bedside and a framed photograph of family members hung by a small, curtain-drawn window. A candlelit lamp sat on a little bedside table, which gave the room a warm, cosy glow.

'Is it true? Did my mother really compete in the games?'

'Did she not tell you? Oh dear! Put my foot firmly in that one.'

She went to Bryn, cupped his face in her hands as if she had known him all his life.

'My dear boy! Your mother was, and probably is, a very fine lady. I haven't seen her since she and your father got married.' She pulled away, sensing Bryn's discomfort. 'They were both so young at the time. Met here, in fact. She only competed once but my lord, all the men adored her. Such a graceful creature. Disappeared after the first competition. Not really sure what happened. I guessed she decided to settle down. You shouldn't be disappointed with her, Bryn. She probably had her reasoning for not telling you.'

She lightened her tone and changed the topic of conversation. Bryn felt she was hiding something but realised it probably wasn't the right time to pursue the matter.

'Let me show you to your room and you can pack away your bits. You might even fancy something to eat. They've started serving dinner in the canteen and the grub's not bad. Then, I recommend an early night. How does that sound?'

It just dawned on Bryn how famished he was. He couldn't remember the last time he had eaten. It must have been back on the trawler, or was it by the geyser? How long ago was that? All he knew was that he needed food.

'That sounds like a good idea, Tilly.' He was finding it hard to string a thought together at this stage, so resigned himself to follow Tilly's recommendations and to start the following morning afresh.

She led him down a long passageway away from her room, stopping at the third door on his left. They passed several trainees en route, who greeted her with a broad smile, standing out of the way to let her pass. Picking a key out of a hefty bundle, she unlocked the door and allowed Bryn to step in ahead of her.

'This will be your room. You will be sharing it with another boy around your own age. I try to pair people up with others who may share similar experiences. It's also his first trial. I hope you'll both become good friends. Should be arriving sometime tomorrow.'

Tilly was still standing at the door as Bryn examined the sparse room. It had two simple cot beds with side tables and a small glass-paned window separating them. There was a chest of drawers by the door with two lamps on top. The day hadn't gotten any darker so Bryn thought he might not have to use them for a while.

Before Tilly made to leave, she called out, 'If you need anything, I'll just be down the hall.'

She gave him a lingering smile before she closed the door behind her. Bryn could hear her footsteps fading in the distance. That was when he noticed his rucksack at the base of one of the beds. There was a note attached to the top of it.

No food or beverage items may be brought in from outside worlds. They contain bacteria that may be harmful to Zhivrah and its people. Therefore, they have been incinerated. We apologise for any inconvenience.
The Council

Bryn almost laughed. He didn't know why he found the note amusing. He dug into his bag. There was a change of clothes and the clothes he had been wearing when he arrived, which had been cleaned and pressed. His mother had also packed away a photograph in the front pocket. He stared at it for a time.

It was taken recently back at the farm. Bryn remembered the day well as his father had bought his mother a camera for her birthday. It had a timer on it that she wanted to try out. So, she lined the three of them up against the front of the house and placed the camera on a bale of hay she had fetched from the barn. After directing Bryn and his father to make cheesy smiles, she set the timer and ran back to be in the frame. After several attempts, she finally claimed she had a result. Bryn, and even his father, couldn't help laughing at her efforts. She had been so animated trying to get the camera to behave. When she did, she looked so full of pride, so happy with the outcome that she almost did a triumphant dance.

He touched their faces, realising how he missed them desperately. He put the photograph to his chest, lay down on the bed and hugged it close. The idea of going to the canteen felt like too much of an effort, though he was still famished. Within moments he fell asleep and dreamt of his parents, but their faces became distorted. He was barely able to make out their features. They were almost unrecognisable, drifting into a blur in the background.

CHAPTER 19

Soft tapping on the door woke Bryn from a deep slumber. Tilly entered the room.

'Good mornin', Bryn. I thought you might like some tea.'

With that, she offered him a hot steaming mug. He sat up and gratefully accepted it. As he absorbed the sweet berry infusion, he thought there was no better way to start a brand-new day. The weariness and strain of the day before's tumultuous excursion had lifted and he was feeling fresh and ready for what lay ahead.

'You'll be glad to know, we had three more check-ins! Arrived last night. They're regulars. Been here quite a few times before,' Tilly said as she watched Bryn relish his cup of tea.

'Have any of them ever qualified?' Bryn asked.

'Not yet, but I admire their tenacity. It's a difficult training regime, never mind the qualifying games. It must be tough to go through all that and have to return without participating in the final tournament. And even if they do, they can tell no one about it when they go home. I don't know how y'all do it.'

Bryn knew this was Tilly's way of telling him not to get his hopes up. He appreciated her sentiment.

'Get yourself up and head on over to the canteen. You'll get a chance to meet some of the others,' Tilly said. 'By the way,' she continued, as she headed for the door, 'I hear your roommate has just landed. Should be here this afternoon.'

Bryn got dressed quickly and went out in search of the canteen at the other end of the courtyard. Once through the doors, he was surprised to find a hub of excitement and revelry in the large dining area. Several small groups of trainees were huddled together, chatting and laughing aloud. However, as he looked around the canteen, he noticed a few older diners sitting alone, playing with their food, lost in their thoughts. Bryn wondered if any of them had ever made the grade, or maybe they were not trainees at all. Putting his thoughts to one side, he made his way to a long serving counter where an array of food was displayed, catering for everyone's tastes.

There was a table of exotic fruit and a choice of bread and meats, which seemed pretty similar to what he was used to back home. There were also a number of hot cereals and drinks to choose from. It all looked very appetising.

Bryn filled his tray with a medley of breakfast offerings and sat by himself at a table near the window. He let his eyes drift around the room at the diverse and bizarre assortment of people enjoying their first meal of the day. Every tribe, apart from the Shiakanas, who were busy plotting at the far end of the room, seemed to mingle like old friends. The Hazurus stood out, as most were exceptionally tall. They also appeared to be less animated and conversational than their counterparts. The Goyteks never seemed to stand in one place for very long, fidgeting and dancing on the spot when they did. Even though the Earthians were less animated, they seemed to do most of the talking – Bryn heard a mixed culture of accents.

He was positive everyone in the room had been somewhat acquainted with their peers, as they spoke to each other like old friends and appeared very at ease in their surroundings.

So engrossed was he in this exhibition of camaraderie, Bryn failed to notice the figure approaching from behind.

'I think we need to talk,' said Samuel, as he tapped him on the shoulder.

CHAPTER 20

Meanwhile, at the Landing Station, Tolk busied himself for the imminent transferral of one of the latest recruits. He had been in his little office when his pager beeped, alerting him that someone had entered the vortex and was en route. Through his monitor, he saw the standard flashing of lights from the arrival suite indicating that someone was about to land. From the dazed expression on the face of the traveller, Tolk knew it was a first timer, so he headed to the suite entrance, clipboard in hand and paced the width of the door frame, occasionally glancing at the list of questions he was about to ask.

When the door slid open, a tall, tanned and extremely blond-haired young man greeted him with a brimming smile.

'Don't tell me… You're a gatekeeper. A Goytek, right? That was some ride, back there. Wasn't expecting to feel so nauseous. I'm okay now. Frasier, Frasier Mullhoney.' Frasier put his hand out to greet Tolk, but Tolk didn't like to be touched, so kept his hands firmly by his sides.

He was immediately aggrieved by this man's gregarious nature and knew he was going to be a talker. The journey ahead was going to be a long and painful one.

By the time they arrived at the station, Tolk learned that Frasier Mullhoney was raised near Melbourne, Australia; his only merit was that his great-grandfather had once qualified to compete in the tournament, and in spite of his family's best efforts they had since failed to produce a warrior of that standard. Frasier told Tolk that he was here to do just that. He was not just here to qualify but hoped to lead his team to victory.

Following in-depth and endless probing, enquiries and unwanted small-talk, Tolk found any excuse not to engage Frasier in conversation, even resorting to feigning the need for complete silence to concentrate on driving the capsule.

At the Embassy, Tolk noticed that Samuel was missing. Someone informed him that he was running late as he was held up at the training camp. The registration was to go ahead without him.

Frasier acted cool and confident but there was a little bead of sweat running down his forehead and a little thumb twitch gave his nerves away. He had rehearsed this interview several times with his father and wanted it to be word perfect. He had been told that this process was just as important as the trials themselves. The committee members not only listened to the interview, but they also watched for weaknesses that may not be so obvious.

His father said that they had specially trained delegates who were able to look beyond the questions and answers, deep into the mind and what it revealed. The interview did not go well. He spoke too fast, was asked questions he wasn't prepared for, which caused him to ramble on about irrelevant subjects. He could see the council were not impressed. They looked disinterested and even started talking amongst themselves. His father would have been disappointed. Frasier was the youngest of four boys and his three older siblings had failed to qualify. He was told that if he didn't make the grade, his father would discontinue the family's birthright to compete.

By the time he left with Sutat, he was downtrodden and spent most of his journey through the forest kicking stones and sticks as he shuffled along, taking absolutely no notice of his walking companion or where they were going.

As he continued his trek through the woodland, he had time to mull over the situation. All was not lost. The training hadn't even begun so there was no point brooding about the situation.

He felt a glimmer of hope, which cultivated a little smile and encouraged him to look up and even swing his arms a little as he hurried to catch up with a very impatient-looking Hazuru standing in the distance.

At the gates, Frasier regarded the scanning machine as 'awesome' and the compound was 'very Gladiator.' He hadn't even noticed Sutat's limited ability to comprehend what he was saying. By the time they reached the dormitory, he knew he was back in form. He had just experienced a temporary glitch, a little chink in his armour. No need to panic, just yet.

After meeting with the delightful Tilly, he was escorted to his room, which he was told he'd be sharing with another recruit. As he unpacked his bag, Tilly presented him with a cup of warm herbal tea and told him that when he was finished he would find his roommate, Bryn, in the canteen. After savouring every drop, Frasier decided that he might as well spend the rest of his first day in this very strange world, enjoying it. There was plenty of time for devising a victory plan, tomorrow.

CHAPTER 21

Back in the canteen, Samuel had just left Bryn with a hell of a lot to think about. He had been very honest about how he felt about Bryn's father's foolish decision to retire early. He could not have made it more apparent how disappointed he was that such a prominent warrior would make such an unwise choice to cut himself off in his prime. There was also an obvious sense of bafflement surrounding Bryn's ignorance of his own father's palpable success.

It felt to Bryn that Samuel was looking for answers that he was hardly in the position to give. He was almost insinuating that Bryn should return home to retrieve him. The whole conversation left Bryn with a slight taste of guilt and shame; not that he had done anything wrong. His mere presence was enough to frustrate this old man.

When Bryn finally got around to talking about his mother, Samuel mentioned how she had partaken in trials once or twice and had competed alongside his father on one occasion. That was all he had to say about her. As he stared at Bryn with a hint of supplication in his eyes, Bryn was unsure of what to do next.

Surely retiring early had been his father's decision to make. On the other hand, was it? The handing down of the entitlement to participate in this esteemed tournament was an age-old family tradition. Maybe his father had not been ready to surrender this opportunity for greatness but did it out of a sense of duty. Nevertheless, he genuinely seemed so excited for Bryn.

Samuel got up from his chair knowing he'd said all that he could to convince the son of the celebrated Lars Jahr to reconsider his participation for a few years. The rightful contender could bring their team to victory.

When Bryn eventually heard this impending request, he wasn't at all surprised. As crestfallen as he was, he still managed to tell Samuel that he would think about it. He just needed a little time. He stood up. Samuel shook his hand and smiled profusely.

'Bryn, you know you'll be doing the right thing. Just go back home and tell him that you never jumped. He'd understand.'

When Samuel left, Bryn began to wish he hadn't come here at all. He had become completely and utterly absorbed in this crazy expedition. What was he to do if he had to leave it all behind? He might have been better off oblivious to this world, travelling on his own instead.

He let his head fall into his hands, to help carry the burden of his heavy mind.

Frasier recognised Bryn from the description Tilly had given him. It helped that there was only a handful of people left in the canteen. He wanted to be certain before he introduced himself.

Bryn was startled by the unexpected table guest, who leant in close, as if inspecting, from the chair across from him. Lost in a world of his own, the last thing he needed was the gawping expression of a stranger, especially when his nose was less than a foot away from his own.

'You must be Bryn. I'm Frasier. Frasier Mullhoney. Very pleased to meet you!' the stranger said, in a boisterous manner. He held out his hand to formalise the introduction. After a slight pause, Bryn accepted it.

'I'm sorry, Frasier. I'm just not really in the mood for company right now.'

Bryn ran his hand through his hair and began playing with the leftover food on his plate. Frasier ignored Bryn's attempt at shunning him away and sat on a chair, facing him.

'I reckon we've both had a really long morning. Come on! Talk to your roommate. We're gonna be spending a whole heap of time together. If it helps, we can compare. I'm guessing my disastrous morning beats yours.'

Bryn looked at Frasier's attempt to encourage him with facial expressions. His eyes begged for his company and his grin was cheesy and boyish. His teeth sparkled, pristine white, contrasting his tanned features but almost on par with his sun-bleached hair.

'Trouble is, Frasier, I might not be here for much longer. Looks like we may not be roommates after all.' With that realisation, Bryn stood up and made his way out of the canteen before Frasier had a chance to get out of his chair.

CHAPTER 22

Just before lunch, an assembly was called. Representatives and hopefuls from each of the four teams gathered on the courtyard, awaiting Samuel and other members of the council to deliver a welcome speech.

Order was instructed and silence fell on the large crowd. Small devices were handed out and instructed to be placed in each ear. They were used for instant translation, so that everyone heard the same words, in the same context. The rules and regulations were to be delivered by the council of the Zhavia Shield. There was to be no favouritism. For they were judge and jury.

Bryn stood near the raised wooden staging area. He was eager to hear how the games were to be played in spite of his conversation with Samuel and the uncertainty he felt. There was a hushed air of excitement and expectancy across the large group.

Samuel moved to the centre of the platform.

'Welcome, athletes,' he began. Bryn noticed a couple of Hazurus adjusting their earpieces. 'It has been nearly two long years since our last competition. We are in the process of narrowing our search to find this year's finalists. It is, as usual, a difficult exercise, as rejection is not easy to accept. You are all here as you may have shown promise and strength. Some of you have competed or may have been through the training before. As you know, that means nothing. Each competition is different. There can be no expectations. For those who have never partaken, it can be a daunting experience. Listen to your trainers and advisors. They can recognise your weaknesses and discover your strengths. Fair play and respect for your team players is essential. Your head trainer will be looking for four talented players who would work well together, four segments of a whole. This is not a place for self-fulfilment.'

Samuel paused for a moment to scan the crowd, taking his time to look each competitor in the eye. He wanted to captivate his audience. He wanted his words to be set deep into the mind of each individual he addressed.

'Every two years we organise these games with one simple objective. Each team must try to reach the Shield before the other teams. Simple idea, really. This year we have added a new dimension. I will now pass you over to Ganesh, our Goytek representative, who will explain this new development.'

Samuel stepped back and the small figure of Ganesh came forward. A voice in the earpiece Bryn was wearing instructed him to change its settings. Bryn complied and then refocused his attention back to the stage.

Ganesh cleared his throat and spoke loud and clear, in his native tongue.

'Competitors.' The translating device echoed his intentions. 'I welcome you to our training camp, ahead of our main event. This year we have devised a new element, which will prove both exciting and challenging. I would like to draw your attention to the gate at the far end of the courtyard.'

Everyone turned as instructed. The gates opened and there was a pause to exaggerate the moment of expectation.

The sound of heavy footsteps reverberated in the courtyard, the resonance escalating as whatever was approaching drew near. Everyone shuffled and craned their necks in anticipation of what was to come.

First to enter through the gate was a herd that appeared similar to raptors of the dinosaur era, but they were of a metallic shell and dark purple colour. All eight were very fast and bore razor-sharp teeth. They stopped and gathered to one side of the open gate, snarling and hissing at the audience. The trainees surged like a wave towards the stage, some with their arms out to protect others or themselves, most looking for their closest door to a sanctuary.

Ganesh's voice called for calm.

Next, two large, ogre-like figures emerged. They bore an uglier and more sinister appearance than those depicted in fairy tales. Their faces and gestures portrayed aggression to an almost vengeful nature, bearing large, mallet-like weapons. They, too, stood to one side of the gate. The crowd could not help but feel nervous at the sight and growling sounds emanating from these ferocious beasts. This parade of formidable creatures was nothing in comparison to what was yet to come. For the footsteps that were heard approaching from afar had now become almost deafening. There was a sense of impending doom and chaos. Bryn could hardly take a breath for fear had taken every muscle from his control.

The large gate and walls did little to conceal the approach. Glimpses of part of a head, or body, or something could be seen before it entered the courtyard. And when it did, there was an audible, collective gasp. Before them, stood a giant. Its face was contorted, with large pointed teeth. Spiralled horns protruded from where its ears should be. The giant's spine curved so it hunched but that didn't take from its sheer enormity. Long, sharp talons made its hands appear larger than they were. Greeting the crowd, it let out a piercing scream, which made everyone recoil even more.

Again, Ganesh called for calm. Then he addressed the creatures, commanding them to be still. They did, pacing the ground under them, eager to attack.

Bryn was almost overwhelmed with fear and oddly enough, excitement.

Eventually, Ganesh managed to coax the attention back toward the stage, though it took a while.

'Don't be afraid. They are completely under control.'

When he was sure he had each head turned in his direction, he spoke again.

'I need a volunteer, someone with weapons training.'

There was an audible reaction of disbelief. After a short pause, an arm went up from behind. Someone shuffled through the crowd and approached the stage.

Frasier, who was a few minutes late for assembly, edged closer to Bryn.

'I think that is Moses, the South African. He is a legend. He is well over fifty with no kids to pass his honorary role to, so he keeps coming back. He has qualified five times and can still outrun an ostrich.'

Frasier was in awe.

Moses climbed onto the stage and Ganesh asked him to choose a weapon from a selection by the backdrop. He opted for a broad sword.

Ganesh asked for more volunteers. It took some time before about a dozen more warriors, from the four tribes, stepped forward. Each wielding a weapon, they awaited further instruction.

'Our volunteers will now fight these creations, to give us a demonstration.'

Moses was running near the back of the audience before the others summoned the nerve to follow. He went straight for the most vicious opponent, the giant.

On cue, the large, menacing figure came to life once more and focused its attention on him. To see Moses attack was incredible. He evaded every strike, almost predicting every move. He would then effortlessly swing his weapon, given any opportunity, at a creature who must have been about five times his size. He was a master fighter and Bryn was awestruck. The other warriors took on the robot raptors and the ogre-like monsters. A great battle ensued but it wasn't long before it inflicted its first casualty. One of the raptors bore its jawbone down on an arm of one of the Hazurus. The Hazuru fought on, killing the raptor, moving onto another. He seemed to have lost the movement of the afflicted arm in the injury, but continued, using his other more than capable one. One raptor sensed his incapacitation and realising his weakness, went for the kill shot, straight for his head. Without any visible injury, the Hazuru dropped to the ground. A Goytek was next to fall by the mallet of one of the ogres but the other ogre was defeated by a Shiakana and a Hazuru working together. They were both attacked by the remaining raptors who had formed a pack to outsmart them. They, too, fell to the ground.

Moses battled on. He had removed one hand from the ferocious beast and was climbing onto its head when its other hand swatted at him, throwing him from his position. The giant huffed and snorted with rage but that didn't deter Moses from his mission. He fought on, as did the remaining warriors. Most of them attacked their foes in pairs, but not Moses. It was a spectacle and he was centre-stage. For the second time, he climbed the monstrous torso, this time making it to his target. Holding on to one of the large horns, the giant's head shaking violently, he lodged his sword into the base of its thick neck, before dismounting onto the ground below. The beast staggered, trying to reach for the embedded sword with its one remaining hand. This effort only lasted second before it succumbed and fell with a large thud, raising a cloud of dust in its wake.

The crowd stood in disbelief. Bryn was in a state of shock. The remaining creatures retreated on Ganesh's command, standing in one spot, almost motionless. Some people started to approach to see if there was anything that could be done to save those volunteers who fell in battle.

Bryn stood alongside Frasier, neither knowing what to say or do. For a moment, even their thoughts stood still. Chatter came from the back of the audience. More people approached the unfortunate casualties. Ganesh called for order. He was being ignored. This disorder was sure to be expected. He called for order again. It was no use. Even Bryn was not going to be distracted from what had just happened.

Suddenly a roar came from the stage, which grabbed everyone's attention. It was a Shiakana. He silenced himself once he had gotten the attention of the crowd, and Ganesh stepped forth again.

'I would like our volunteers to come forward.'

On command, the six volunteers slowly got to their feet from where they had fallen and approached the stage. The group of warriors returned their weapons and returned to the flabbergasted crowd. It was the greatest magic trick Bryn had ever seen. He wanted to applaud.

After a moment of stunned silence, the crowd erupted into an array of excitement and approval. The council congratulated Ganesh on such a spectacular display of modern innovation. After a time, Ganesh once again brought the courtyard to order, this time relatively quickly.

'Competitors!' The crowd hushed. 'What you have seen today has been under development for many years. The creatures you have just witnessed are a combination of holographic imagery and complicated nano-robotic technology, far beyond anything ever produced before. The subjects used carry mass, in other words, they can be used as solid units, as and when we desire. We are in full control of every action they take. When they strike, the holographic imagery over-rides the force of the impact but will leave an anaesthetic substance on the area affected. A quantity of anaesthesia is released, depending on how successful their strike is, or if several strikes have been inflicted, the casualty is temporarily paralysed and rendered unconscious for a short time. For the sake of the demonstration, we kept the dose to its lowest strength. On the field, expect to lose consciousness for several hours. This contender is then deemed out of the game.'

Ganesh continued to explain how safe the use of these holographic forms was. There was no risk of permanent paralysis or injury. Any strikes delivered to the creatures would be perceived as real.

'Let me conclude my demonstration by saying that this is just a taste of what we have planned. This is going to be an exciting year for the Zhavia Shield.'

CHAPTER 23

After the crowd dispersed, Frasier found Bryn in their room packing his belongings. Bryn didn't look up when he walked in. He had made up his mind. How could he remain here, when he knew he wasn't wanted? If he stayed any longer, he would only find it harder to leave.

'What's going on, Bryn? Why are you moving out? Look, I know I can be a bit full-on, but…'

Frasier just rambled on.

Bryn was barely listening. He had almost packed everything when he noticed that the photograph he had slept with, was still under his pillow. He fished it out, stared at it for a moment and found himself slowing lowering himself, to sit on the edge of the bed.

'My father would have made an excellent soldier. Loyal, commanding, strong. It seems he was pretty popular around here. I can't compete with that. They reckon he was too young to retire.'

Although they had only just met, Bryn felt he had little choice but to confide in Frasier, so he told him what Samuel had said, how he should go home and let his father compete instead. When he was through, Frasier regarded him for a moment.

'Bryn, you don't know me from Adam, but you also don't know this Samuel bloke.'

He sat down beside him.

'I guess you need to figure out what your father was feeling when he asked you to become a part of this,' he continued. 'Did he really want to come back? Did he look like he was about to regret sending you here? Bryn, you don't want to resent going home when your father could be disappointed to see you. You could have this all wrong. Now, unpack your things as you're certainly not leaving today. It's my first day here and I feel a little exploring is in order!'

Bryn knew Frasier was right. There was no need to make a decision straight away. Another day wouldn't hurt. The training didn't officially start for another few days. All he had to do was go back to Iceland and make a phone call. He had plenty of time to do that.

Outside, a scuffle had broken out in the courtyard. A Goytek was having an intense argument with an oversized Shiakana in a language both Bryn and Frasier could not understand. The Goytek started to shout, hands flailing, head shaking and in response the Shiakana picked him up, walked to the fountain, and sat him in the basin of water. It was the perfect piece of visual comedy the two young men needed to snap them out of their pensive moods. After a moment of quiet, self-indulgent laughter, they went to the fountain to help the drenched, sulking Goytek out of its centre.

'Thank you,' the Goytek said meekly. 'I could have taken him on, you know. I'm stronger than I look.' Bryn and Frasier were not convinced.

'He could have pulverised you with his baby finger,' Frasier said.

'Or, had you for lunch,' Bryn continued. 'What were you thinking?'

The Goytek looked defeated. 'Those Shiakanas think they can get away with anything just because they're big. It's not right, you know! We're smarter and faster. Most of them live in caves! Did you know that? They have the nerve to think they can bully their way around here. Well, I'm not standing for it any longer and I'm going to report him.' He turned to leave.

'Could you tell us what that particular Shiakana did to offend you so much?' Frasier asked.

'That oaf ate the last of the wet wheat. He came up from his table for second helpings and jumped ahead of me at the counter. I have a good mind to… and, I'm starving.'

'Why didn't you have something else?' Frasier continued.

'I'm a Goytek,' he replied, as a matter of fact. 'We have a restricted diet,' he explained before he walked away.

'What strange creatures,' Frasier remarked when he was out of listening range.

'They're not that bad. Did you meet Tolk? He was all right.'

'He didn't like me so much. Must say I didn't help myself by being so full of it,' Frasier said with a hint of regret.

'Never mind. Come on, we should have a look around. They might have a map we could borrow from someone. We should have a look by the entrance gate. I thought I spotted an office of some sort there yesterday.'

A small wooden shack stood to the right of the entrance gate. Inside, a Hazuru was busy organising shelves of paraphernalia.

'What do you want?' the Hazuru asked in the same monotoned, robotic voice Sutat had used when he was introducing himself as Bryn's escort at the Embassy.

'A map? Would you have a map of the area we could use?' Bryn asked, avoiding eye contact as he still found the mere appearance of these beings remarkable and almost overpowering.

'I have a map but you need a vehicle to help cover ground. I will see if I have something that you can use. Please wait here.'

The large Hazuru made his way out of the office, which seemed too small to contain his lofty stature, returning shortly to inform the young men that he had just what they needed, outside.

When they peered through the door Frasier's face lit up. He walked around the vehicle examining it in closer detail. Bryn stood back in awe. They couldn't believe their luck.

'It's like a hovering jet ski. How cool is that?' Frasier commented.

'This vehicle is propelled by hydraulics, enabling it to free-move without the use of a carrier system. I think you will find it useful,' the Hazuru informed them.

Bryn and Frasier spent a few minutes studying the map. The area was larger than Bryn had expected, but not difficult to navigate. The terrain to the north seemed mountainous, with parts labelled as having limited access. Bryn was curious but not enough to distract him from today's adventure.

'I'm driving,' Frasier announced, while Bryn was still concentrating on the layout of the map, not giving him a chance to argue. Bryn didn't mind too much. After a quick demonstration on its use, they were ready to set off on their journey. After a few false starts, they were outside the gates, driving alongside the seemingly endless wall. The more confident Frasier became, the faster he drove. Although Bryn said nothing, he was visibly relieved when they eventually reached the wall's extremity, where Frasier slowed almost to a halt.

'That's the longest wall I've ever seen. It must stretch for miles,' Bryn remarked.

Looking around the corner, they saw that the wall continued ahead of them, as far as the eye could see. Frasier pulled out the map from his pocket, taking a moment to study it.

'I know where we need to go.'

CHAPTER 24

They had travelled for almost an hour west of the compound through lush forest, veering around trees and scrub, rarely slowing down. Frasier was in his element and Bryn was becoming more tolerant of his driving skills. Finally, Frasier decelerated, surveyed the area and consulted his map to check if they were close to their destination. They could both hear a distant rumbling and although Bryn was completely oblivious to what they were listening to, Frasier concluded the sound was confirmation that they were getting close.

They travelled toward the resounding din slowly and purposefully, until it grew so loud Bryn was convinced they had stumbled upon some sort of volcanic or glacial eruption. He wasn't too far off the mark.

Continuing on foot, Bryn was reminded of the lightning storm he experienced in the vortex, the thunder so deafening that he eventually passed out. As he cleared the last of the trees blocking his view, Bryn realised he had relatively little to fear.

The two of them were standing on a perch overlooking the most magnificent and ferocious waterfall they could ever have imagined. Above them the water fell at speed, from a height Bryn was barely able to see. Below, there was a large lake with small tributaries and rivulets leading away from the core, like a splayed spider. Near the top, large birds flew close to the spray hoping to catch any fish that may have been carried into the stream. They were less than fifty feet from the base, which explained the deafening, explosive resonance.

With the help of a few hand signals, they decided to climb down to explore the foundation. Grabbing anything they could get hold of, they gradually made it down the rock face, making sure not to get too near the gushing water. Apart from where the water fell, the rest of the lake appeared to be quite peaceful. Bryn was surprised. They carried on along one of its tributaries leading them to where they could hear themselves speak. It led to a large pond.

'Fancy a swim?' Frasier asked Bryn.

It was as though Bryn could read his mind. They both stripped down to their underwear and plunged into the inviting water, emerging re-energised from its depths.

'What an amazing find. If you're trying to get me to stay, you're doing a rather good job,' Bryn told Frasier.

'How could you even consider leaving now?' Frasier asked and without waiting for an answer he dived under again, resurfacing at the edge of the pond.

Bryn appraised his surroundings from every angle. He admired the majestic trees towering into the skyline. The smaller shrubs were just as impressive, with an array of vibrantly coloured blossoms and rich, green foliage. Small birds threaded the top of the water, dipping their little talons in the underneath to cool off. In the distance, calls of larger animals could be heard but Bryn didn't feel nervous in the least. He was right where he wanted to be. Forgetting all his worries of the past few days, he absorbed this breath-taking landscape, lying on his back, floating in this heavenly abyss.

Bryn had almost fallen asleep when Frasier broke his meditative state.

'Have you seen some of these critters? They're fascinating.' He had dressed and been exploring their surroundings.

Bryn raised his head to see Frasier at the water's edge, playing with some large insect on his hand. He swam closer to see that it resembled an oversized, rainbow-coloured centipede, crawling up and around Frasier's arm, adorning it like a piece of jewellery. When it reached his neck, suddenly and without expectation Frasier recoiled, cursed and unwound the creature from his arm, throwing it as far away from him as he could.

'The damn thing bit me,' he explained as he jumped to his feet.

'Are you all right?' Bryn asked, getting out of the water, concerned about his friend.

'Yeah, I'm fine! I wasn't expecting that. It's always the pretty ones.' Frasier laughed it off, but Bryn thought he might have been a little embarrassed for overreacting.

As Bryn was deciding whether to go back into the water again or get out to explore a little, he noticed Frasier stumbling slightly where he stood.

'Are you sure you're okay?' he asked again, as he got back into his clothes.

'I don't know… Feeling a little queasy.'

Bryn approached him. The colour had drained from Frasier's face and he faltered again, this time landing on the ground.

'Frasier!'

Frasier was barely conscious when Bryn bent down to check him.

'Don't worry, I'll get you out of here,' he told him, not sure if he could hear his words.

'It'll be quicker if you went and got help. I'd only slow you…' His voice faded away. Bryn knew he had no time to lose. He picked Frasier up and threw him over his shoulder as if he was a small child. Running as fast as his legs could carry them both, it wasn't long before he had reached the base of the waterfall.

After quickly assessing the height he must reach and securing Frasier as well as he could, he scaled the rock face like a large feline. At the top, and without hesitating, he disappeared into the dense forest in search of the hovering jet-ski-type vehicle, jumping bushes and dodging trees along the way. When he spotted it, he felt relieved until he realised that he was barely paying any attention when they were shown how to operate it.

That didn't stop him though. He threw Frasier across the front of it, not even stopping to check if he was okay. As he climbed on behind, the contraption turned on automatically. This provided a bit of relief and now all he had to do was decide which button made it move. He tried the blue one.

As they lurched backwards and hit a tree, Bryn wasted no time and pressed the red one. The jet ski struggled a little, not appreciating being so badly abused and then slowly moved forward with a lot less pace than Bryn hoped for. What was he doing wrong? Of course, like a motorbike, the power was controlled by the handlebars. With the slightest movement, the jet ski took off with great speed.

CHAPTER 25

Not knowing if he was on the right path, Bryn continued his journey as fast as the vehicle could carry them both. He had forgotten his nerves. All he cared about was Frasier's welfare, and whether he could get his limp and motionless body back to the training camp in time. He drove so fast that the scenery around him merged into a haze of green light. When at last he exited the forest, he instinctively veered to avoid hitting the immense wall. As he reached the gate he motioned at the scanner, frantically waiting to gain access. The Hazuru from the wooden shack greeted Bryn as he entered and immediately radioed for help. He helped lift Frasier's limp and fading body off the vehicle and carried him towards the dormitories. Bystanders stood back, some offering help, but the Hazuru drove on with intent.

Tilly was waiting for them in the courtyard. After a quick examination, she instructed them to take Frasier to his room and she would follow. She needed supplies. Bryn watched as the Hazuru gently lowered Frasier onto his bed. Frasier was motionless and sweating profusely. The colour had drained completely from his face at this stage, turning it an ashen grey. Within moments, Tilly burst through the bedroom door and asked Bryn what had happened. He told her how Frasier was bitten and described the creature in detail. As she rummaged through the large satchel she had brought with her, she asked to be left alone with Frasier. Though Bryn was hesitant, the Hazuru laid a hand on his shoulder and slowly led him out of the room. He had never been remotely close to losing anyone he knew before; the fear that he might was stifling.

He paced up and down the long corridor, occasionally sitting on the floor against the wall, never far from the door where Tilly was desperately trying to save Frasier's life.

After a time, a small group of well-wishers – or gossipmongers – had gathered, waiting to hear news of the fate of the young man inside. They came and went until Bryn was left on his own again, and for over an hour no one else entered the building.

Eventually, Bryn heard heavy footsteps approaching.

'What the hell happened here?' Gregor boomed as he approached Bryn. 'Is Frasier all right?'

'I don't know, Gregor!' Bryn replied, relieved to see a familiar face, yet still sick with worry. He explained what had happened at the waterfall to Gregor.

After another hour of pacing and fretting, they began to hear weak and muffled sounds of moaning and whimpering from Bryn's room. Gregor put his ear against the door, hoping to get a better idea of what was going on. Minutes later, the hallway fell silent again. Bryn feared the worst.

Gregor sent an envoy to fetch Samuel. He was getting more anxious and looking more impatient by the minute.

'Is there anyone else who could help? Surely, there must be a doctor or some form of qualified medical practitioner nearby,' Bryn pleaded with Gregor.

'You must have faith in Tilly. She is a great healer,' Gregor said firmly, but then his features softened as he looked into Bryn's fearful and despondent eyes.

Just then, the door to the bedroom opened, revealing a dark candlelit room and in the doorway stood an exhausted and dishevelled Tilly.

'The child will be fine,' she said and managed a weak smile. 'He still has a bit of a fever and needs rest,' she continued.

'Can I see him?' Bryn asked, looking visibly relieved.

'Only for a moment, but be sure not to wake him,' Tilly said.

Bryn entered the darkened room and sat in silence beside Frasier, who was in a deep and soundless sleep. He reflected on how close to death he was and wished him a speedy recovery. It wasn't long before his thoughts drifted back to the encounter he had with Samuel earlier that day. He had made up his mind. All he had to do now was let Samuel know his decision.

CHAPTER 26

Bryn stayed at Frasier's side for over an hour before collapsing onto his bed. Apart from getting up twice to check on his friend's welfare and occasionally hearing Tilly coming and going, he slept rather well. When he finally sensed it was time to get up, he was more than a little surprised to find Frasier sitting up in his bed, sipping a cup of tea.

'You're awake!' he said, rubbing his eyes of sleep and also because he could barely believe what he was seeing.

'You just missed Tilly,' Frasier said, nodding towards the door. 'You were out cold. If you hadn't saved my life, I might have requested a new roommate because of your snoring,' he said, smiling at Bryn.

Although he looked a little drained, he was in good spirits.

'You'd better get used to it,' Bryn said as he got up. 'I am not planning to go anywhere for a while.'

'So, you've decided to stay? Good for you,' Frasier responded.

'Well, who else is going to save you from the local wildlife?' Bryn replied jokingly. 'I'm going to head out for breakfast. Want anything?'

'Yes, please. I'm starving! Just don't get me any of that wet wheat stuff. Tried it yesterday and it was just like eating cardboard,' Frasier said, as Bryn left the room.

Crossing the courtyard, Bryn was in high spirits due to Frasier's quick recovery and his decision not to leave.

In the cafeteria, he spotted Gregor sitting with Samuel at a table not far from the counter. They sat across from each other with their heads so close together and their facial expressions so serious that Bryn knew it wasn't the right time to approach either one of them. He tried his best to keep out of their line of sight in case they beckoned for him, hiding discreetly behind the large Shiakana standing in front of him in the queue. Between the conversation he had with Samuel and his exploits with Fraiser the day before, he had a fairly strong feeling that his name had come up in their conversation.

Filling his tray with random items from the breakfast counter, his only thought was to leave the cafeteria fast and unnoticed. When he was satisfied that he had ample supplies, he left and crossing the courtyard, he breathed a sigh of relief. He certainly wasn't ready for a confrontation with either one of them on an empty stomach.

'Bryn!'

He heard his name being called from behind and stopped dead in his tracks.

'I don't believe it!' he muttered to himself, under his breath.

He turned around to see Gregor approaching him from the cafeteria.

'How's Frasier? Any improvement today? I was just about to call Tilly for an update,' Gregor said with genuine concern.

'A lot better, Gregor. I went to get him something to eat.' He gestured at the tray and felt a little embarrassed at the sheer volume of food on it.

'He must be doing very well if you expect him to eat all of that.'

'Oh, that's not all for—'

'Bryn!' Gregor cut him off. 'When you're done playing nurse, I want to see you at the meeting room. A matter of considerable importance has been brought to my attention. I'll be waiting, so don't take too long.' He was walking away as he uttered the last few words.

As he entered their room, Frasier's delight at seeing so much food quickly turned to concern at seeing Bryn's glum expression.

'I saw Gregor and Samuel talking. I thought I'd managed to escape when Gregor caught up with me. He wants to talk. I've suddenly lost my appetite. You might as well have this,' Bryn said as he handed Frasier the tray.

'I thought you wanted to sort this mess out?'

'I did. I do… but…' Bryn pondered for a moment. 'I guess there's no time like the present. You'd better wish me luck.' He turned to go.

'Bryn, thanks for the grub. You'll be fine. Remember why you're here,' Frasier said, as he tucked into some sort of dried meat dish.

CHAPTER 27

The meeting room was furnished with six low-standing benches, which formed a hexagon in the centre of the room, a large table at one end near the door, and two large wooden trunks at the far end. A large chalkboard hung on the white-washed wall near the table. Bryn had knocked several times on the open door before entering and seeing that it was vacant, decided to wait for Gregor inside.

He was under no illusion as to what their conversation would entail. After yesterday's elaborate and slightly unfortunate misadventure, Bryn was certain that Gregor would support Samuel's notion, to ask him to surrender his position to his father. However, Bryn also knew that his family was bestowed the right to compete for a place in the tournament, so he would do everything in his power to fight for it.

After a few long and contemplative minutes, Gregor walked in. Samuel followed in his wake, like a bad smell. Bryn was not impressed. They invited him to sit, which Bryn declined, opting instead to stand. He wasn't giving them the opportunity to look down on him.

'Bryn, Samuel has brought what he considers a rather serious matter to my attention,' Gregor began. Bryn swallowed hard but tried to appear unfazed.

'Are you sure you're ready for the trials? You can always postpone until the next tournament.'

Bryn kept his composure. 'I am ready,' was all he said.

Samuel stood beside Gregor keeping a watchful eye in case of hesitation. Bryn wasn't going to give him any satisfaction.

'Samuel has explained to you that your father was an exceptional warrior. With his participation, we would have a good chance of beating our opponents this year,' Gregor continued. 'Would you be willing to return home and send your father in your stead?' he asked.

Why was Gregor doing this? He had brought him here to compete. He knew his father's wishes. Bryn thought for a moment before replying.

'With all due respect, Gregor, my father had his opportunity and now this is mine. I am not willing to return home unless I am forced. I hope I will have your support with this decision.'

His eyes were fixed on Gregor's. He behaved as though Samuel wasn't even in the room.

'Is that your final decision?' asked Samuel.

'Yes!' replied Bryn.

'Well, in that case…' Samuel paused for a moment, 'it seems you have just passed your first test. Training starts in the morning.'

Samuel forced a smile, appearing satisfied with the response, bid his farewells and left, leaving Bryn and Gregor alone. Bryn was dumbfounded, dubious of Samuel's intentions. Gregor suddenly let out a bellow of laughter before giving him a congratulatory whack on the shoulder, which nearly sent Bryn flying.

'You should see your face, Bryn. You can relax now. You're officially part of the training camp,' he said and followed Samuel out of the door.

Bryn needed to sit down for a moment to gather his thoughts. He couldn't believe they had no intention of sending him home. He felt a medley of emotions all at once – confusion, anger, relief, excitement. The most important realisation was that he was staying, and that got him back to his feet. He went back to the dormitory to share his good news.

When he got back to his room, Frasier was dressed, sitting at the edge of his bed, anxiously waiting for Bryn's return.

'Well, mate, how did it go?' he asked.

'It was a test! I had no idea,' Bryn replied.

Frasier didn't seem at all surprised.

'Did you pass?' he asked.

'With flying colours, apparently,' Bryn said. 'I have to say, it was the last thing I expected. I truly believed that I wasn't worthy and now I actually feel accepted. Can't tell you how relieved I am.'

Frasier stood up and shook his friend's hand. 'Good to have you here, Bryn. Well done for passing the test.'

'You don't seem at all surprised that this whole business was contrived,' Bryn questioned.

'Bryn, you don't think you're the only one assessed as part of their first test, do you? I had mine this morning while you were still counting sheep. When Tilly brought me my tea, she was adamant that I should go home to make a full recovery. The discussion got a bit heated so I was surprised you didn't wake up. You have to understand. I have learned from my family that here, everything you do is a test.'

Bryn couldn't believe the trials had begun already.

'Anyway,' Frasier continued, 'she finally backed down, and when you went to get breakfast, she told me that I passed the first test. I was dying to tell you but I had to swear to secrecy. She told me that each candidate is tested by his or her weakness, a trait picked up on at the registration meeting. I'm sorry I couldn't warn you, but I was told they would boot me out if I did,' he explained.

But... Bryn thought. He wasn't at the registration meeting long enough for anyone to figure out his strengths or weaknesses, or to evaluate any aspect of his personality. It was Samuel who cut the meeting short. Why was Samuel so focused on him? What did he not want the other members of the council to see?

He was probably overthinking. It had been an incredible couple of days.

Bryn and Frasier left their room, following the sounds of bustle and voices in the corridor. By the doorway, they were met by three large figures trying to get by. Along the corridor, more men and women were making their way to their rooms, some quite confidently and others led by Tilly. She stopped for a moment to speak to Bryn and Frasier.

'Tolk just brought us the last of the trainees. Held up in Reykjavik by bad weather. They've arrived in bulk so I'm hoping you might take these two under your wing and show them around.' She turned sideways so that Bryn and Frasier could see to whom she was referring.

The first would have been impossible to miss, for his frame filled their vision. He was immensely large, standing at least a foot above Bryn and had to stoop slightly, otherwise his head would have touched the ceiling. People passing struggled to get by, because as well as being remarkably tall, he was also excessively wide and front heavy. His shovel-like hands were clasped together around his swollen belly, thumbs twiddling as he stood; the rest of his body possibly unable to move due to lack of space. He had a large bulbous nose and small rounded ears, which stood out from the side of his head, one slightly higher than the other. His eyes were also small, quite close together and dwarfed by his mammoth eyebrows. There didn't seem to be one feature that would be considered to be of normal proportion. The giant of a man didn't say a word, just smiled nervously, as Bryn and Frasier stood in awe.

From behind came a young woman, who was tall and slender with long, black hair tied in a braid. She stood in military attention as Tilly spoke, also not uttering a word, though Bryn doubted that had anything to do with nerves.

CHAPTER 28

Tilly introduced them. 'Bryn and Frasier, this is Stefan. He's from the Netherlands, and this is Madison from New York. I trust you'll make them feel right at home. Make sure you fill them in on anything they may have missed.'

Bryn shook Stefan's hand, which was nearly twice the size of his own. It was hot and sweaty, grip like a vice. Bryn had to rub the clammy residue off on his trouser leg before offering his hand again to greet Madison.

'Nice to meet you,' he said to both of them.

Frasier followed suit but held on to Madison's hand a bit longer than was considered etiquette. She barely acknowledged him. It became apparent within minutes that she didn't enjoy small-talk. On the other hand, Stefan couldn't be more forthcoming, once he got out of his uncomfortable stance in the corridor.

Crossing the courtyard to the cafeteria, Bryn heard all about Stefan's large family in Amsterdam. He had five brothers and two sisters, who were all very close in age. They drew lots to see who would be first to compete. It was a little unorthodox and not in keeping with tradition but that was the way it had been done for generations. Stefan knew they were all very surprised when he won. His father didn't have very high expectations of his qualifying chances but Stefan thought he'd give it a go. He didn't give Bryn and Frasier the impression he was too bothered either way.

They ordered coffee at the counter and sat at an empty table by the door. Madison had yet to utter a word. She was the last to sit down, all the while scanning the room, watching people coming and going, paying particular attention to the foreign characters congregating in groups around the room. Bryn noticed that Frasier was also watching her every move, and assumed he found her behaviour as odd as he did.

Meanwhile, Stefan, who seemed completely oblivious to Madison's strange conduct, slowly sipped his thick, tar-like coffee substitute, all the while grimacing with the bitterness of every mouthful.

'Will you chill a bit!' Frasier finally addressed Madison. 'You're making me think we could be under attack.'

'Do you think we're on some sort of summer vacation? You… with your highlighted hair and… Is that fake tan? Unlike you, I happen to take this competition very seriously.' Madison offered Frasier such an ugly glare, it made everyone at the table uncomfortable, even Stefan, who had been busy looking over at the food counter until then.

There was a moment of strained silence before Frasier, who stared at her with such disdain, finally spoke.

'Well, if you want to me to prove to you that I am serious about this competition, and if it might stop you scanning the room like a meerkat, I can tell you who's who,' he said.

The lack of response was his cue.

Frasier turned to face the room.

'See that Goytek sitting two tables behind me, the one with the red strap tied to his right arm…?' The four of them looked around. 'He's Tumlock, the Goyteks' strongest competitor. He's faster than anyone else on his team and agile as a Russian gymnast. There is no doubt that he'll be competing in the tournament again this year, probably as team leader.'

Frasier motioned to the far end of the room.

'See that giant Shiakana? You can't miss him. He's the largest living thing in the room. His name is Marchek. Stronger than an elephant and despite his appearance, as sly as a fox. Team leader for the last two tournaments.'

He returned his attention to Madison.

'Gima doesn't seem to be here. She's the forerunner in the Hazuru camp. She has competed in every tournament most people can remember. Some say she's a guru in the martial arts field, and always coming up with a new way to outsmart an opponent.'

Madison was taken aback. Bryn could tell that she was also a little impressed. He was certainly very impressed, as well as a little surprised. Frasier was a lot more serious about this tournament than he was letting on. Bryn began to wish he had more time to prime himself for this competition, but was also glad to have Frasier as a mentor.

Madison started to relax a bit, the tension in her shoulders lifting slightly. Frasier had also momentarily captured Stefan's attention but that didn't last long as he had disappeared to the food counter, unable to abstain from temptation any longer.

'So what about our camp? Who do you reckon is the strongest player?' Madison quizzed Frasier.

'The situation in our camp is a little different.' Frasier's tone softened a little. He didn't come across as defensive and treated Madison as though he forgot the distasteful remarks she uttered only minutes before. 'We have a few really strong contenders. Ollie from the West Indies and Orisa from Nigeria, to name two. Then there's Moses from South Africa and possibly Kenta from Japan… The list goes on. The competition is very much an open book.'

'Are any of them in the room?' asked Bryn, looking around.

'I can see Moses and Kenta, talking together by the door. Bryn and I were lucky enough to see Moses in action. He's been competing for years. I've heard he has no children, no heir, so just keeps coming back.'

'How do you know all this?' Madison queried.

'That, right there, is where you've made your first mistake, Madison. Never judge a surfer by the colour of their hair.' Frasier smiled.

Stefan returned to the table with a tray full of grub.

'You could feed a starving country with all that food,' Madison commented.

Stefan was too preoccupied with his stockpile of exotic cuisine to take any notice. His chair creaked slightly under the pressure of his weight as he sat down. He gorged himself for the next few minutes, occasionally pausing for a moment to remark on some new taste experience.

Frasier, Madison and Bryn sat in complete silence, watching in absolute fascination at the sheer volume of food he was putting away. When he was done, he belched so loudly that it captured the attention of the whole room. He excused himself. Surprisingly, Madison was the first to laugh before Frasier and Bryn joined in.

CHAPTER 29

'This competition is not just about brawn or muscle. It also requires speed, stamina, brains and backbone,' Gregor said, once he had all the trainees gathered in the yard behind the meeting room, the following morning. Anyone wanting to try out for the tournament was obliged to complete the training program, whether he or she had competed before or not.

Bryn was standing in line with the other hopefuls, twenty-four in all, not including the seemingly confident Orisa and Ollie, who had yet to show their faces. There was complete silence as they listened intently to every word Gregor had to say.

'You are expected to attend each class. Any absence must have a damn good excuse or else you should expect to be sent home. I will not tolerate tardiness or disrespect.'

Gregor continued to explain the rules and regulations for the next twenty minutes or so, until he was interrupted by the late arrivals, striding towards the group at no great speed, talking and giggling to each other in an obvious flirtatious manner. Bryn needed no introductions. He knew they were Orisa and Ollie, the contenders Frasier had described in the cafeteria the day before. They eventually stood in line with the trainees, as they had done many times before, spending the last leg of journey discussing – a little too loudly – how they felt the training camp was a complete waste of time for accomplished warriors, insinuating that it would be better for all concerned if they just showed up on the day, competed in the tournament and then went home.

Gregor was not impressed by their smug disposition. He was trying to control his brewing temper by chewing on the inside of his mouth. He had even managed to draw blood and that wasn't helping.

'Orisa and Ollie,' he said in a firm tone. 'You have finally graced us with your presence. Did you not know that you were supposed to be here yesterday?' he asked them, firmly.

Orisa spoke up.

'Gregor! It's good to see you, old man. You're looking well.' She was trying, without sounding too insincere, to sound respectful.

There was a certain hint of sarcasm in her tone that bit on Gregor's temper even more. It didn't help that she was stealing glances at the equally complacent Ollie, who was smirking self-confidently, foolishly unaware that Gregor's face had turned crimson.

'To show you how serious I am about compliance,' Gregor addressed the group, showing some semblance of composure, 'I will now demonstrate what happens if one fails to adhere to said rules. Orisa and Ollie, step forward!'

Both contenders reluctantly did what they were told.

'I am grateful to you both for making your return journey to Zhivrah. Your strength and bravery as warriors is to be commended.'

Gregor paused long enough for the two of them to regain their poise before he delivered the killer blow.

'However, your blatant disregard for the rules of this competition and lack of discipline regarding your training efforts has tainted your efforts. Therefore, you are not welcome here. You may try out again when you have remembered how to conduct yourselves.'

There was a deathly silence and no one moved a muscle. It was as though someone had paused the scene for a dramatic purpose. After a few uncomfortable minutes, both Orisa and Ollie broke formation and walked away, unable to say anything to defend themselves or protest the decision.

Once they were clear of earshot, Gregor spoke again, addressing the rest of his recruits, who had suddenly gained the deportment of an army brigade.

'Let that be a lesson to all of you!' he said. 'Now, time for a warm-up exercise. Laps first!'

He motioned with his finger around the enclosure.

'Start jogging. I'll tell you when to stop.'

Bryn was amazed at the sheer simplicity of the first exercise. He certainly was not expecting this and following what had just happened with Ollie and Orisa, he was relieved to hear it.

The row of fourteen men and twelve women immediately and without protest, moved to the periphery wall and commenced a slow sprint, as instructed.

Frasier and Bryn jogged side by side for a while, but after a short time, Frasier moved ahead, gaining momentum and speed and it wasn't long before he was leading the pack. Madison followed suit, matching him stride for stride. They broke the unit into two groups and before long four others, frantically competing for a place at the finishing post, joined them. Little did they realise that Gregor had gone.

Bryn had noticed Gregor's absence before they completed the first lap and got a vague impression that he wasn't coming back anytime soon. He was quite content to maintain a relative speed, not so fast that he would tire out quickly and not so slow as to be seen right at the back. Stefan joined him and moved with ease, in spite of his large stomach rising and falling as he ran.

An hour later, most of the group stood their ground, with only a few showing signs of tiring. Frasier and Madison still stayed in front but the gap was closing in. Bryn guessed that they had realised they were in for the long haul and may have decided to pace themselves.

After another hour, the pack reunited as one and started to shout words of encouragement at each other to keep going. Stefan was complaining about how they had missed lunch and that wasn't good for his low blood sugar complaint. His stomach also grumbled in protest, which was heard by everyone, causing him to blush.

After the third hour, the group broke in two again. Some, including Frasier and Madison, received a burst of energy, convinced that the exercise would be ending soon. Others were getting weary and stayed at the very back. Bryn kept up with the second group with ease. This was where most of the experienced competitors banded. He considered joining the leaders but decided after some careful deliberation that he would stay where he was. Gregor may not return for hours. He didn't feel that it was worth the risk.

Within another twenty minutes, almost everyone showed signs of struggling. Even some were throwing up the breakfast they had hours before.

But not long after, Gregor arrived through the large entrance and he was not alone. Hovering above him was an orb, which made a rather low humming sound. It was in polished metal and reflected light, distracting the runners to nearly a standstill.

'Pay no attention,' Gregor directed, sensing their attention. 'This is a test of stamina. It is not a race,' he said, as he noticed that some had gathered speed.

The orb left Gregor's company and headed straight for the two groups of runners. Although there were obvious signs of apprehension, everyone tried to ignore its low drone as it approached. When it reached the leading group, it took a moment to configure before a beam of red light left its core, scanning each participant from head to foot. Once done, it waited for the second group to pass by and did the same.

'Okay, you can stop now!' Gregor ordered and everyone collapsed to the ground. The only person left standing was Bryn. He was relieved that everyone was too overwhelmed with exhaustion to notice, except for Gregor. He certainly had noticed. Bryn sat down beside Stefan who looked close to having a cardiac failure. He was sure he could hear him quietly calling for his mother as he lay flat on his back, arms spread-eagled.

The orb returned to Gregor, who stood close as it dispatched its data through a small holographic screen. It was too far away for Bryn to read what it displayed but he had a fair idea. He was certain the machine had somehow determined the contenders' physical condition on finishing the exercise. That was the most logical explanation.

Once the orb finished relaying its findings, it hovered away, leaving Gregor briefly alone with his thoughts.

He approached the group, who were slowly regaining composure.

'As I said,' he began, 'that was a test of stamina.' They rose to their feet and stood in line. 'I have rarely seen all participants finish this marathon run, so I must commend you all on that achievement.'

He paused as he paced the row of dishevelled men and women.

'Unfortunately, this is the end of the line for one of you. The orb did a complete medical check at the end of the run to evaluate your body's response to this sort of stimulus and I am afraid that one of you did not make the grade.'

Stefan shifted uncomfortably where he stood, but Gregor wasn't looking at him. He was walking in the opposite direction, to where Frasier and Madison stood.

'Madison, step forward!'

There was a muffled gasp from some of the others as Madison did what she was told.

'Madison, the orb came back with some interesting results from your scan. I must say that I am very disappointed.' He was only inches away from her and she barely flinched. 'Traces of anabolic steroids were found in your system,' he said sternly. 'I do not need you to explain yourself or offer any excuses. I just want you at the departure gate later this evening with all your belongings. You are going home. If you wish to return and join this competition at a future event, make sure you're clean.'

CHAPTER 30

Gregor dismissed the group but turned his attention to Stefan when everyone else had walked past.

'I will need to see you later this evening to discuss a suitable diet for you to have any chance to complete this training program. The results of your health check also concern me, for different reasons. Come and see me after dinner, before lights out.'

Stefan looked slightly embarrassed and all he could manage was an obliging nod. He sauntered away to the canteen, where he had a relatively smaller heap of food piled on his tray for lunch.

Meanwhile, Bryn and Frasier decided to follow Madison. She had wasted no time disappearing to the sanctuary of her room, where they could only assume she was packing. On their way, they spoke of their shock and utter disappointment, both finding it difficult to believe Madison would be capable of cheating.

They knocked on her door repeatedly before Frasier decided to walk in. Inside, Madison was sitting on the side of her bed, packed bag in hand.

'That was quick,' Frasier said, gesturing at the full rucksack. Madison didn't comment and refused to avert her gaze from a blank spot on the floor by her shoes.

Bryn, though saddened by Madison's sudden dismissal was more disgusted by her audacity, so stayed in the shadows knowing full well that Frasier had begun to have feelings for her.

'I can't believe you felt you needed to resort to taking steroids,' Frasier said, as he sat down beside her.

Madison turned to face Frasier. 'I can't see how that has anything to do with you,' she barked. 'It's fine for you two, built like machines. You barely broke a sweat on the training field,' she said, turning her gaze to Bryn. 'I saw you. How was that even possible? How am I supposed to compete with that?' She was angry, spiteful. 'Well, I have been training for years and that was never going to be enough. I knew that. I would never have made it here if I didn't get a bit of help. So, don't patronise me! I knew what I was doing. I am only sorry I got caught,' she said as she got to her feet and stormed out the door.

Frasier was stunned and looked to Bryn for his reaction.

'I reckon she may have been a little too fiery for you, Frasier,' he said, trying to console his friend with a little humour.

'You're probably right, mate,' he said, slightly downhearted, as he got to his feet.

That evening, Bryn and Frasier went off to the canteen and, after a light supper, decided to retire early. They had no idea what to expect for their second day of training so thought they should get a good night's rest. Tilly called to their room with mugs of warm herbal tea, which they gratefully accepted. They felt lucky to have someone with such a kind heart looking after them.

Bryn slept as soon as his head hit the pillow and was awoken after some time by Frasier calling his name and nudging at his arm.

'Bryn, get up! You're not going to believe this!' he said.

Bryn came round and quickly grasped that there was something odd going on. Something very strange indeed. Instead of being curled up in his bed, he was lying at the base of a tree, fully dressed. He glanced at his woodland surroundings and then at Frasier, who looked as puzzled as he felt.

'What's going on?' he asked.

'I have no idea, mate,' Frasier replied. 'But I think the likelihood of both of us sleepwalking out to the middle of woodland is pretty slim, don't you think?'

Bryn stood up and slowly turned a full three hundred and sixty degrees to take in the heavily dense forest they happened upon, in a seemingly unconscious state. He was completely mystified as to how they arrived at such a destination and was even more perplexed by the fact that he had no idea where they were. Meanwhile, Frasier was shouting hellos with ever-increasing volume, hoping for some evidence of life close by.

'I have this sinking feeling that we may be on our own, Frasier,' Bryn said in despair. 'I may be wrong, but I think we have been set a challenge.'

'What makes you think that?' Frasier wondered with a tone of sarcasm, as he turned to find his friend had disappeared.

Bryn's voice came from behind a large tree, which blocked his view. 'I think you should come and take a look for yourself,' he said. Frasier walked around the great obstacle to find Bryn staring at a piece of parchment posted on it. At the base of the tree there lay a canvas satchel.

Every good warrior needs the ability to find their way home. You have been provided with adequate supplies for this task. Your journey should take no more than two days. Good luck.

'You've got to be kidding me!' Frasier ran his hands through his hair in frustration.

Bryn was kneeling, emptying the satchel of its contents. He found two blankets, a compass, a large hunting knife and a leather-bound pocketbook. Flicking through it, he saw that it was a guidebook of local flora and fauna, mainly focusing on what to eat and even more importantly, what not to eat on their journey.

'It was Tilly's tea,' Frasier said with certainty.

'What was Tilly's tea?' Bryn asked with little interest – he was immersed in the deadly consequences of eating the wrong-coloured berry.

'It must have acted as a strong sedative. They drugged us and hauled us off to the middle of nowhere. How the hell are we supposed to prepare for that?'

'It's quite brilliant actually,' Bryn said enthusiastically. 'So simple, yet effective.' He kept out the compass and the guidebook, tucked the knife into his belt and quickly repacked the blankets into the canvas bag. He took the parchment from the tree and studied it very carefully.

'What are you doing now?' Frasier asked inquisitively.

'I don't think they would leave us out here without some sort of clue to where we are. The compass would be no good to us if we don't know where we're going.'

He handed the piece of parchment to Frasier for further inspection while he started to scrutinise the guidebook, page by page.

'You may as well sit down, Frasier. This might take a while.'

Some time later, Frasier had closely examined the bag and its contents and scoured the area for a sign of their whereabouts in relation to the training camp. Bryn was still engrossed in the guidebook looking for any cryptic or blatant indications to which direction they should be heading.

'I think I have it!' Bryn exclaimed, eyes wide with delight.

Frasier had been kicking a tree in a moment of pure frustration when he was interrupted by Bryn's triumphant holler. He stopped mid-motion.

'Don't tell me the directions were written in the guidebook all along?' Frasier asked him.

'Not quite. Come, have a look for yourself,' Bryn offered.

CHAPTER 31

Frasier approached Bryn and stood beside him to peek at the page of the guidebook he had been studying. 'There's nothing here but bushes and berries,' he said, disappointed.

'Not just any bushes and berries. It seems most vegetation grow in specific areas, depending on the localised climate. It varies more than it does back home. These particular berries happen to only grow in the northern regions,' he said, showing Frasier the contents of his hand. He quickly flicked through a few pages. 'However, these large red ones only grow in the south,' he said, pointing to a diagram. 'Do they look familiar?' he asked.

Frasier came closer to get a better view. 'Not really,' he replied.

'They grew in clusters alongside the waterfall,' Bryn told him. 'We need to look around and confirm my theory. If true, we need to head south. It'll be a good starting point.'

The two young men didn't hesitate and quickly began exploring the area.

'Found something,' Frasier called out to Bryn from a nearby ditch. Bryn climbed down to find him examining a blue berry between his thumb and index finger. Bryn quickly referred to the guidebook.

'Nope, try again. Those are found everywhere. Whatever you do, though, don't eat it.' He read the description. 'They are severely hallucinogenic.' He read on. 'May also cause intense migraine and diarrhoea.'

Frasier dropped the berry, rubbed his hands on his trousers and carried on rummaging through the next bush. Moments later, he emerged with another berry. This one was small and mustard in colour. Bryn scrutinised it before flicking a few pages and reading the findings.

'It's actually a seed… Very good for cooking with… Spicy.' He read on. 'Found primarily in the western region.' He looked up. 'That's good enough for me. I think we should head south and possibly veer east tomorrow.'

After getting an accurate reading from the compass, Bryn and Frasier began their journey back to the training camp. Drinking fresh water from a small stream brought relief from hours of trudging through forested terrain. With the onset of darkness approaching, they needed to think about eating and resting for the night. When the time felt right and they thought they couldn't travel much farther, they found a small, sheltered ravine and sat beneath a burly tree.

Bryn referred to the guidebook for more clues, to see if they were trekking the right course and to find something to forage for supper. Frasier scoured the area for berries and seeds, bringing them back to Bryn for closer examination. Bryn thoroughly scrutinised each morsel of food he was brought, frequently consulting the guidebook and slowly building two piles at either side of him. He told Frasier that the pile on his right side was edible and the pile on his left was not to be touched. Frasier was glad to see that the fruit from a nearby tree had qualified, as it would provide them with more sustenance than consuming just berries and seeds. What he desperately wanted was some red meat. It had been a staple part of his daily diet for as long as he could remember. He felt anaemic without it.

As a distraction from his rumbling stomach, Bryn gathered twigs and small branches, and began his attempt to make a fire by rolling a stick between his hands against a stone. After a few false starts, he found his rhythm and managed to create a little flame on a small number of leaves he had placed between the stick and stone. He fed them to a neatly organised mound of kindling and then guarded his efforts for fear of it being extinguished.

'I'm guessing that you were a boy scout,' Frasier said. He was glad of the heat. It was becoming colder as the sunset.

'No. We hiked a lot. Sometimes we walked so far, we'd set up camp under the stars. I guess I'm used to it,' Bryn told him, satisfied with his now blazing fire. Sitting close to it, they both ate their rations of scavenged fodder in relative silence.

'I think we're on the right track,' Bryn said, eventually.

'It's still a little vague, don't you think?' Frasier asked, in between picking at little morsels of food stuck in his teeth with splinter of wood.

'Well, we've been following the berry trail and that seems to be pointing us along the right path, so far,' Bryn insisted.

'I understand your theory about the berries, but it's hardly going to give us a direct route back to camp. We need something more specific.'

Bryn could understand Frasier's scepticism, however he felt confident.

'Do you remember the map, Frasier? The one you found the waterfall on?' Bryn didn't wait for an answer. 'If you remember, the landing station was in the southeast. To get to the training camp, the capsule travelled west, along the mountain range to the south. The waterfall was in the southwest. The berries tell us we're in the northwest, so I reckon if we keep heading south, we would reach the waterfall. But that's not where we need to go. It's too far away.'

'But how do we know if we have gone too far east?' Frasier asked.

'Simple,' Bryn replied. 'The mountain range will come into view. If we can aim to get to somewhere between the waterfall and the mountain range, then it'll be close enough. We'll end up either near the training camp, or the town. I'm sure we'll figure that out when we get there.'

Frasier was impressed with Bryn's logic but a little disappointed in himself for not paying close attention to the map in question. It was a real rookie mistake, but not one Bryn made. He would feel resentful towards his friend if it wasn't for a niggling feeling he had, telling him that there was more to this challenge than just finding their way home. He would keep a sharp lookout for anything suspicious and hopefully have the opportunity to save them both. He knew they would be watching. Bryn didn't need to hear of his concerns. He just needed a chance to prove himself, a chance to give him a head start in the competition.

CHAPTER 32

As they slept, an orb, identical to the one they saw at the training camp, hovered over the surrounding trees and came to their campsite. It silently floated above each of them briefly and rose again, whizzing away at great speed to a position nearby, somewhere it wouldn't be seen.

Early the following morning, Frasier woke as Bryn was busying himself putting their supplies into the canvas bag. He left out a small stash of food and handed Frasier half, instructing him that they had better eat on the go, as he feared they may have fallen behind. At that moment, Frasier wished he was the one who had woken earlier and given instructions. He always seemed to be one step behind. That needed to change.

Bryn thought Frasier was unusually quiet. He had been since the night before. Probably hungry, he assumed. Bryn didn't mind. He was used to trekking in silence. His father thought it was a great way to appreciate his surroundings, be at one with nature.

The woodland was thinning out, enough to let in ample light and give them a view of what type of terrain lay up ahead. No sign of the mountains yet, or the waterfall. Bryn reckoned there was a fair distance left to travel.

By afternoon, hunger had started to deliver its usual pangs and Frasier was feeling the need for some real food. He couldn't bear to feed on any more insipid plant life. It all started to taste the same. He kept a watchful eye on nearby shrubbery, hoping to find some game they could feast on that evening. He also kept watch for any unusual activity, a hint that there may be more to this trek than expected.

An hour later, in a nearby bush, he heard rustling and hoped its source may provide sustainable nourishment for the remainder of their journey. He appealed to Bryn to be still and slowly approached the origin, aware that any sound may frighten whatever it was away.

Bryn followed a short distance behind and quietly handed Frasier the hunting knife. There was another movement in the bush and as if acting on a cue, Frasier pounced, hoisting his full body weight off the ground, targeting whatever scurried beneath.

Bryn looked on, unaware that someone had been scouting their movements for some time, waiting for a chance to strike. And, as the ominous figure rose into the air from the dark woodland behind, Frasier quickly sensed a presence and evaded impact by sidestepping out of its path. Bryn was less fortunate, and only had time to turn and face his assailant's feet, as they skyrocketed into his solar plexus, winding him badly. Giving himself a moment to recover, he regained his stance and followed Frasier's eyeline to their attacker, who faced them both in a position of impending combat.

Expecting the worst, Bryn was surprised to see that the blow that knocked him off his feet was delivered by a slight young woman, who must have been close to his age. She was tall. Similar, but not the same skin tone as a Hazuru. Her long, black hair was tied with a leather strap and flowed down her spine reaching the base of her back. She wore a natural suede dress, with a leather belt. It appeared to be handmade and fit her beautifully. Her eyes were dark, close to mahogany in colour, abnormally large but suited the symmetry of her face. Tiny blue jewels curved around her eyes and along her temples. She had the most intricate black body art following her neckline down her arms to her fingers. She stood several feet before them both and Bryn was transfixed. He thought she was magnificent, was lost in her beauty; and that was when she lunged herself into full battle mode again – when he least expected it.

This time she went for Bryn first. As her frame was significantly more slender than his, and as his attention was somewhat distracted, he made the mistake of not reacting to her advancement. She spun and Bryn felt the full effect of the back of her right arm across his cheekbone. She then skilfully lowered herself to the ground and swiped both of his legs from under him with the foul swoop of her right leg. Bryn fell flat on his back with his ego suffering more of a bruising than any physical pain he endured.

Her intentions shifted to Frasier, who was now posed in a martial arts position, ready for battle. Bryn noticed how she appeared neither threatened nor concerned by the sight of this giant of a man about to engage in hand-to-hand combat with her. If anything, she seemed slightly amused and he was the one who looked concerned.

She didn't waste any time. Bryn watched as she leapt into the air and somersaulted, landing on Frasier's shoulders. She wrapped her legs around his neck and held them in that position, even though he struggled like a fish out of water. He eventually collapsed to the ground.

Bryn rose. He had seriously underestimated her. Catching the sly glint in her eye as she climbed off a semi-conscious Frasier, he figured out at that precise moment that she knew this too.

She was swift with her attack. Bryn moved quickly to avoid her but wasn't quite fast enough. Although graceful, her limbs flayed with such erratic motion, he had no idea what part of his body she was targeting.

Just as he braced for impact, he sidestepped left, so when she leapt into the air to land her full body weight on him, she only managed to strike his right shoulder. He used the opportunity to grab her around the waist and throw her from him. She went far enough to fly past Frasier, who was stirring, and was swallowed by the dense forest a formidable distance away.

Frasier sat bolt upright, seemingly impressed by the sheer strength of his new comrade.

'That was quite a pitch, Bryn,' he said, shaking his head to revitalise. Bryn couldn't help but feel slightly pleased with himself. He went to help his friend off the ground.

'We'd better think of heading off before she comes around,' Bryn suggested.

They suddenly heard shrill from the forest. It was almost animal but not quite. Whatever it was had a temper.

'I think it might be too late, mate.'

'Who was that?' Bryn asked, almost to himself.

'That was a Panak, I'm guessing. Don't know what her problem was though. They are said to be a pretty tame race.'

They both stared into the forest waiting to see if she emerged anytime soon. They stood together, ready for anything.

Then they saw her. She was fast, running at them with speed and agility, somersaulting and flipping. She looked furious.

This time Bryn was ready. He braced himself.

She stopped, just a few feet in front of them. They noticed she now bore a weapon, a stick; sturdy but not exactly deadly, Bryn thought.

She soared into the air as if she had bounced off a trampoline. Their eyes followed every movement. Then, she came like a cannonball back down. They stepped away but she predicted that, so when she landed, she was spinning the stick like a baton, striking Bryn first on the neck and then Frasier at the back of his head. They were both momentarily stunned. She was hoping for that.

She took that chance to lambast them with everything she had. Within moments they fell, as predicted. They were inexperienced. She knew she had won. Her eyes turned bright blue as she stood alongside the two strong warriors laid out on the rough.

A voice came from above her.

'That may have been a little harsh, Kyra,' said Gregor, from a hovering orb above her head. 'Come back to base. I need a full report.'

Kyra took one last look at her opponents, paying particular attention to the one who almost made the ambush intriguing. She rarely, if ever, had anyone overpower her, even for a moment. *This competition may prove interesting,* she thought to herself before making her way back to camp.

CHAPTER 33

It took Bryn and Frasier a while to fully recover from what had just happened. Although they suffered no serious physical injuries, their pride incurred quite a dent. They spoke little as they continued their journey and as they approached the camp the following morning, their accomplishment was dampened slightly by their spirit.

As they entered through the gate they were instructed to go straight to the dorms where they had a chance to rest and recuperate.

Tilly greeted them in the hallway with two mugs of what could only be tea of some description. They both refused her offer, slightly wary of her intentions, but she persevered with promises of innocence and following orders. She insisted the tea she was giving them would heal all wounds and they would awake to feel refreshed and reinvigorated. They were eventually persuaded.

In their room, they spoke for the first time about the thrashing they endured at the hands of their equally young opponent. She beat them both, and they fought together. Frasier thought it made them look weak and unworthy. With some persuasion, Bryn agreed not to share what happened with anyone and not to speak of it again. They drank their tea and both fell into a deep dreamless sleep.

Tilly was right. Both Bryn and Frasier woke after their nap feeling energised. Their sombre moods had also lifted. Food appeared to be the only thing occupying their thoughts at that moment.

The cafeteria was almost empty apart from a large group of Shiakanas at the back, discussing tactics and disputing strengths and weaknesses of each team player. Of course, Bryn and Frasier had no comprehension of what they were saying due to a significant language barrier, but that didn't stop the Shiakanas from lowering their voices to a dull drone.

'I wonder if we were one of the first back?' Bryn mused.

'We could be one of the last and everyone else could have moved on to their next task,' followed Frasier.

'We should check the meeting room once we're done, and then the training ground. We're bound to find somebody.'

With the plan decided, they finished their meal and headed out to the courtyard where they could see a small group huddled by the gate. They went to investigate.

Lying on the cobbles was Stefan. He was twisting and convulsing with his eyes rolled back in his head. He was foaming at the mouth and spouting random words, which were barely audible. Crouching beside him was a man in his thirties who Bryn recognised from the training ground. He was a seasoned competitor and appeared genuinely concerned for Stefan's wellbeing.

Tilly arrived, examined Stefan and asked what had happened. His assigned partner told her, in a pronounced French accent, that he had been tracking his way back to camp with Stefan. Although he had warned him of the implications of eating certain vegetation, it did not stop Stefan gorging on anything that looked in any way fit for consumption.

Tilly reached into Stefan's pockets and fished out a handful of fruits and berries, which she stored away in her bag to be examined later. She ordered him to be moved to the dorm, where she could examine and treat him accordingly. It took Bryn, Frasier and two others all of their effort to carry him there by stretcher.

Tilly stayed with Stefan for most of the day. She told all concerned to get on with their business as there was nothing they could do to help. She had little sense of urgency and a calm demeanour as she closed the door to onlookers.

Bryn and Frasier decided it was time to find the rest of the group and see how they were fairing, beginning their search at the meeting room.

Gregor barely greeted them as they entered the otherwise empty room. He appeared distracted. As they approached, they noticed he was not looking directly at them but was gazing below their eye level.

On closer inspection, they found that he was monitoring what could only be described as a form of holographic imagery. It appeared that it could only be observed from where he was standing and from there the picture was as clear as day. Bryn and Frasier were taken aback and stood in silence as they watched this technology unfold what was taking place outside the walls of the encampment. Competitors were being surveyed making their way back. There seemed to be several scenes portrayed at once.

The images of each pair of competitors stood about half a foot from where they rested on the table in front of Gregor. They all appeared exhausted and some slightly wounded. None were badly injured. Gregor studied each scene intensely. Bryn was curious to know what he was thinking.

Frasier broke the silence.

'Are those the last of the trainees in the field?' he asked Gregor.

'Yes, Frasier,' he replied, all the while not lifting his eyes from the holograms. 'They are not far from the gate now.'

Bryn noticed a fatherly concern in Gregor's voice, and it felt reassuring.

'We will reconvene in the morning in the training room. Don't forget your weapons. Tomorrow you will hopefully learn to use them.'

They were dismissed.

'As we were asked to bring our weapons tomorrow, I'm guessing we must have passed the orienteering challenge,' Frasier remarked, feeling satisfied with the result.

'I wouldn't be so sure of anything in this competition, Frasier,' Bryn responded.

CHAPTER 34

The following morning started early for both Bryn and Frasier. Frasier went for a run and then on to the cafeteria for breakfast, while Bryn spent most of it alone in his room, unsuccessfully trying to operate the scheda his father had passed on to him. He first examined the wooden body, playing close attention to the inscriptions. The etchings portrayed primeval images of hunters and animal prey. However, instead of the hunter bearing an ancient spear or axe, he held a similar if not the same weapon Bryn now had in his grasp.

The rim at each end had been painted black at some stage, though the colour had faded to a charcoal grey. There were other black markings, but they had faded too much to decipher.

Holding the centre, he gripped the scheda and squeezed his fists as Gregor did, making sure there was enough room at either end for the blades. Nothing happened. The last thing Bryn wanted was to turn up at weapons training without even being able to operate the one bestowed to him. He felt disappointed and frustrated, gave up his failed attempt after forty-five minutes, rewrapped it in its canvas and put it on the bed.

When Frasier returned from breakfast, Bryn couldn't bring himself to admit how unprepared he felt for this morning's training session.

'Are you ready for a bit of action on the training field?' Frasier asked him.

'As I'll ever be, I guess,' Bryn replied, not feeling very enthusiastic.

Frasier scrambled under his bed and from the far end he pulled out a box, about a foot long, made from dark wood. It appeared old, with scuffed edges. There were black markings, in a language Bryn didn't understand. He was intrigued. 'Can I see inside?' He gestured at the metal clasp.

'Yeah, sure,' Frasier replied, 'but it's nothing very exciting really.' He seemed a little coy and that made Bryn feel a little more curious.

Frasier set the box down and opened the two clasps holding it closed. Inside, set neatly in moulds, were a selection of metal ring blades. One was large, about a half-foot in diameter, the inner circumference thicker than the outside. A small section of the ring was bound with leather.

'I'm guessing the leather part is the handle,' Frasier remarked as Bryn tried to pick it up.

The rest of the box contained rings of various sizes, all with a form of protective sheath to cover the sharp blades. In one of the moulds, there was a tiny leather box, a cube, about an inch wide. Frasier picked it up, opened it, and showed Bryn the ring inside. It was so small it would fit a finger.

'What's that for?' Bryn asked.

'I have no idea. In all honesty, I haven't a clue about any of it. All I know is that my great-grandparents brought it over from Pakistan, at a time when there were only a handful of Pakistani immigrants in the country. It's an old weapon, not used today, but had been for centuries. The large ring is called a chakram and the smaller ones are chakri. I was given the box when I left. I wasn't allowed to practice with it back home, which is a bit of a bummer, as I have no idea how to use any of it.'

Bryn smiled. He didn't feel so bad now. As an act of appreciation and understanding, Bryn unwrapped his weapon from its canvas cloth again and showed Frasier his scheda, letting him know of his failed attempts at operating it that morning.

Both feeling a little relieved, they picked up their ambiguous weaponry and headed for the training field.

CHAPTER 35

Bryn and Frasier lined up alongside ten others. The numbers had halved. Stefan was there. That surprised them, after him appearing to be on the verge of death the day before. There were eight who appeared to be experienced and apart from Bryn, Frasier and Stefan, there was one other who wasn't. The group was made up of seven men and five women, every contestant looking fierce and eager. The competition unnerved Bryn slightly but to everyone else, it appeared that he was holding his own.

Each trainee had a satchel or a box of some description. Not one weapon had yet been exposed. They stood side by side, waiting for Gregor. Luckily, they didn't have to wait for long.

As he approached, the group stood to military attention. As he walked past, he studied each trainee, making a mental note of each one. He stood in a central position, ten paces in front and addressed them with such strength of voice that he may have been heard at the other side of the encampment.

'Congratulations on getting this far in the training program. Don't get too confident. There is a lot left to do. Today, we will concentrate on your weapons. Most of you have some training experience. Those who have will be assigned to me. Those who haven't will be spending the day with our weapons expert. Learn what you can for there is limited time for you to get advice or the assistance you need.'

Gregor gestured at the entrance gate. A figure drew closer. Nobody turned to look, as they held their position and their attention towards Gregor.

'All those who have been here before, follow me to the training field,' he continued. 'Stefan, Frasier, Bryn and Giselle stay here.'

As the others left, the anonymous figure walked into their line of sight.

All four trainees were noticeably taken aback.

'My name is Kyra,' she said, pacing with her hands clenched behind her back. With a wry smile, she continued, 'I will be your instructor today.'

CHAPTER 36

Kyra knew she had surprised two of her trainees. They stood looking at her with expressions of disbelief. She had to appear composed. It was proving to be more difficult than she imagined. This was her first time instructing competitors and she needed to prove herself worthy. Her youthful looks may play as a disadvantage but that was why Gregor had insisted she take part in the last training session. It certainly boosted her confidence, but only just. She was also fully aware of her capabilities and so was Gregor. He wouldn't have come to her village to persuade her to instruct if he didn't believe in her. Gregor always thought everything through to the finest detail.

'We are here today to introduce you to your weapons that have been passed on to you,' she began. 'I know I have met some of you already under less friendly circumstances, but let's put that behind us now. We need to move on, and we haven't much time.'

The four young trainees seemed to relax a little but still hadn't budged from their stance.

'I want you to unveil your weapons and place them by your feet.'

They did as they were told without question. She knew if she asked them to hop about on one leg, they probably would. That would change, she hoped. She was used to fighting on instinct and their rigid ways would have to change if they hoped to qualify.

She examined each weapon thoroughly, asking the name of each trainee without raising her eyes from each piece.

Giselle had a crossbow. The bow was two feet in length, beautifully crafted and the arrows were slender and plentiful.

Stefan had a large axe. The wood used to craft it was tough and roughly shaped. There was a six-inch spike raised from its head. She knew with a well-placed wallop from this, his foe wouldn't stand a chance. The question was, how good was his aim?

Frasier had a chakram. For such a rare piece of weaponry, he appeared to be disappointed. She was certain he hadn't discovered the embedded, retractable spikes yet. His attitude was sure to change by the end of the day.

Finally, she reached Bryn. She remembered his face. How could she forget? He nearly had her. She certainly wouldn't be standing where she was if she had been defeated by them. She felt slightly apologetic for leaving him unconscious, but needed to show strength. They would never have taken her seriously if she had held back as Gregor instructed. She needed to prove her worth. Being the youngest instructor ever enlisted, she felt every bit as challenged as the trainees.

Bryn had a binary blade. She had only seen one of its kind before. It was a difficult weapon, taking her more time than others to master.

It belonged to her father's friend, Lars. He called it a scheda. She knew he was passing his legacy to his son. This must be him. He had the same powerful, athletic build as his father, but his facial features were softer, younger.

She held the weapon in both hands for a moment before passing it back to its keeper.

'Welcome to your first weapon training session,' she said, after her inspection. 'I doubt any of you have had much experience with your weapons as the use of such devices is forbidden outside of Zhivrah.'

Bryn was now beginning to understand why his father had never revealed this undiscovered world or its hidden secrets.

'I would like you to form a circle around me and stand about fifteen paces apart. I will come to each of you and demonstrate each of your weapons. Pay attention, everyone. You will learn to master your weapons, but you need to be familiar with everyone else's too.'

She went to Giselle first and took her crossbow. She loaded it with ease and familiarity. Pointing it at a far post, she let the arrow fly. It hit the target, dead centre.

'This is the action of a simple crossbow, but like each of your weapons, this is not just a simple crossbow.'

She reloaded. With a couple of quick, minor adjustments, she took the shot again. This time, a telescopic lens released from the centre of the bow. The arrow Kyra shot split into four independent arrows and when they hit the same target, they formed a line – spaced two inches apart.

'That shows you shouldn't underestimate your opportunities.' She addressed the small group. 'These weapons have been designed for maximum effect.'

Next, she turned to Frasier. He barely looked at her when he passed her his box of metal rings. Bryn wasn't sure whether he was a bit sheepish after a humiliating defeat outside the training arena or maybe he felt unimpressed by this bequest from his father. Kyra took out the large ring, holding on to the leather grip, and slowly examined the piece. Then, she took the smallest ring from its box and placed it over the thumb on her right hand. With a slight adjustment of her left hand on the grip of the large ring, it split in two. Now there were two rings. Frasier suddenly became fascinated. Eyes on a target, she let one of the rings fly. It cut the post in half. With a gentle tap on Frasier's thumb ring, by her forefinger, the discharged weapon lifted from where it fell and flew back, landing over her outstretched arm. When Kyra threw the second half of the ring, she launched it in a vertical position. This time, spikes penetrated the outer layer. It hit its target; the blade wedged in the piece of wood. Kyra summoned it back. The smaller rings, she demonstrated, circled each arm like wrist bands. They had a protective cover to prevent accidental self-harm, and when a piece of it was removed, each paper-thin ring blade could be launched with a simple, but effective finger movement. Kyra demonstrated, and again recalled the blades.

'Wow!' gasped Frasier. 'That was the coolest thing I have ever seen.' He was grinning from ear to ear.

'These larger rings can also be very effective in hand-to-hand combat. These are not the simplest of weapons to master. Significant practising will be required,' Kyra informed Frasier. She then moved on to Stefan's axe.

Unlike Frasier's previous disregard for his chakram, Stefan showed great pride in his axe. It was a suitable symbol of his strength and power. Its head was metallic and polished as bright as the day it was forged. When handed to Kyra, it took a moment for her to grasp its full weight, although she didn't seem burdened. Standing by a nearby rock and grasping the axe with both hands, she swung it above her head and shifting her entire body for better leverage, she hit the fairly substantial rock, splitting it in two. Kyra ended her short demonstration with the body of the axe lying horizontally. With one quick twist of her wrist, its blade extended over three feet long. Again, the four trainees were suitably impressed.

It was time for Bryn to get his introduction to his intricately carved piece of wood, which somehow could transform into another impressive piece of weaponry. Kyra took it from his grasp and momentarily studied its etchings. She moved it slowly across her body, switched hands and mirrored the same motion with her other hand. She built a rhythm and soon she was treating it like a stick used in martial arts during a performance. Without pausing, she made the blades appear from either side and suddenly she was transformed into to a deadly assassin. Effortlessly, she managed to separate the scheda through its centre and now brandished two swords. She sliced through the air with her performance, entrancing the young hopefuls with her grace. She was both fierce and elegant, supple and intimidating.

Once finished her demonstration, she skilfully reattached the swords and retracted the blades. She handed it back to Bryn and addressed her captive audience.

'By the end of this week, I want each one of you showing true potential with your weapons. It is my job to make you familiar with them. It is your job to make them work to the best of your abilities. I can only send two of you on to the next level, so make every effort to impress.'

She looked into the eyes of each of the contenders.

'I have basic holograms for you to work with. These images are programmed to get hurt when struck and die if you manage to kill one. They will also beep if they inflict injury and a siren will be set off if they have hit a kill zone. You are welcome to come here to train as often as you like. You can approach me or any of the trainers regarding the use of an orb. These devices project the holographic technology used in training and will be used to release the more advanced technology in the tournament. Get familiar with the different programmes and settings. Let nothing take you by surprise.' Every word was spoken with clarity and vigour. 'Today I need to spend time with each of you so that you can learn how to use your weapon efficiently and safely. Giselle, you will be first. The rest of you may wait outside the gate by the courtyard. I will call you in turn.'

Frasier, Stefan and Bryn were dismissed. As they headed for the gate, Bryn turned for a moment so that he could absorb what he considered to be a vision of brilliance. He had never seen or heard of anyone quite like her. She was exceptional in every sense of the word.

All he wanted to do was impress her, get himself noticed. Frasier watched as he paced in anticipation. Bryn caught him grinning in his direction.

'What?' he asked Frasier.

'I think I may be sensing a little crush, Bryn,' Frasier remarked.

'No… maybe… I don't know.' Bryn found it difficult to deny but was relieved Frasier was called into the training grounds before he probed any further.

CHAPTER 37

When it was time for Bryn's tutorial, he was a little disappointed by the lack of conversation. His communication skills were a little awkward, but he thought he had at least made an effort. Kyra was very professional and courteous but there was no time for small-talk. It was considered a very serious affair.

Kyra thought Bryn showed promise but he seemed to be distracted. He was lacking concentration and that needed to change.

He was also heavier on his feet than she would have liked. She guessed he hadn't much experience in dancing, though she was hardly going to suggest classes as part of his regime. He possibly needed boxing lessons as part of his training. That could help with his footwork. She made a mental note to recommend for later.

Bryn held the rod. Kyra told him to study the etchings, as every image told a story. With both hands grasping the centre of the scheda, she instructed him to twist them in opposite directions. The blades released instantly. When he used the same motion with his hands separated, he was grasping two swords.

By the end of the hour, Bryn's technique was beginning to come along. He knew he had a great deal of work to do, but at that moment he wasn't too worried. His main concern was a personal one.

Kyra had captivated him. She had awoken feelings in him that were both distracting and frustrating. It was affecting his concentration. At least, he realised with a tinge of disappointment, the sentiment wasn't being reciprocated. If there was any chance, it could make things very complicated.

He needed to focus, to snap himself out of this stupor. He couldn't afford the distraction.

CHAPTER 38

The time spent weapons training was exhausting, but exhilarating. Bryn found himself growing stronger every day, physically and mentally. There was little consideration for anything else.

As well as trying to master his double-blade, he was advised to participate in boxing and martial arts classes, and because of his previous experience, he was placed with seasoned contenders. This was an unfamiliar undertaking as he had spent little time with anyone, other than Frasier and a few other fresh faces. Some of these men and women were far superior to him in many ways. It would be a difficult task to not appear immature and a little green. However, it allowed him to prove himself able, and that was what he was determined to do.

He began every morning, before dawn, with tai chi alongside the other contestants in the training arena. This was followed by a group run around the walls of the encampment and a hearty breakfast. Afterwards, an hour was spent on practical theory and the teaching and reinforcement of the rules of the games. The penalty for breaking one of the rules was an automatic disqualification.

The afternoon was used for mastering weaponry. This was Bryn's favourite part as the holographic images were so lifelike. It was captivating. He could spend hours working on his swing, perfecting each sway of the blades until they became extensions of his limbs.

His rhythm and footwork improved dramatically with the boxing and martial arts classes he had every evening. Not only had he reached an equal status with the more experienced players, in a very short time he had also surpassed some of them. They became his peers and he had gained some respect and due regard.

By nightfall, Bryn fell into his bed dog-tired and weary. Most nights Frasier was asleep ahead of him. They hadn't seen each other very often recently, occasionally passing on the running track. Not long enough to allow for conversation or even to acknowledge each other. They were both consumed with their efforts, both realising how much they wanted this opportunity – to the point that Bryn finally regarded Frasier as competition. They had gained so much knowledge and skill during training that neither one was going to find it easy to let go. Neither one was going to fail, without carrying out everything in their power to make sure that that wouldn't happen.

The day came when their fate was to be told. Bryn, Frasier, Stefan and Giselle were summoned to the training grounds to compete for the chance to become one of the four representatives in the Zhavia Shield. They knew by the end of that day, two of them would be sent home.

All four made the effort to sit side by side for breakfast that morning. It was the first time they had been together since they were given their assignments five weeks before. The transformation in each of them was incredible. Not only had they become physically robust, their naivety had also been consumed by confidence, stemmed from their training and their lust for accomplishment. In such a short time it may have seemed impossible, but not with their inherent abilities, strict regime and Tilly's special brew.

The biggest surprise at the table, was Stefan. Most of the fat he had carried seemed to have been converted to muscle. His weight was probably much the same but now instead of appearing as if he enjoyed an abundance of food, he looked fierce and Herculean.

'What the hell happened to you?' Frasier exclaimed as he studied with disbelief the size of Stefan's small breakfast portion.

'What can I say? I am a dedicated student,' Stefan responded with a mouth full of food.

They were equally aware of how much effort was needed to earn a place to compete. Although they sat and tried to enjoy each other's company, there was a niggling desire in all of them to suss out their opponents, which in this case, were sitting alongside them.

'So, Frasier, how is your chakram training coming along?' Giselle asked.

'Great, Giselle, but it all really depends on the one who is throwing it,' he replied, with a hint of sarcasm. 'Lucky for me, I'm a damn good shot.'

Giselle rolled her eyes at Frasier's remark.

'How about you, Bryn?' she continued. 'How is that double-bladed what-ya-ma-call-it working out?'

'Better than I expected.' Bryn sensed Giselle was developing a barefaced competitive streak, and either she was beginning to feel a risen confidence, or an element of doubt. Questioning her sincerity, he kept his answer short and vague.

There was an awkward silence that intervened until the last contents of their plates were devoured.

Stefan grew restless and fidgety.

'Are you okay there, big man?' Frasier asked, genuinely concerned.

'Of course I am not!' claimed Stefan. 'I am still starving.'

The building cloud of tension was suddenly defused by Stefan's blatant remark and the topic of conversation quickly turned to idle chatter, anything to distract them from the day ahead.

CHAPTER 39

When they reached the training ground, Kyra was waiting and it seemed like she had been there a while. Four orbs floated in wide circles above her head, ready to be put to work.

The four young contenders stood side by side awaiting her instruction.

'Today is the final day in the competition for two of you. Your fate will be determined by a simple test. You will each do battle with a hologram and I will choose two of you to go forward to the final round.'

Kyra had delivered the final challenge. Each competitor took a corner of the training ground and an orb hovered above them as they moved into position. When they were ready, she produced four large shields from a canvas bag by her feet and handed them out.

'Today, you will need these. You will be fighting a creature you have not experienced yet. These shields will prove vital.'

Bryn felt the weight of his shield and tested a few positions with it to find one that might prove most effective.

'Be careful with your aim. I have purposefully kept distance between you so that you won't accidentally kill each other.'

Kyra felt confident they were ready for the final challenge. She was impressed with their poise and stature. These were not the same trainees she introduced herself to five weeks ago. They were now warriors. She just hoped they would prove worthy of a role in this year's games because she was fully aware of how much effort each of them put in to get this far.

'When you are ready, we shall begin,' she said and took position in the centre of the arena. In her hand was a small black gadget. As the hopefuls bore their shields in expectation, she pressed the central control button.

CHAPTER 40

The orbs released four large, powerful and extremely irate dragons. They stood over twenty feet tall and seemed more lifelike than any of the creatures projected before. It took Bryn a moment to remember that these were just creations, figments of someone's imagination portrayed by a complicated and advanced technology.

His dragon was coloured a crimson red, with a striking yellow underbelly. It was an impressive sight and Bryn would have appreciated its vibrancy more if it wasn't trying to demolish him. His shield kept him in good stead. It gave him a moment so he could plan an attack manoeuvre. He was getting blasted by fake heat, but that knowledge did nothing to wane the intensity of the situation.

He took a quick peek at his other competitors. They appeared to have charged straight in. He heard a couple of beeps to indicate that one or more of the other dragons had inflicted some pseudo injuries, however he couldn't ascertain the condition of the beasts themselves – whether they had been wounded at this early stage or were still battling at full force.

All this contemplating did nothing to help his chances of outwitting this fierce creature, who was now trying to remove the shield from his grasp.

Then, he had a moment of what he regarded as brilliance. There was little point him trying to fight face to face with this dragon. It had too much leverage. The better option was to go in low. If he could get under it, he could inflict more damage and possibly have the upper hand. The dragon may be partially blindsided and that could play to his advantage. However, if he landed on him or managed to strike when he was at such proximity, that would quickly be the end of any chance of competing in the games.

A siren went off. That meant someone was out. Yet he had no idea who. He had no time to waste. Now was his chance.

He lifted himself. He could almost smell the dragon's breath on him though he knew that was not possible. With his shield held above for protection, he lurched forward already wielding his scheda, with a blade protruding from one end. The bellow from the beast was resounding. Bryn was afraid to look beyond anything but his target. The hind legs of the dragon danced from one to the other and apart from raising slightly when it flexed its wings, they were the most reliable point of attack.

He fended off the beast's head with his shield and when he got to the legs, he wasted no time and speared one with all his might. Even though he was hitting air, the experience felt real. Before he heard the beep to acknowledge his affliction, he split the binary spear in two and went straight for the beast's other hind leg.

That was when he emerged from under the dragon. It stumbled backwards and Bryn used the chance to run at it with unrelenting speed, abnormally fast. As he approached, he leapt into the air – vaulting higher than he could imagine – and using the separated blades, he aimed for the throat, slicing through it like paper. The beast was beheaded.

Bryn would have loved to hear the thud of the body as it hit the ground, but instead, the image simply disappeared. The holographic depiction had ended, and Bryn had beaten it. He couldn't believe his achievement and sat on the sawdust-coated ground to take it all in.

CHAPTER 41

When he turned, he saw that Stefan was the last man standing in battle, putting up a ferocious fight against his rival dragon. Giselle seemed to be in the middle of a heated argument with herself and Frasier was standing at his assigned position, staring over at Bryn, with a facial expression that Bryn found difficult to read.

What had just occurred had such an element of surrealism that Bryn was slightly overwhelmed. It didn't help that his ears were still ringing from the sheer volume that had radiated from the technology used to create such a fierce creature. It took a moment for him to collect his thoughts and to return to the reality of the situation.

When he stood, his hearing improved dramatically. He didn't feel drained or tired from what he had just experienced. He began to feel invigorated. It was fun. Even if he didn't make it, he knew that it was a memory he would always cherish. Not many people get to fight a dragon, even if it wasn't a real one.

Kyra's attention was fully focused on Stefan. His dragon was stumbling, ready to drop. So was Stefan. He put in one final effort and gathered all his might. He charged at it, roaring something in his native Dutch tongue. He lodged the axe deep into its belly and it fell; so did Stefan. He had completely exhausted himself.

Before long, all four stood once again in front of Kyra, waiting to hear their fate. She gave no impression that she was pleased or disappointed with how the event had played out.

'Giselle, step forward,' she said without hesitating. 'Frasier, step forward. I'm afraid this is the end of the trials for you both.'

Bryn was shocked that a decision like that could be made with little consideration and delivered so bluntly.

Giselle and Frasier didn't even have time to react before she turned on her heels and headed for the gates. They turned to their fellow competitors and looked physically gutted.

Nobody spoke as they made their way back to their rooms. Neither Bryn nor Stefan felt like celebrating their elevation to the next level of the competition. It didn't seem appropriate and they barely had enough energy to make it across the courtyard. They were both now physically and mentally drained and the next day was time enough to consider their next challenge and to revel in their achievements.

Back at the dormitories, Bryn watched as Frasier packed his belongings.

'Don't even know why I'm doing this,' he said, pointing at his rucksack. 'The portal isn't being activated until just before the games begin. It's bad enough being knocked out so close to the end, now I have to wait around this godawful place with no way of getting home.'

Bryn knew that Frasier didn't mean what he said about Zhivrah. Of all the contestants, he settled in the quickest, made the most effort to make it home away from home, and spent any spare minute off exploring.

'I miss the beach, you know. The waves crashing, the weather… the women.' He feigned a smile.

'Frasier, I don't know what happened out in the training grounds. I don't know why Kyra chose me over you. Honestly, it could easily have been you,' Bryn offered.

'That was no toss-up,' Frasier interjected. 'You should have seen yourself out there. I was dead long before you emerged from that shield. What you did… let me just say that I have never seen anything like that. You were on fire! You deserved that place. Hell, you deserve a place on the team.'

Frasier's remark was heartfelt and genuine.

'I am almost tempted to hang around to see what happens,' he added, perking up a bit.

Bryn was dumbfounded for a moment.

'I'm sorry you didn't make the team,' he said, just before Frasier unexpectedly fell asleep. When he heard no response, he looked over towards Frasier's side of the room where he was passed out on his bed. That's when Bryn noticed an empty cup on the bedside table. Tilly had worked her magic again tonight. Frasier appeared to be having his best night's sleep in weeks.

CHAPTER 42

Frasier was still sleeping when Bryn left for training the following morning. The six final contenders ran at great speed around the boundary walls, none feeling its toll, their strength and stamina evident.

Gregor had approached them before they set off, to inform them that a decision had been made on the final four – the team that would represent the human race, the Earthians. It was to be announced after lunch. The four men and two women had decided to continue training. It was easier than waiting around for the verdict on their fate.

When Bryn returned to his room, Frasier was just rousing from his slumber. Bryn's nervous energy was driven into the floor as he paced it, not sure how to break his news to Frasier, who appeared surprisingly nonchalant.

'The team has been picked. They are assembling everyone to the training ground after lunch,' Bryn blurted out.

'That was quick. Do you know who you are you up against?'

Bryn thought for a minute. 'Well, there's me and Stefan. Moses's through too, but that's no surprise. There's Alisi from Fiji and Zora, the Serbian. Kenta, from Japan is the sixth and final contender.' He paused for a moment. 'They're the best of the best, Frasier. Chances are that we will be both watching the games from the stands. I haven't a hope.'

'Bryn, you are as good as anyone I've seen. You have as much of a chance as any of the others. You just need to believe it.' Frasier sounded sincere. 'Anyhow, the team has been picked so you might as well show up.' He smiled.

Bryn knew that in spite of Frasier being knocked out of the

competition, it was generous of him to encourage his former rival. Although, deep down, he always considered Frasier more of a friend than an opponent.

Lunchtime brought little appetite for Bryn. He sat in the canteen with Frasier and Stefan. Giselle sat close by but wasn't in the mood for talking, as she was still rather disappointed at being ousted from the competition. No one spoke much. Even Stefan ate less than his normal smaller, but still large, helping.

In spite of most competitors being knocked out, the canteen was unusually busy. Bryn learned that the majority of contenders who didn't qualify for the final go exploring Zhivrah, or take a break in the town near the encampment before some set off on their return journey. Most stay for the games as the experience itself can be one to treasure. For others, the time is used as grounds for learning and tactical appreciation for the next opportunity to participate.

After what little lunch Bryn could digest, he wandered out to the courtyard, where a platform had been erected and a crowd had started to gather. Across the yard, he spotted Gregor talking with Samuel. They appeared to be immersed in a heated discussion. Curiosity was a welcome distraction, but as he drew closer to get a better sense of what was causing such debate, Frasier pulled him right back into the hub of the building excitement surrounding him.

'No more waiting, Bryn,' he said, with an encouraging smile. 'You should make your way over to the podium. Your destiny awaits.'

CHAPTER 43

The contenders from each tribe were to be announced from the podium. The captive audience was large and bustling with excited chatter. Bryn, Stefan and the others were led behind a curtain alongside the finalists from the other three teams. Although they were foreign to each other, they displayed the same nervous energy, natural to such an event.

The crowd hushed and everyone was handed out earpieces like the last gathering. Bryn installed his, just as the first speaker was getting started. It was Samuel, so a translation wasn't necessary.

Samuel welcomed the crowd of enthusiasts who had gathered, his voice travelling with vigour as far as to back wall of the courtyard. He spoke of how well the contenders fought to ascertain a place in the team, which would represent their race, in the most anticipated event on the calendar. He commended the instructors and dedicated staff at the training facility. Everyone applauded on cue, apart from the Shiakanas, who believed that clapping made no sense. It was just another ridiculous ritual brought to Zhivrah by these senseless beings.

Once the introduction speech was delivered, he gestured to another speaker, a Goytek member of the council, who spoke at length about the introduction of new technology that superseded any creative power imaginable. His pride in their development of these upgraded nanotech instruments far outweighed his regard for the participating Goytek team. It was well beyond the outdated holographic technology used for previous competitions, adding depth, versatility and imagination. They were excited to see what this dynamic would bring to this year's games.

By the time the other two members of the council addressed the audience, the crowd was becoming impatient. Bryn was busy chewing a fingernail and the rest of the participants behind the curtain were becoming so restless that they could be heard on the stage floor.

'Would the final six competitors from the Hazuru team please come forward?' Bryn heard through his earpiece.

Everyone went silent as the six teammates mounted the stage.

One by one the names of the final four team members were called out, followed by a cheering consensus from the courtyard.

The Shiakana team were announced next. The final four were celebrated with a frenzy of grunting sounds, which resembled feeding time at a zoo. It was accompanied by the stamping of feet and raising of fists.

Bryn's team was called next. He exchanged a nervous glance with Stefan, took a deep breath, and followed him onto the stage. Samuel greeted each of them like a proud father, although he paused slightly as he was about to embrace Bryn. At that moment, Bryn realised that the argument earlier between Samuel and Gregor was about him. He had to put that thought aside for the moment and as he scanned the crowd, searching for familiar faces, it hit him how important these games were to the inhabitants of Zhivrah and how privileged he was to get this chance to be a part of them. The audience had become larger than he could have anticipated. There were people gathered from all of Zhivrah – including a few outside guests crammed together, trying to get a look at the six finalists. Bryn had no idea where they had all come from. His nervous smile grew into a broad grin. He spotted Frasier close to the stage, cheering and chanting his and Stefan's names.

As he continued to take in this spectacle, two people fought their way through the crowd to get closer to where he stood. When he saw their faces, he fought every urge in his body not to run to greet them. It was his parents. He could not believe what he was seeing. They came all the way here just to see if he would qualify.

They struck Bryn as being proud, especially his father. His mother waved and smiled, yet seemed distracted, her eyes diverting to the crowd. Maybe she had been here before. Maybe she had competed alongside his father. It didn't matter now. That conversation could wait. This moment was the greatest in Bryn's life and even if he didn't make the team, he would always have this to remember. He stood tall though uncertain as he awaited his fate.

Samuel called for order as he was about to deliver the decision made by the council and the instructors. The first name called was Moses. He smiled graciously, shook hands with Samuel and waved at his many supporters.

Next name to be called was Kenta. He appeared unfazed and respectfully bowed at Samuel and the spectators.

Bryn's hands were sweating. He swallowed hard. The enormity of what he had achieved and what he could achieve hit him suddenly.

'Next to make it through is Alisi,' announced Samuel. The Fijian leapt into the air with delight and then tried to compose herself quickly, as if she may have made a mistake celebrating so boisterously. However, she couldn't hide her broad smile.

The last contestants were Bryn, Stefan and Serbian Zora.

CHAPTER 44

Bryn stood alongside his fellow competitors, vying for the last spot on the team. The crowd were pleased with the choices made by the council so far. These were experienced warriors. Moses and Kenta had participated previously and Alisi had stood on stage twice before, however had not been picked. It was no wonder that she jumped for joy when her name was read out.

Unbeknownst to most new contenders, all orb feeds of trials were displayed on screens around Zhivrah for the citizens to follow. That was the main reason for the vast crowd gathered for the team selection. Most had their favourites picked by the time the vote was cast. The majority seemed satisfied so far.

'The final contestant will be…'

Samuel hesitated for a moment, Bryn wasn't sure whether it was for dramatic effect or a moment of doubt.

'…Bryn Jahr.'

Bryn couldn't believe it. Neither could the crowd. Some cheered straight away. Others had to confer with their neighbours before they applauded and the rest stood with indifference, not sure what to make of this newcomer who had robbed the more experienced in the final rounds of the competition.

This didn't bother Bryn. He hardly noticed as he only had eyes for his parents, who both gleamed with pride, his father even shedding a few tears.

After Bryn and his other team members were led backstage, the Goytek finalists were summoned. Behind the curtain Stefan congratulated his friend, putting on a brave face to show that he wasn't too crestfallen. Zora had disappeared without saying a word. The ceremony continued and Bryn was becoming agitated as all he wanted to do was see his parents.

Moses approached him, followed by Kenta and Alisi.

'Welcome to the team, Bryn.' Moses offered his hand and Bryn shook it. 'You'd better be as good as Gregor thinks you are!'

He made sure that no one heard his follow-up remark, except Bryn. It was obvious that Moses resented the council's final candidate for the team.

'Well done, Bryn. Looking forward to the opportunity of training together. We'll get to see what you're truly made of!' Alisi reached over Moses' broad shoulder and offered a wink and a sincere handshake to Bryn, who welcomed it gratefully. Kenta didn't say a word, which was not surprising as it was rumoured that he only spoke Japanese. Watching him train, it was clear he certainly understood English, but whether he couldn't speak it or didn't want to, Bryn wasn't sure. As Bryn looked at him and took in all those years etched on his face, he realised that he must be close to sixty, outnumbering most of his competitors, apart from Moses, by over thirty years.

All those weeks training, he never really spoke to these contenders. He considered them higher ranking, more worthy opponents. The idea of competing alongside them had never entered his mind. The notion of competing at all was never a true realisation, until now.

CHAPTER 45

Sanne waited behind the podium for Bryn to step down. Their reunion was one of pride and emotion. Lars knew that there was a chance that Bryn would do well in the training arena but had no idea of his true potential. He held back, until Sanne released their son from her embrace, to shake his hand. Entering him into the competition was a gamble but it seemed to have paid off. Lars sensed that Samuel was watching them. That never changed. He decided to lead his family away from the crowd, so they could talk in peace.

They moved to the edge of the courtyard, near the doors to the canteen. Most of the crowd had started to disperse. There was a celebratory meal about to start inside but the Jahr family needed a moment alone. It was the first time they had seen each other in over two months, the most extraordinary two months in Bryn's life.

'I am so proud of you, son!' His father was glowing with pride. 'I thought you might do well, but I never expected that you would qualify at your first trials. You have surpassed every hope I had. I really am very pleased.'

'Thanks, Dad,' Bryn responded, slightly abashed.

After a moment of contented silence, Sanne exchanged glances with Lars. She had rehearsed a conversation on the journey over, one she knew she needed to have with Bryn. Realising there was no way to broach the subject softly, she decided to discuss it with him as soon as they saw each other. She had no idea how he was going to react.

'Bryn, I know your father told you how he has been competing here since before you were born. We thought it best not to disclose too much information to you before you left, as it can be overwhelming. Your father and I didn't want to frighten you off the idea of competing. Anyway, now that you're settled in, I… we thought it best that you know that I have competed here once. It was well before you were born.'

'Mum, I know. Samuel told me. I didn't know that it was true until now, but I'm fine with you not telling me. I get it. I completely understand.' Bryn's response was a testament to how much he had matured since he arrived. Sanne smiled with relief. 'Though, I am curious as to why you decided to leave and not return to compete?' Bryn asked.

'Not everyone comes back, Bryn. Don't get me wrong, I love it here. But, it just wasn't for me. I passed the legacy on to a distant cousin before we moved to England. It felt like the right thing to do.'

'I know a spread has been laid out for the feast,' Lars interrupted, 'and I'm starving. Sanne, you must be too. We have been travelling all day, Bryn. Do you two mind if we move this inside?'

Bryn wasn't surprised his father cut the discussion short. He always had the attitude to not dwell or elaborate on conversation.

The canteen was packed. Bryn had never seen it so full. Frasier had kept places for them to sit. Stefan and Giselle were seated alongside. Giselle had come round from her defeat in the training field and even Stefan was surprisingly happy. Introductions were made to Bryn's parents and they welcomed them warmly.

The large banquet had already been set, a selection of meats waiting to be carved with large bowls of vegetables and bread rolls. Everyone tucked in. The room was filled with the bustle of excited chit-chat. Every tribe sat separately, each feasting on dishes native to their homelands.

Bryn told his parents about his journey with Gregor, the crossing to Iceland on the fishing boat, the hesitation at the geyser and a short account of his experiences so far in Zhivrah. Frasier, Stefan and Giselle also described their passage and experience, and in return, Lars relayed some of his anecdotes. Circumstances prevented Bryn from hearing these stories as a child. He was captivated. It was also a relief for him to see his father talk about his past so enthusiastically, especially in front of Bryn's friends.

But suddenly mid-conversation, spotting Samuel entering the canteen, Lars excused himself from the table. Bryn watched as his father confronted him at the other end of the room. It didn't seem to be a most cordial reunion. Giselle, sensing Bryn's distraction, suggested that she, Frasier and Stefan leave Bryn and his mother catch up. It was also getting late.

'You'd never guess that they were friends once,' Sanne said, indicating Lars and Samuel. It was just Bryn and her left at the table. 'The tension between them has been building for years. Best you not get involved.'

Bryn didn't realise his mum was watching him.

'On my second day, Samuel approached me and tried to convince me to go home; that I wasn't ready. He wanted Dad back. I was told later, it was a test to see if I was committed enough, if I was ready to compete. For a moment, I thought I wasn't welcome. I thought he admired Dad. It's just strange to see them behave that way with each other,' Bryn said.

Sanne hid her surprise well. They never had mind games like that back when she did her training. She did her best to hide her rising anger.

'Bryn, you need to listen to me. Respect Samuel for who he is. He is an admired member of the council and he has a lot of influence. But, stay out of his way. You may not understand why, you just have to remember it has nothing to do with anything you have done or said. I promise, one day, I will talk to you about it. Today is not that day. You have more important challenges ahead of you,' she said.

Bryn wanted answers but understood that their quarrel most likely had nothing to do with him. He knew better than to push the subject.

Sanne and Bryn spent the next ten minutes discussing the farm as though they were back in their kitchen, like nothing had ever changed. Lars returned to the table braving a calm demeanour, shaking off the heated discussion he just had with Samuel. He didn't offer any explanation or reason, and Bryn knew better than to ask.

'I am so glad you came.' Bryn addressed his parents. 'It means a lot to have you both here.'

Sanne reached across the table, reaching for her son's hand. Lars held both hands in his.

'Journeys of self-discovery are important, son,' he said. 'They provide an opportunity to explore and learn. It is important for you to choose your path wisely. Grow your confidence slowly. From now on, you will not be on your own, but part of a team. Don't let ambition cloud your judgement. Confidence is certainly an attribute but focus on the whole picture, the loyalty to your teammates, the duty you have to those watching.'

Lars knew this would be the last time they saw Bryn before the tournament. He wanted to encourage him, to give the advice given to him at his age. 'When we meet again, you will no longer be an apprentice, but a warrior. This is a rite of passage like no other, very few people are given this chance. Don't waste it.'

This tournament meant a lot to Lars. Bryn knew this. Thinking back to how he had prepared him his entire life for this moment, it all made sense now. There was no emotion in his words though they were reassuring, like a teacher encouraging a student. Bryn was constantly reminded of his father's aversion to displayed affection, his difficulty expressing emotion. He often wondered how his parents had maintained such a solid relationship. There must have been some attribute that attracted his mother to him, some softness in his manner Bryn hadn't seen. Yes, Bryn appreciated all the training Lars had drilled into him his entire life. He respected him for that and the advice he gave now. But, he doubted they could ever connect fully as father and son. He didn't want to disappoint him, wanted to make him proud. The question he had to ask himself now was, was he participating in the tournament to achieve self-attained glory or was it to gain his father's recognition?

'I will do my best to make you proud,' Bryn responded, after a pause.

Lars smiled at him.

'I think it's time for bed. It has been a long day for all of us,' his mother said.

'Yes, of course,' Lars added. 'We shall see you after the competition, son. Best of luck.' They shook hands. Bryn hugged his mother and didn't want to let go.

CHAPTER 46

The four teammates were called to the training ground at sunrise. Gregor greeted them at the gate. His face was difficult to read. He was serious by nature, usually lacking any visible expression of emotion or otherwise; much like Bryn's father. The only difference was Gregor, at times, could become unexpectedly animated, whether it was anger, passion or humour. Most of the time he was exceptionally professional. Because of this, he was highly respected by recruits and his peers. Few crossed him, even less had a bad word to say in his regard. He was the warrior to the warriors, mentor to the wise and scholar to the students.

He walked alongside them with long, proud strides. His head was high and his air was confident.

Bryn was trying to keep a cool façade, mimicking the others. They surpassed him in years and in experience and he didn't want his unseasoned background to mar his capability. He strode into the training ground behind Gregor, holding his weapon with purpose. Was this the part of the competition when everything came apart and it became evident that he should be watching with Stefan, Frasier and the others from the side-line?

Moses had a sword, one that wouldn't have looked out of place in a medieval setting. It crossed his back, held by a sheath strapped around his broad torso. Alisi had a rifle, which Bryn could only describe as a double-barrelled shotgun. It looked like it could be made from silver or a similar metal, with a leather handle. It hung over her shoulder. She also carried two side-arms, holstered around her waist.

Kenta didn't seem to have a weapon, which was a bit unusual, but Bryn was sure that there was a perfectly reasonable explanation for this.

Gregor stopped and they formed a line. He stood facing them.

'You four are the chosen ones, who will represent our world. You will bring honour and pride to our lands. Doing your best will not win this tournament. Being the best is what we need to achieve. You are no longer competing against each other. You are a team and from now on will behave like one. That will mean spending every waking moment together for the next three days. Each one of you will know your teammates' strengths and weaknesses. Individually you each possess certain capabilities that when bonded should potentially create the perfect balance, giving us the greatest hope for victory. It is up to you to make this happen.'

Gregor spoke with clarity, defining every word, barely a trace of his German accent, his intonation neutral. The four competitors hung on to every word, standing to attention, not even moving a muscle as they listened.

'We have three days, three days to mould you into a force to be reckoned with. The preparation for this event is as important as the participation. Believe me!'

Just then, Kyra entered the arena, followed by a mammoth of a man wearing a sleeveless tunic, exposing biceps as large as Kyra's head. They stood side by side with Gregor without saying a word.

'I think we have a little time to see what these warriors are made of,' Gregor challenged, his tone becoming suddenly lighter. 'Kenta, Moses, stand down for now. I want to see what the other two are capable of first. Alisi, you can take on Kyra. I know Bryn has had some experience with her in the field. Bryn, you can take on the might of Hercule.'

Bryn was visibly bemused.

'Before you ask, Hercule is my real name. It suits me, no?' Hercule commented with a broad French accent, his manner having a hint of condescension.

Bryn accompanied him to the centre of the arena, knowing his blades were probably no match for Hercule's brawn. They faced each other in battle mode, although it took longer than expected for Hercule to administer eye contact. His mind seemed elsewhere and unfocused. He was distracted by his environment. Bryn realised that he could use this to his advantage. There may be a little hope after all.

Hercule and Kyra were each handed Gregor's choice of weapons. Two wooden rods for Hercule and a long staff for Kyra. They seemed unfazed and confident with this selection. Bryn faced Hercule ready to unleash his blades but Gregor handed him two wooden sticks in their stead. Alisi was also given a long staff.

'You can inflict bruises but everyone is leaving here today with limbs intact.'

CHAPTER 47

Bryn became so focused on his target that he managed to block all surrounding activity from his attention. He noticed that Hercule had been vying for Kyra's attention with glances, even as she positioned herself for her challenge. He also occasionally glanced at Gregor, maybe hoping for his approval or awaiting direction. He even managed to swat at some flies near his face as the countdown was about to begin.

'On my mark. Three, two, one... engage!'

Hercule diverted his eyes momentarily, delivering Bryn a self-assured grin, before settling his hands on his rods to gain a comfortable grasp. Bryn slowly made a guarded approach, wielding Gregor's choice of benign weaponry. He watched how Hercule favoured his left arm. That was important as a blow could be delivered from an angle that he may not have foreseen. He was also heavy-footed and that could be advantageous if correctly exploited.

The distance between the two combatants lessened slowly and as it seemed that Hercule was expecting a hesitant start, Bryn took the opportunity to launch a full-speed assault. His surprise tactic wasn't wasted as he delivered a double-footed punch straight into his opponent's chest, winding him and knocking him to the ground.

Hercule quickly recovered and took a moment to regain composure along with some of his pride. He became focused, thoroughly concentrated on his target, one who would pay dearly for making a fool of him.

Hercule struck a blow with one of his batons, which would have caused significant damage if Bryn hadn't predicted that it would come from his preferred left arm. He ducked and danced around the large man trying to disorient him to gain an advantage. What he hadn't expected was a backhand from Hercule's right hand that caught him on his left cheekbone. He could already feel it swelling from the force. He stumbled backwards but only for a moment. He shook off the searing pain that was expanding from the point of contact.

The battle took a different tangent once Bryn engaged Hercule with both rods. The sound of wood on wood became rhythmic as the beats grew in tempo and force. Gregor watched as both participants engaged as if competing in a duel of honour. Bryn had the youth and speed but Hercule's strength and experience easily matched, if not surpassed it.

Kyra had just delivered Alisi a final blow, ending a fairly non-stimulating match by comparison. She was expecting an approving nod from Gregor but turned to find that Moses, Kenta and Gregor were not looking in her direction, but were immersed in what appeared to be a full battle being played out at the far end of the arena. Although somewhat vexed, she had to admit that within moments she was impressed. She had never seen Hercule this worked up before, even when they sparred together. Every move he made, Bryn was one step ahead. They fought like true warriors, as if their lives depended on it. It was truly mesmerising.

Apart from an odd blow, Bryn had not been having much luck getting past Hercule's defence. However, with one swift and bold move he managed to twist both batons away from him and they landed several feet away. Hercule was stunned and then mad. He became so mad, he looked fit to explode. He stood and stared at Bryn with wild eyes. Bryn felt triumphant but had to bend forward with his hands on his knees to catch his breath. In that short moment he looked away, he could hear the stomping of feet closing in on him. He could see small grains of sand vibrating on the ground below. By the time he straightened up, it was too late. Hercule had taken him full force, like a tackle in a sports game. He charged at him from over a hundred feet at tremendous speed, straight into a wall, pinning him so that he could barely catch a breath.

With his face so close that Bryn could smell garlic emanating from his pores, Hercule whispered in his ear. 'Not a bad fight, Bryn, but there was no way I would let you beat me, garçon. Time for you to go to sleep now.'

Hercule applied so much pressure to Bryn's chest that in less than a minute he passed out, maintaining eye contact until the very last moment.

CHAPTER 48

Bryn woke in his room expecting to see Tilly there with a cup of tea flavoured with whatever it took to heal wounded pride. Instead, he was alone. Getting out of bed was a slow process due to his tender ribs but he was eager to find Gregor. He needed another chance to prove his worth in the field and wanted to schedule a rematch when it was physically possible. He could really do with a day or two to heal first.

As it happened, Gregor wasn't difficult to find. He was standing out in the courtyard having a heated discussion with one of the instructors from the Goytek camp. Bryn approached as they broke conversation, and both headed their separate ways.

'You look a little bruised there, young Bryn.'

Gregor had caught sight of Bryn as he neared.

'Are you talking about me or my ego?' Bryn even managed a smile as he flinched with a stab of pain.

'You should be resting.'

'What was that about?' Bryn asked, regarding the disagreement he just witnessed. 'Anything we need to worry about?'

'It's nothing, as usual. When the Goyteks release new tech, they think other races can't fathom it. The older tech we use in the training field was holographically designed. Simpler. We knew what we were fighting wasn't real. There was no physical structure. It was based on imagery. This generation is more complex, more absolute. You will be fighting an enemy that can fight back. And, though they cannot inflict pain, just paralytics, we need to be sure there isn't room for error. We don't want anyone to be seriously hurt. He just didn't understand why I would question the safety aspect. Pure arrogance. Typical Goytek behaviour.'

'Are we going to have a chance to train with this new technology?' Bryn queried.

'As it happens, we'll be spending the afternoon discussing other team members; their strengths and weaknesses, but more importantly we'll talk about possible course challenges and the finer intricacies of this tech and how it will affect our chances. Tomorrow, on your last day of training, you'll get a chance to see what we're up against.' Bryn's intrigue distracted him as Gregor walked away. He never had a chance to inquire about a possible rematch. It didn't seem important anymore.

After lunch Bryn, Alisi, Kenta and Moses sat on a bench facing Gregor in the meeting room. They were there to discuss tactics, gameplay and the strengths and possible weaknesses of their opponents.

The ultimate goal of the Zhavia Shield was pretty straight forward. The first team to get their hands on the Shield wins. Team participants would be equidistant from its position but starting from four separate locations: north, south, east and west.

Each team would endure separate obstacles, based on the strengths and weaknesses of their race. This tactic was employed to display fairness in competition. Each fabricated opponent had relevant skills to meet each competing team. That was why the teams never crossed paths. It would be deemed unfair.

Because the Goytek cabinet gained approval for technology beyond anything the committee had seen before, this year's event was sure to draw most, if not all Zhivrah nationals. Also, past competitors would visit just to bear witness to the nanotechnology and the effect it would have on future tournaments. Although each team member had their individual talents and skills, the challenge was to work as one entity, to understand and identify each warrior's strengths and weaknesses; for you cannot have one without the other.

Bryn was the only link that suffered from inexperience, but Gregor pointed out that that may not necessarily be a negative attribute, considering the traditional hurdles that impeded their route had become obsolete. They had been replaced with technology beyond anything the other three had ever seen.

Kenta's weakness was his obvious lack of communication skills. They would have to overcome that by adapting to hand signals and subtle facial expressions, both techniques familiar to Alisi and Moses from experience.

Moses' arrogance was widely regarded as bravado. Since they began to work as a team, his large ego had been replaced by sheer determination and kinsmanship, and a loyalty Bryn had only ever experienced from his own family. Moses knew his weaknesses and understood that he must let go of the frivolous ones.

This was the furthest Alisi had come in her years of training and she had ultimately reached her goal, the chance to participate. Had she exhausted herself in order to get this far or did she have a lot more to give? Gregor was confident. She just needed the encouragement to reach the next level.

Gregor was fully aware that each warrior here was not perfect but as a team they might be the best collaboration he had seen in his lifetime. He was proud and by the end of the tournament, he was sure that they would be too. Yes, there were significant risks involved, but there was incredible potential. He was both excited and nervous about the prospect.

CHAPTER 49

The Goytek team was led by Bortal, a distant cousin to Tolk – Bryn's primary caregiver when he first arrived in Zhivrah. They looked similar, Bortal being modestly taller. However, they could not be more different in persona. He had travelled, like most competitors, from his native world and although familiar with Zhivrah, it was not his home. Although he had competed previously, this was his first role as the team leader. Gregor explained that through observation he had come to realise that Bortal was not putting the same effort into his team as previous leaders, being more of a lone ranger. This would not bode well for the Goyteks' chances this year and that was a pity, for both them and the competition itself.

Their weaponry was based on laser technology. However, they were only permitted a certain voltage so as not to create an unfair advantage.

The Shiakanas were a force to be reckoned with. Although appearing clumsy and heavy-footed, their sheer strength in battle had supporters of all teams jumping and cheering their favour. They were regarded as a force, like thunder, struck hard and seemed impossible to take down. Their weapons were archaic and simple but were all they needed to create a substantial impact. Gregor explained, it was simple to predict their team leader in every competition. It was always the one that appeared the largest and the strongest. This year the chosen one was at least a foot taller and a foot wider than the others. Moses added that they should not underestimate the tactics from the Shiakana team. They were far more clever than most gave them credit for.

Finally, the Hazuru team was to be led by Gima. Her name directly translated as 'the slayer'. She had maintained this illustrious position for many years and their trainers had yet to find anyone who would even come close to filling her role. She was the reason the Hazuru tribe had remained unbeaten for the last four tournaments.

This year, Gregor wanted to change that. Their weapons were most similar, their physicality was proportionately not too far apart. He told them how they had certain advantages, especially with regard to speed and agility. Their course was probably the toughest. It would usually wind around mountains or difficult terrain. It wasn't unheard of for the council to manipulate each course, provide extra hurdles to make the tournament more interesting for the audience and competitors alike.

This year, it was up to Moses to bond his team and become a leader and not just a teammate. That strength alone may determine this year's winner. But could Moses' arrogance stay abated long enough to command the respect needed for this alliance to be a force of solidarity and fortitude? With one day left of training, Gregor was still unsure.

CHAPTER 50

On the last morning of training, Gregor sent the team on a two-hour coordinated trek through woodland and marshlands, eventually being directed to a large meadow, about four acres, lined with leaf-laden trees. On arrival, with no sign of further instructions, Kenta travelled to the far end of the pasture to meditate, while the others sat and snacked on leftover breakfast from the canteen. Moses ate in silence, while Bryn and Alisi discussed the anticipation of their final, imminent exercise. Moses interjected to surmise that the final day would be Gregor's opportunity to throw a drove of hostile entities onto the field, then stand back and watch what would happen.

With that, Alisi and Bryn decided to get up and scout the territory, for it would be sensible to ascertain plausible areas of cover and escape routes. Bryn wanted to find a higher vantage point if needed, so climbed a tree to search for hills or mounds, but none came to view. All the while, Moses lay on the grass, his head pillowed by his satchel, appearing relaxed and unfazed.

Kenta stretched in a fluid motion, slowly moving from one position to another until he froze momentarily. With one quick movement, he turned and ran effortlessly with great speed back to Moses, where he simply pointed to the sky. Moses rose. Bryn and Alisi returned to where he stood and all four readied themselves for a battle, which seemed from Kenta's expression, to be imminently approaching.

Bryn spotted a small cluster of orbs advancing from the east, and then another from the west. Each cluster divided, creating a patterned formation across the skies, where they hovered for a time.

'Spread out. Leave enough distance to drive whatever's coming back to the far trees, where we will circle what's left and finish them off,' Moses instructed.

The range between them was too far apart, Bryn thought. For a team effort, he felt very much alone. He was on the left side of the pasture, Alisi barely visible at the other end. Suddenly, he became acutely aware of his rapid breathing and did his best to slow it down.

Gregor had explained that the orbs carried micro-machines, so small that they were barely visible to the naked eye. Pin coding, a technique used to carry software and hardware augmentation, formulated a transmogrification within the devices. This led to the creation of whatever opponent the council – or in this case Gregor – deemed suitable for the team below. The orbs were about to release their consignment into the trees, just at the end of the meadow. The scenery in front of them flickered, and the trees swayed with movement as figures began to take form within the darkened woodland.

With a momentary glitch of imagery, one by one, creatures emerged from afar, and Bryn was able to observe the entire scene, a building army coming to life. This was neither a force of man nor machine, but beasts. More specifically massively oversized insects. Ants, cockroaches, centipedes, scorpions, black beetles; all standing several feet tall, some close to ten, with a flurry of wasps or hornets flying just overhead.

Bryn looked toward Kenta and Moses; Kenta focused on the job ahead, while Moses, catching Bryn's glimpse, grinned with satisfaction as though he was satisfied with the hurdles Gregor had laid before them.

The creatures were coming to life, almost like they were waking from a stupor. Bryn was unsure what to do next until Moses as if predictably reading his mind, gave his order.

'Charge!'

And that was that. Three of the warriors gripped their weapons, ready for battle. During the last day of training, Bryn had discovered Kenta's arsenal. He had two hidden daggers strategically incorporated into the lining of his sleeves. Also, in the inner pockets of his robe, there was a reasonable selection of small throwing blades. Kenta's incredible skills in martial arts meant he rarely needed any assistance as he was deemed a weapon in his own right. Bryn believed that he was the most incredible and disciplined fighter he had encountered since he arrived in Zhivrah. If not for the fact that he could not articulate commands and converse with his teammates, Bryn was convinced that he would have been leader, and a great one at that.

CHAPTER 51

As they rushed head-on into combat, Bryn heard a battle cry in the distance. Realising it was Alisi, he couldn't help but smile and it lifted his spirits. Ahead of them, the swarm were getting riled, sensing the oncoming threat. First to advance were the ants. The scene replicated a chessboard, pawns being dispatched first. They were smaller than the creatures behind, but they were larger in numbers.

Kenta, being the fastest, engaged first, followed simultaneously by the other three. Bryn already had his two blades exposed, beheading two of the murky-brown, waist-high ants on his first draw. Their deaths were registered by the immediate disintegration of their corpses. If they became wounded, they simply battled on until they were delivered their final blow. However, if a competitor was wounded, the area affected lost functionality due to body sensors relayed from the orb. It may be temporary or last the tournament. Being killed rendered the competitor unconscious, and they would be out of the competition.

The ants were not fierce, and Bryn suspected they were being used to tire his team before the larger force were deployed. He wanted to bypass the herd and attack the mightier of the beasts before he lost his strength to do so with force. He pushed and fought his way forward, determined to get farther toward the trees to his left, in case there was a need for cover. Just when he thought he was going to drown in this sea of ants, he noticed he was suddenly under a cloak of shadow. He looked up only to find a locust staring down, threatening to drool on him. Bryn, still running at full speed, leapt onto a charging ant and with his blades pointing upwards, sliced the locust from chest to tail. And then the locust was gone. He unexpectedly realised he had lost his teammates. All he saw were spindly legs, which rose to a height of over five feet, and large bulbous bodies of various shapes and sizes. The more insects he defeated, the more they came. He had to get to the trees.

Sweat poured from his brow, salt stinging his eyes. Sharp fangs snapped at him, sharp stingers tried to stab him, and he almost got trampled once or twice, but on he fought. The trees were close. He wasn't about to give up.

At last, he got to cover. He took the opportunity to climb the tallest of the trees nearby, to get a better view of down below. First, he spotted Alisi. He heard the gunfire before he could see her on the far side of the field. She was letting loose a litany of bullets, each having the desired impact but what she may not have been aware of was — for every row of insects she killed, there were five more behind, drawn in by the noise.

Moses was stuck right in the centre fighting an oversized centipede, possibly the largest beast of all, but that was not surprising. What Moses didn't know was that there was a queen ant not too far from where he was standing. Bryn wondered what would happen if the queen was killed. Would it bear consequence for the rest of the colony?

Kenta was fighting the largest horde. Bryn thought he should have joined his efforts but felt his decision to climb the tree was worthwhile because now he had a plan.

He lowered himself to a sturdy branch below and used the opportunity to launch himself from its tip, right into the thicket of insects below. Blades splayed, he beheaded a wasp and split two ants on his way down. He fought his way to Moses and when he saw him through the corner of his eye, he veered left. And there she was, the queen, and she was larger and stronger than her subjects. They stood in force surrounding her, protecting her from harm.

Bryn wasted no time. He needed to defeat the wall of soldiers and cripple its matriarch.

CHAPTER 52

Bryn used one of his blades to point, mouthing the word *queen* to Moses. The noise from the swarm was deafening and they didn't have the luxury of time for conversation, so when Moses quickly nodded back his direction, while attempting to stand his ground, Bryn was sure he understood. However, Moses wasn't thoroughly convinced, and didn't take Bryn's gesture seriously until he witnessed what happened as Bryn closed in on her.

The entire colony of ants shifted their attention towards their queen. It was like they instinctively knew that she may be in danger. With a feeling that he had nothing to lose, Moses pursued Bryn and worked to help clear the path to their target. They skilfully used their swords, outmanoeuvring their opponents, working together, guarding each other as they made their approach.

Bryn leapt on the back of one of the ants and used the closest ones as steppingstones. Neighbouring ants clawed at him, but Moses slaughtered them before they got too near. The queen was becoming nervous, it seemed, commanding her army forward while she began her retreat. It didn't matter. Bryn was fully focused on the target ahead. With a blade in each hand and direct eye contact, he launched himself from a lone black beetle, and as she raised herself on hind legs to demonstrate a power play, her position made it possible for him to inject a blade into either side of her neck. He hung there for a moment until she collapsed to the ground and within moments, disappeared.

Bryn got to his feet and turned his head to see the colony of ants staring straight at him. He was afraid he may have made a mistake and instead of bringing them closer to victory, he had quashed any hope of completing this challenge. Within seconds, each ant began to pop like inflated balloons, one by one, with Moses' figure emerging as they vanished, expressing his appreciation with a simple thumbs-up and a half-smile grin.

The army of insects had been quartered within seconds. In the distance he spotted Kenta and Alisi. Moses beckoned at them to join him. He had devised a plan of his own.

'This seems to be the centre-point of the battle. We need to start here and work our way outward. By my count, there are about six scorpions. They are large and will do more damage than any other species. We need to attack these in pairs.'

Noticing that Alisi was limping, he asked if she was okay to carry on.

Alisi didn't even flinch. She was wrapped up in battle mode and eager to carry on regardless. Kenta seemed frustrated to be pulled momentarily from the battle, but it was hard to tell as he didn't say a word. They set themselves back-to-back, in a close formation. Weapons drawn, they were ready to finish this.

CHAPTER 53

The insects had created their own battle plan, on instinct or by their constant chatter, encircling the warriors and slowly, cautiously, moving forward. The giant forms appeared much larger with the absence of the smaller ants. Although they were lower in numbers, they still stood four rows deep and didn't give the impression of tiring anytime soon. As they closed in, the four teammates held their ground. They raised their weapons and waited until Moses gave the order to strike.

It was then that Alisi began to fumble. The adrenaline from the fight had caused the paralysing agent to react slower than expected. She fell to the ground in a heap, her legs collapsing from underneath.

'Go! I will hold them off as best I can from here!' She reloaded her rifle, putting extra cartridges to her side. That was their cue. Moses gave the order to charge again, but this time they had a planned attack.

Alisi kept her position and fired using a sniper's eyepiece for faultless aim. The others proceeded from their positions, covering all four of the quadrants they had forged. Kenta propelled himself from a ground position, launching at least five metres as he rose. Bryn had caught his movement through the corner of his eye, as he ran, and couldn't help but be impressed. Ahead of him were black beetles, at least one locust and he was sure that he caught the glimpse of a scorpion's tail somewhere behind. He wasn't afraid. He was caught up with the excitement and the rush he felt as he approached. It was a game after all – and it was time he started to enjoy it. Striking low, he first hit the legs of a beetle with both blades, sending it crashing to the ground with just enough time so it wouldn't land on him. As he rose, he struck another under the jaw, both blades exiting through its eyes.

As the battle continued, their opponents fell one by one. They were purposely leaving the scorpions until last. Although the other species were large and imposing, they were also disorganised and cumbersome. This didn't seem to be the case with the scorpions. They appeared to be working as a team, happily staying behind so that they would combat together in the final battle if the warriors made it that far.

Bryn was on the back of a locust when he realised it felt as though they were succeeding. He let out a loud battle cry, drawing attention from the other fighters, before he decapitated a locust, spraying a clear jellied substance on his face. Moses laughed and Kenta just shook his head, still focused on their task but feeling encouraged. The scorpions were circling the perimeter as though they were warming up, eager to pounce.

Kenta killed the last of the beetles with a series of throwing blades of various shapes and sizes. The scorpions were the last standing. They were yet to make a move, apart from pacing the formation they had created that surrounded Bryn, Moses, Kenta, and Alisi who was trying desperately, yet failing, to get on her feet. Now that the other insects were defeated, they realised how ferocious and predatory these creatures were. With their large black-red, granular-textured pincers and long curved stingers, their menacing dark figures began to edge forward. Bryn retreated to the position they had embarked from on the previous battle, and without taking their eyes off their opponents, they began discussing a plan of attack.

While Bryn and Moses' main focus was to fend them off, it was Kenta's task to somehow get behind them without gaining attention. So, huddled down, as if planning the final details, they suddenly rose to launch Kenta into the air with force. Unwavering and with speed, Moses and Bryn rushed out toward their ultimate campaign with the intent of creating a distraction so that Kenta could escape unseen. All Alisi could do was arm herself like before, this time propped up by Kenta's empty satchel. The trouble was, both Kenta and Alisi were running low on ammunition and the team worried that they might not have the advantage they had started the day with. Also, they were becoming tired, as this training session was heading into nightfall and they hadn't a moment to rest. They were all now hungry, surviving on flasks of water and nothing else since breakfast. Sustenance was needed and it didn't feel like they would be receiving that anytime soon.

Following Moses' lead, Bryn advanced on the first scorpion. They needed to defeat it quickly before the others joined forces. It was too late. With a rapid pace, the remaining five broke their encircling positions and made their way towards them. As the scorpions hadn't noticed Kenta's movements, it created an opportunity for him to make a surprise attack from behind. He had scavenged the area for any throwing weapons that he could reuse and launched his bounty into the tail ends of his targets as they moved from his direction. With their hard shells, they were proving more difficult to defeat than expected but Kenta's efforts didn't go unrewarded as he managed to dismember two stinging tails and one of the scorpions' hind legs. Their focus as a group was temporarily hindered, unsure which direction they should pursue, which target they should be focusing their attention on. One of the stingerless scorpions joined another to help the one Moses and Bryn battled and the rest diverted their attention to Kenta. Meanwhile, Kenta used his few seconds of grace time to indicate to Alisi the areas of vulnerability on their armoured bodies, insinuating that there was little point aiming elsewhere. Apart from their heads and extremities the rest of the body seemed almost impenetrable. Alisi had only three cartridges left and needed to make them count. Her first shot skimmed past the head of the lead scorpion, which was heading for Kenta. The trouble was that they were moving too fast and their heads consisted of a pair of eyes and a barely visible mouth, protected by large pincers at either side, hindering a clear shot. She needed to attract attention as she would have a better chance if one headed straight for her. As luck would have it the gunshot was enough to distract the second in line heading for Kenta. It changed course, veering in Alisi's direction. The third and last scorpion stumbled over his lost hind legs and had difficulty keeping balance.

Bryn and Moses played defence as neither of them could get close enough for a fatal blow.

'Aim for the tail tip! We need to weaken his weaponry,' Moses shouted to Bryn when they had a moment of respite.

It was at that point they were joined by the other two scorpions and instead of defending themselves against one, Bryn and Moses now had to battle three.

'Don't lose focus, Bryn!'

Fortunately, Bryn, who had taken his advice, used an opportunity when the stinger was pointed at Moses to climb on its bent tail and drive a blade through its tip. Within a second he used the other blade to drive through a minute gap in the armour of its neck. One down, five to go.

CHAPTER 54

As Bryn and Moses faced their two remaining opponents, Kenta was finding it a challenge to deal with one on his own. Trouble was, it was too close to throw at and not close enough for him to use his daggers. His adeptness at martial arts and his ability to leap long distances was an attempt at exhausting it. But he found that was tiring him as well. At the same time, Alisi was striving to slow her breathing to almost a standstill so she wouldn't miss her next shot. With two cartridges left, she hadn't time for miscalculations. With one last slow exhale she pulled the trigger. Metres from where she sat, and a bit too close for comfort, the face of her assailant exploded, erupting from the bullet that had landed between the eyes. She exhaled again, this time with a sigh of relief, disappointed that she had doubted her abilities in the first place, but also realising that there was never room for error.

At this stage, Kenta was fighting one scorpion on his own, Bryn and Moses had two; there was one scorpion still struggling to stand, with Alisi feeling just as redundant. As only one of the scorpions Bryn was fighting had a stinger, he intended to eliminate that threat first. It wasn't an easy feat as these beasts were fast and they seemed able to predict every oncoming threat. Moses was kept busy fending off the second scorpion but simultaneously attempting to get his sword through the defending pincers to wield a killing blow. He felt that every swing was hitting rock until, without intent, he managed to strike a sliver of exposed muscle and sliced one of the pincers clean off. His second strike went cleanly behind the second pincer and in, under the shell of its back, where Moses pushed as far as the blade would go. Without a moment's hesitation, he turned to join Bryn, feeling more confident than before, outnumbering their attackers rather than being outnumbered. They were on the home stretch.

Kenta had climbed the tail of his contender and was near the tip, trying in earnest to hack it off. Alisi had her eyepiece focused in the same direction, waiting for an opportunity to take her final shot. The scorpion was flaying and thrashing about, trying to shake him off, but Kenta was holding it like an experienced rider breaking a stallion. He was almost successful but as he jabbed the hard shell, he lost grip and the dagger fell, landing on the scorpion's back. Every time the tail lowered to the point that Kenta felt he could grab it, the tail rose again, pulling him far from reach. Kenta was becoming frustrated and just as he made his last attempt before he had to rethink his efforts, he heard a whistle close to his ear and then the end of the tail exploded. He turned around to catch a thumbs-up from Alisi, who was about two hundred metres away.

Bryn and Moses were standing separately with the plan that they would attack from opposing angles. The venomous tail jabbed from side to side, hitting the ground and lifting sand. This was the last scorpion with the ability to fight, and it was now playing defence. Kenta quickly checked on Alisi, before joining the other two for the final battle. The scorpion that had been injured by him, gave up attempting to stand on its remaining limbs and lay in wait, already defeated, for whatever fate had in store. Kenta stood between Bryn and Moses, awaiting final instructions. Bryn had an idea, which Moses felt could work, but there was a significant risk involved.

'Now!' shouted Moses.

They replicated an earlier strategy, launching Kenta into the air from a hunkered position. As predicted, the scorpion watched Kenta's flight and was ready to attack as he landed. With tail and pincers directed towards the sky, the other two used the distraction to attack from below. They jammed their blades into any fragment of soft tissue they could find. A piercing shrill emanated from the beast but luckily it suffered a quick and timely death, just as Kenta made his predicted landing on its back.

All three fighters collapsed to the ground, suddenly overcome by exhaustion. They were too worn out for celebrations, and although they knew they still had to tackle their final, fast-fading opponent, they just needed a moment of calm. They were surprised to see that Alisi had mostly recovered and joined them, remaining in a standing position, glad to have the use of her legs again.

'Alisi, would you do the honourable thing and deal with that?' Moses requested, pointing to the last scorpion, which was barely moving, a pool of jelly-like matter emanating from where its limbs once were.

Kenta handed her a dagger. As Alisi approached, she wasn't sure if the scorpion was still alive. It lay motionless. She felt a bit cheated with the lack of effort involved, but she was not complaining. Closing in, dagger in hand, she was surprised that the scorpion opened an eye. She hadn't the time to feel any form of disbelief with what was about to happen next, and although they had the impression the scorpions were shrewder than the other creatures, she was completely caught unaware. The others were paying absolutely no attention as Alisi fell to the ground, stabbed in the chest by the tip of the scorpion's tail. Although the vision of the victorious creature vanished from sight, it wasn't because it had died. It was because they had lost. They were a team after all. And on this training exercise, they were to survive as just that. It was Moses who first noticed the absence of their final combatant, but it was Kenta who saw their teammate lying motionless on the ground. It took a moment before the realisation of what had happened sank in. Bryn was first to rise, running to Alisi's side to check on her welfare. Relieved to see that she was soundly sleeping, snoring slightly, he sat beside her dumbfounded by the dawning awareness that they had made such a foolish error in judgement. They underestimated what they had thought was their weakest opponent and it cost them profoundly. No words were spoken between them. They sat in utter silence until a scouting vehicle came for them, about an hour later.

CHAPTER 55

Bryn reflected on their day while he showered, pushing the water to as hot as he could cope with, doing his best to wash away the disappointment he felt after an otherwise glorious day. He was reminiscing, and even relishing the challenges they endured and battles they won. However, they were reckless at the end and it cost them dearly. Gregor had met the team at the gate when they arrived back, sending them in separate directions, not giving away any feelings on how he thought their last training day had gone. Alisi was carried by stretcher to her room, accompanied by Tilly. She was starting to stir but had yet to open her eyes.

They were due to meet at the canteen shortly. Bryn was starving but the thought of Gregor's judgement was making his stomach a little queasy. Once dressed, he spent a little time cleaning and sharpening his blades, and then slowly made his way across the courtyard.

He was the last to sit at the team's table in the canteen. The room was more subdued than usual, only teams and council members present. Gregor was conversing with the trainer of the Hazuru team at the far end of the room. While the other three teams huddled together, chatting excitedly, Bryn's team appeared as though they had lost the tournament already. It wasn't the welcome he was hoping to receive at the table, but it was understandable, considering how unfortunate their last day of training concluded. Although sedate, Alisi seemed to have fully recovered, which was a relief.

'Bryn! Grab some food. Gregor could be a while,' Moses suggested.

Picking at the small meal he brought back to the table, Bryn couldn't help but wonder if they were ready for tomorrow.

'This new technology is more challenging than I was expecting.' Alisi broke Bryn's train of thought. 'Though the idea of the scorpions seems a little familiar. Wasn't there an old movie based on Greek gods, the one where the guy chops off Medusa's head?'

'That was Perseus,' Bryn suggested. 'But I don't think he fought any scorpions. No mention of it in the Greek mythology books I read.'

'I know the one you're talking about. The half son of Zeus. A kraken was going to eat the princess and Perseus saved her. Good movie,' Moses interjected.

'That was a cetus. I'm pretty sure Perseus saved Andromeda from a cetus. The kraken was mainly featured in Norse mythology,' Bryn added, starting to feel doubtful.

'It was a movie, Bryn. Have you ever heard of artistic licence?' Alisi asked rhetorically.

'The point is that the exercise was obviously inspired. That's interesting.' Moses felt a little enlightened.

'It was fun though.' Bryn wanted to change the conversation. Watching films wasn't a luxury he was often afforded, growing up.

His three teammates looked at him, each slowly producing a smile, even one from Kenta.

'Focusing on the queen ant was a good call, Bryn,' Moses stated. 'I was hoping there was a good reason you were sitting in a tree.'

Smiles turned to laughter and the mood suddenly lifted.

*

Moses was talking tactical errors and improvements when Gregor joined them. He appeared distracted but regained focus once he sat down.

'I have to be honest here, I felt today's exercise went pretty well.'

Bryn was surprised.

'You knew it wasn't going to be easy and you nearly had it.' Gregor pinched his thumb and forefinger to about an inch from each other.

'Did any team beat them?' Bryn asked.

'The Goyteks,' Gregor answered.

'That's hardly surprising. It's their technology. Who knows how long they've been training on their planet?' Gregor's response had frustrated Moses.

'We have been assured by the council that there was no unfair advantage. The technology is certainly theirs, but the software program was designed by the council, to ensure there is no advantage. Though, I found their endeavour remarkable considering the lack of effort from their team leader,' Gregor added.

Bryn was curious.

'How can a species that… weak compete alongside everyone else? Surely, they must have a huge disadvantage?'

Moses interjected. 'The Goyteks have the use of limited technology on the field. Their strength is their technology and they can use that to even the odds. Remember they'll be running a separate course and I have to admit, it can be just as exciting as everyone else's.'

'Laser guns, small mobility units… But their true strength is their minds. You cannot underestimate their capabilities, Bryn,' Gregor added.

The canteen slowly emptied until the only table left occupied was theirs. They had no idea what variety of beasts they were to encounter at the tournament but Gregor and Moses worked on rebuilding the team's confidence, to the point that Bryn felt they could take on whatever was put in their way. The events of that day were taken as a tool that they had learned from, and, with a new perspective, the feeling of disappointment was replaced with encouragement. Nothing was to be taken at face value from that moment on. They had moulded into the team Gregor needed to inspire victory.

As they readied themselves to leave, Gregor drew their attention.

'Tomorrow, on the field, be careful. Watch out for anything out of the ordinary. I know the technology is new but I feel there is something more at play. Call it a gut instinct. It might be nothing, and

I hope that is the case. But, if there is a chance that a team is cheating, or taking advantage, talk to me. Remember I'll be watching.' He brushed off his seriousness in an instant. 'Now, get some rest. We will meet in the courtyard at sunrise.'

Outside, Bryn caught a glimpse of Kyra, who was sitting alone by the fountain. He said his goodnights and veered in her direction. It seemed like she was waiting for him, or them. He wasn't sure. They maintained eye contact until he sat on the fountain's ledge, beside her. Only then did she look away.

'You're up late, Bryn. If you and your team were prepared, you would be asleep by now.' Kyra was being her professional self. Bryn had hoped that she would have softened by now, even a little.

'We had a long training day. Everything got delayed. Doesn't mean we're not ready.'

Bryn got up to leave, disappointed that he could not reach her at a personal level; although, on reflection, he had hardly made an effort. It was easier to talk to her when Frasier was with him. Now that he was alone, it was difficult to think of the right thing to say. He dismissed his lack of effort and his affections, as he couldn't afford the distraction anyway.

'Will you be watching tomorrow?' he asked, as he began to walk away.

'Not sure, Bryn. I would rather be participating than watching from the sidelines. And that is never going to happen.'

Without a 'goodnight', Bryn continued his way back to the dormitories.

He felt a moment of sadness for Kyra's lack of opportunity and believed she would better him or possibly any of his teammates. She was the most incredible fighter. It was not his problem though, he told himself. He needed to put all his focus and effort into tomorrow's tournament. It was to be the most important event of his lifetime, one that may never be repeated. However, it didn't stop his feelings of sympathy, and even a twinge of guilt, that perhaps he may have taken a position in the team she felt was rightfully hers.

He went to bed, anxious about not getting a good night's sleep. He was both excited and nervous, endless possibilities of what lay ahead playing around in his head. Even so, the events of the day had worn him out. It wasn't long before he fell into a deep and restful slumber.

CHAPTER 56

'Everyone take your seats, please!' instructed one of the two Panak announcers, who sat in a hot-air balloon above an exceptionally large amphitheatre stadium.

The venue was horseshoe in shape, had four small wooden gates at the curved end, just under the seating, reserved for council members and trainers, and a prodigious, impressively distinctive gate opposite, which stood over one hundred feet high – with equally large concrete pillars at either side. A band played in the centre of the arena and food stalls were set up at the base of the seating area, which was filling rapidly. Flags and banners were being waved and displayed by excited crowds, all chanting well-versed anthems or shouting out the names of their favourite teams or contestants. A long day lay ahead. The first day of the tournament would certainly stretch into the night. Some of the crowd would go home and come back the following morning. Others brought provisions and blankets. Children ran freely through the seats, entertained by performing acrobats and jesters making them laugh and squeal in delight.

Team supporters were not segregated as this was a day of fun for all, the one day that every citizen of Zhivrah was guaranteed to attend. Though the competition was fierce, the nature of the Zhavia Shield was to entertain and celebrate the all-encompassing gathering of tribes and their cultural identities. Even the Shiakanas, known in the training grounds for their grumpy and bad-tempered demeanour, were dancing to drumbeats and chanting songs from their homeland in unison.

Council members took their seats, dressed all in white to show that they were an independent entity within the games. They had not only designed the program, but were also umpires, rule-makers and moderators. It was important for them to remain impartial and speak with one voice, promoting fairness and unbiased opinion.

Bryn's parents were seated with old friends; some who were visiting, like themselves, and others who had lived on Zhivrah their entire lives. They expressed their congratulations on Bryn making it onto the team. Lars and Sanne, though naturally humble, were both brimming with pride.

Frasier sat with all the trainees who hadn't qualified for the team. His disappointment had been replaced by the infectious excitement overwhelming the arena. There was always next time, he had conceded. He just needed to convince his father to let him compete again. For now, he was more enticed by the prospect of this tournament and the days that lay ahead. Stefan sat beside him, gorging a large sandwich, its contents spilling to the ground as he tried to fit too much in his mouth at one time. This made Frasier laugh out loud.

Large screens were suspended high above the arena, there to display the efforts of the teams throughout the tournament, which could last up to four days. In the meantime, the audience was becoming familiar with their heroes. Their faces filled the screens; snippets of them in action on the training field were shown for all to see. Bets were discreetly made by pundits, vying their favourites, playing the odds, hoping to profit from their projections. It wasn't a promoted activity at the games; scorned upon, but not illegal.

Security was lax. There was never a cause for trouble. It was a family occasion, not one for hijinks or malice. The competition was in the field and sporting rivalry was encouraged. However, disdain and arrogance were not. In saying that, it was difficult for the Shiakanas to remain composed, but that was only to be expected. It was part of their nature and allowances were made.

It was still relatively early in the morning. The sun was already bright and warming the crowds. Some had arrived before the sun had even hinted the horizon; some had arrived the night before, camping outside the gates, hoping to attain desired seating. And some were still arriving, grateful for any seats that remained.

The band paused momentarily. There was a hushed silenced as all eyes fixed on the platform above where the council members sat. A large, circular metal plate hung from a wooden frame, and beside it stood a muscular Shiakana in ceremonial garb. As he awaited instruction from his earpiece, he picked up a large club and readied himself. The crowd remained silent in fettered anticipation. Once the gong was struck, it signified the players were about to make their way from the training ground to the arena.

CHAPTER 57

Moments earlier, back at the training ground, Gregor was emphasising the important elements of the rulebook of play. There was to be no attacking, tracking or affiliating with players from another team. Tempers needed to stay restrained, no matter how frustrated or impatient a player may become. Participants could use any means available to defeat their opponents. Sometimes, creativity could garner extra points. The privilege of partaking in such an event was just that, a privilege. No one could hope to win the tournament with arrogance, as that would often lead to shame and embarrassment. The list went on.

Kyra was there, alongside Hercule. Bryn recalled her words from the night before, her resentment. He found himself wondering how she must be feeling about today, knowing that if she had only been born true blood, she would most likely be taking his place.

'Bryn,' Gregor boomed. 'Are you paying attention?'

Bryn mumbled a low-toned, embarrassed apology and realigned his gaze toward his mentor. He felt nervous but not so much that it affected him physically. Moses had spent the hour before reassuring and energising the team. Alisi had regained her confidence after her pride had been blemished in the last training event. Kenta seemed calm, which was almost predictable. Bryn doubted that anything could faze him. It was oddly comforting.

Each team member was given a compass and a map in a pack, which also contained three days' food rations and a flask of water. They were dressed in matching garb, dark red, with a tanned leather belt. Kenta wore a long robe, but the others had simple tunics. All four wore basic leather sandals.

There came a point when Gregor had no more advice to give and they knew it was only a matter of moments before they would be called to the arena. The time was used for a moment of quiet reflection, Bryn focusing on Moses' earlier advice about the challenge being one not just about speed, but of endurance and wit. He also reflected on his life before the games, the simplicity of it and how he would never be that boy again. What was he to do after it was all over? Was he expected to return to life like before? He shook those concerns from his mind. Those thoughts were not for today.

The gate opened into the training arena, disturbing Bryn's thoughts and grounding him back to reality and the building excitement for the day ahead. A messenger approached Gregor, announcing that it was time to travel to the arena. The crowds were ready. The tournament was about to begin.

On Gregor's orders, they followed him to a door that stood perpendicular to the entrance gates, a door Bryn had never noticed before. Behind the door, a long staircase led to tunnels down below. The walls were lit with flaming torches but the light was dim and Bryn could barely see the others, even though they were only a foot or two apart. In the distance, a whirring sound disturbed the silence and a gush of warm air hit them from behind. Within seconds the tunnel began to light up and Bryn was surprised to see a pod approaching with Tolk sitting in the driver's seat. It halted near their feet and the doors slid open. They embarked. Bryn chose a seat close enough to Tolk that he might get his attention. Kyra, Gregor and Hercule sat near the back, Kyra in a seat that was positioned farthest from Bryn. Everyone was quiet. Tolk never averted his gaze from the track ahead, even as they boarded.

'Tolk...' He was close enough to tap his shoulder. Tolk reacted quickly but it took a moment before he realised who he was talking to.

'Ah, it is the son of Lars! I don't believe you made it through,' he said sincerely.

'I thought you might have heard the news by now, Tolk.' Bryn was genuinely surprised, as all the contenders' statistics had been displayed on screens everywhere since they were selected.

'I'm not one for being idle and wasting time watching screens, but I have to admit, I am impressed. Hardly surprised though. Your father was the most incredible sportsman, and from what I hear, your mother was also a force to be reckoned with. I didn't really know her very well.'

Bryn had forgotten that Tolk must have been well acquainted with his father, and even his mother, over the years.

'Furthermore, although I was young at the time and not in the job very long, I do remember your father arriving here for the first time. It must be customary for your family to arrive on Zhivrah in ignorant bliss. You'd be surprised how many contenders arrive here all prepared, like they have been here many times, and know exactly what to expect. But not the Jahrs.' He laughed as though this family trait was the most ridiculous notion.

'But seriously… from what I hear, Bryn, your lineage is a strong one. You and your family must be doing something right.'

Tolk stole a glance at Bryn; his eyes became sincere and the token was heartfelt.

'Thanks, Tolk,' Bryn responded.

The end of the tunnel was in sight, just up ahead. Bryn stood in anticipation and was quickly joined by Alisi, who also wanted a better view.

'This is it, Bryn. You ready?'

'As I'll ever be. You?'

'Too late to turn back now.' Alisi winked at Bryn and flashed a large, toothy grin.

CHAPTER 58

The crowds in the stadium had been going wild since the gong was struck by the Shiakana tasked with the job. Bryn and his teammates could hear them as soon as they had disembarked the capsule, in a tunnel under the stadium. The Goytek team had arrived just before them and Bryn could hear another capsule approaching. It didn't seem too far away. The tunnel they stepped into had a large platform, intricately decorated with mosaic tiles forming images of previous games and victors. It was adorned with more flamed torches than the one they had just left and the lights from the capsules lit its large, caverned, cobblestoned roof. Gregor gestured to Kyra and Hercule to go ahead.

Hercule blasted a loud, 'Bonne chance, mes amis.' Kyra managed a meagre wave as they headed into the darkness.

It wasn't long before the other capsules arrived and all four teams lined up outside them, with their head trainers, waiting for a signal to enter the stadium. All competitors waited with bated breath and in silence, although the Shiakana team were beginning to get restless. Just as it was becoming distracting, a light switched on in front of each team. Then another light ignited in front of that one, and then another. Within a moment, four tunnels lit up, one facing each team. With Gregor in the lead, they followed one by one into their designated underground passageway. The light seemed more artificial now. It glowed with a white luminescence that flickered, casting shadows on a grey-tiled wall. There was a gradual inclination of the ground as they walked, steeper as they went on. The noise from the crowd above grew louder. Bryn stayed focused but became more nervous than excited, his mouth losing moisture to the palms of his hands. This day had finally come, and he felt he may have needed more time to train, to gain more insight to fully understand the rules. Moses had said that no one truly understands the games until they participate. With the new technology, the game design had gained a new development and a changed format, which affected all participating. But the goal remained the same. Get to the Zhavia Shield before any other team.

A large wooden door became visible at the end of the corridor. Light ebbed through cracks along its sides, and from a gap of about an inch from the base. The radiance of the morning sun warmed the artificial, incandescent lighting of the exiting tunnel. Gregor stood facing the door, followed by Moses, then Kenta, Alisi and finally Bryn. The thunderous cheering and chanting prevented any chance of sharing any last words of encouragement. It would have been lost on deaf ears. They just needed to wait for the door to open.

Suddenly, from above his head, Bryn heard what he thought were trumpets blowing. There was an instant calm, as the crowd was silenced. A muffled voice could be heard making an announcement, but Bryn could not determine what was being said. Within a minute, the crowds erupted again, and someone could be heard outside the door, unlocking a bolt. The door opened in two vertical halves and without hesitation, Gregor walked through and out into the arena. Bryn was eager to move forward to catch a glimpse of what lay ahead. Moses didn't move as it was customary for the head trainers to meet at the centre of the arena and shake hands before introducing their team.

Bryn's nerves were replaced by excitement once again, though he kept his feelings contained. Moses was waiting on his cue and he could see Gregor from his position perfectly well; Bryn's view was hindered by his position behind the others. He couldn't keep his eyes off the back of Moses' head, wishing him to move forward. With one last blast from the trumpets, Moses followed his cue, leaving the enclosure of the tunnels to greet the euphoric fans outside.

CHAPTER 59

Bryn could hear a chorus of voices calling Moses by his name, the audience instantly recognising him from previous competitions. One by one, as they entered the arena, the contenders waved to the crowds. First Moses, then Kenta, Alisi and finally Bryn. The glare from the sun was momentarily blinding, but as Bryn's eyes adjusted, and as he absorbed the enormity of the arena, he found it was truly incredulous. It was larger than any venue Bryn had ever witnessed. The din he had heard from below, matched the spectacle from the crowds. The stalls, which must have been nearly twenty rows high, stretched out on either side before him. As he continued to wave, he turned around to see the council members and other significant guests sitting in stalls behind him, in an arc-shaped gallery with a section near the base where the trumpeters and other orchestral musicians were standing on ceremony. Ahead of them was a gate. It must have been over one hundred feet high and appeared similar to the door they had just entered from, but formidable in stature. At each side, there stood a stone-carved statue depicting two warriors: one male and one female. Both stretched to the apex of the gate and each depicted a fighting pose; the male held a sword above his head and the female had a spear, firmly grasped and ready to use.

The structure of the arena itself was made with large block-stone. Wooden staircases divided it into accessible sections, and by the sound from the crowds – stamping as they cheered – below them was most likely constructed from wood as well. The ground beneath Bryn's feet was a mixture of red sand and gravel, with flowers, streamers and bunting being strewn about.

The three other teams had entered the stadium from adjacent doors at the same time as Bryn and his teammates. They too waved to the crowds, cheered on by fans. The head trainers waited for their teams at the centre of the stadium, joined by what Bryn assumed were four adjudicators. One from each tribe, all dressed in grey. When they reached Gregor, he gave them each a translating earpiece, to be used also as an emergency communication device for the duration of the games. He instructed them to form an arc of a circle, and when the other teams fell in, the circle was completed. In the centre stood the four adjudicators, facing the four trainers. Before anyone spoke, Bryn discreetly attached his earpiece.

'Today, we mark another year of the Zhavia Shield,' began the Shiakana representative, speaking her native language. The crowd went silent, listening in on the address. 'This year, the games have been updated and I know you have all been informed of any rule changes. What none of you are probably aware of is, we have included a new element that we are all very excited about. We have added our new tech into the scenery to manipulate the environment, just a bit. Don't be complacent as you might find it difficult, at times, to decipher what's real and what isn't. Best to accept that everything you encounter is real. That will prevent unwanted injuries.'

She took a moment to survey the competitors in silence, to emphasise the importance of what she just said. Bryn wasn't expecting this development, and by the faces of the other competitors, neither were they. The audience reacted with applause upon hearing the news.

'You have had a little time to prepare yourself with the new technology. We feel it will heighten excitement, especially for those of us watching,' continued the Goytek representative, who seemed very proud of their newly added tech-ware.

'Anyone found cheating or behaving in a manner deemed unfit for competition will be disqualified from the games for life and will have a two-generational ban placed on their participation,' added the Hazuru representative.

'Don't forget to enjoy yourselves over the next few days. It's going to be a long one, so stay hydrated, take breaks when you can, and don't forget to eat,' said the Earthian tribe's representative, who was someone Bryn had never met. He must have been in his mid-fifties and had the confidence of someone who had being doing this for some time. He was certainly addressing all of the teams when he spoke, as were the other adjudicators, none showing any favouritism towards their associated tribes.

With the speech over, the trumpeting began again. They were instructed to turn to face the crowds, and then to do a circuit of the stadium. The audience went wild, no fear of their vigour starting to fade. Bryn tried to catch sight of his parents in the stalls, but there were just too many people. He waved and smiled, absorbing the commotion. He was never going to be able to relive a day like today. Even if he did manage to compete again, it'd never be the same.

Bryn was lost in the ambience when he caught sight of Gregor stopping just up ahead. They were gathering at the gate. It was time. The games were about to start.

CHAPTER 60

There was a roll and clatter of drums as the large doors opened. Bryn was surprised that just beyond, four transport capsules were positioned alongside each other, doors open, ready to take the participants to a destination that was yet to be revealed. There was a platform below each one, wide enough to allow each person to embark in single file. One last wave to the crowd and they made their way to their assigned vehicle. Tolk was standing outside the driver's seat waiting to guide them on board.

The capsule was smaller than the one they had arrived on, just enough to seat the five of them, with a narrow, raised platform to one side, which displayed a vertical holographic image of what appeared to be a map.

Once seated, everyone took a minute to study the image before Gregor spoke up.

'It looks like we are going north. You will be dropped at these coordinates.' He pointed at the screen. 'You will need to enter those into your compass, and follow that with the destination coordinates, which you can see is down here.' He pointed farther down the screen. 'You will see from the map that all four teams represent a point on a square, each equidistant from the centre. You can also see that each team has the task of clearing geological obstacles – in your case, it seems to be an area of woodland or tropical forest. The distance from point A to point B is about 70 kilometres. It may not seem extensive but, don't forget, there will be plenty of delays along the way.'

Bryn was concentrating on every word of Gregor's instructions but was conscious of the orb that followed them onto the capsule and was currently over his head, monitoring every word and image, which it relayed back to the big screens in the arena. Although he spotted his teammates catching an odd glimpse of it, it seemed they had forgotten it was there already.

As they entered the data into their compasses, they were also instructed to check their supplies, to ensure they were ample. Outside, another orb was circling the capsule, capturing images and the momentum before departure. Some of the spectators spilled out from the gates, waving frantically. Alisi waved back, nudging Bryn to do the same.

Tolk was dressed in full regalia of navy-blue and black, seated upright, facing forward and awaiting instructions.

'You four have as good a chance as any other team to win this year, but if you work as well together as you did on the last training exercise, you have a great chance of beating them all,' Gregor said, in encouragement.

'I'd like to wipe the smiles from the smug faces of the Hazuru team. They have been impossible to be around after winning the last three,' Moses added quietly so that the orb couldn't decipher what was said.

'I can tell you that they are just as impossible when they lose,' Gregor responded in a whisper, followed by a loud chuckle.

Just then, a beeping sound came from the orb and on it, a small black screen initiated a countdown from sixty seconds in red font.

'This is it,' Alisi stated as she rubbed her hands in anticipation, smiling broadly. The excitement was gathering, Alisi's smile becoming infectious. Bryn noticed his foot tapping unconsciously and he instinctively put his hand on his knee to steady it. He decided to do one last check of his bag to make sure everything was securely in place. If he had forgotten anything, it was now too late.

12… 11… 10… The countdown began.

CHAPTER 61

Through his earpiece, Bryn could hear the countdown starting from ten. Tolk had his hand on a lever, ready to initiate.

3… 2… 1…

All four capsules suddenly took off and travelled together for a few seconds, before branching off in different directions. Their capsule veered left, and they could see one other following the same direction but farther on up the track. After another minute, the capsule turned left again, where they entered a forest brimming with trees and then they lost sight of the trailing capsule completely.

The forest grew dark, but not too dark, as Bryn noticed a brook running alongside the track. It wasn't that deep, but he caught sight of silvery lights breaking the water, most likely fish swimming downstream. Ahead, light broke the horizon and within moments they were out of the darkness and travelling through a meadow of wildflowers. A herd of ostrich-like birds bolted, startled by the sudden emergence of such an evasive presence. Hills rose from the horizon, seemingly low in stature but as they neared, they grew so large they blocked the view of the sun. It certainly didn't faze Tolk, as he maintained speed on his approach. As the hill, now resembling a mountain, became more obtrusive, Bryn was curious about how they were going to travel around it. However, just as he was considering options a small tunnel entrance became visible in front of them and it wasn't long before they were enveloped in darkness once again.

The capsule meandered through the mountain for over thirty minutes, and when they eventually exited, Bryn was momentarily blinded by the strength and extremity of light from the sun. As his eyes adjusted, he became aware that the terrain and foliage had changed. The environment was luscious green, with unusually bright floral accompaniments. It felt as though they had entered tropical lands, with large, palm-like trees and lily pads on the river that had rejoined them along the track. Jumbo-sized dragonflies hovered over the lilies, darting from one to another. Although the capsule was soundproof, Bryn imagined their surroundings were alive with the callings of strange and wonderful creatures.

These views unfazed the others, apart from Alisi who appeared just as transfixed on the local flora.

The calm was suddenly broken by Gregor's booming announcement.

'Gather your gear. We are almost there,' he delivered.

A scrolled map was handed to Moses, who passed it to Kenta for consideration, before putting it in a side pocket of his satchel. Bryn quickly realised that although the journey was mapped in each compass, it would be up to Moses, and possibly Kenta to determine the ultimate course they would take.

Gregor handed each of them a ration of bread to consume before they landed. The food and water supplies in their satchels would be rationed once they made good headway, but until then, this would be their last meal before the competition officially began. Bryn relished every bit.

Tolk began to slow down. It felt as though they would begin their campaign in a jungle. Whether the entire tournament would take place in this environment, Bryn wasn't sure. It wasn't the terrain they had trained on, but this was never going to be a simple task. The foliage was dense and that was going to slow their journey. Hopefully, there would be a clearing ahead. However, Bryn had learned to expect anything. Even the most seasoned competitor could not predict the day that lay before them.

The capsule stopped dead on the track. Everyone was on their feet now, looking out at their destination. Without a platform to climb down onto, it felt a bit like they had arrived in no-man's-land. Bryn double-checked he had his compass and this was indeed where they were supposed to be.

The sun shone from above, but only a shimmer of light could be seen through the dense jungle and tall trees that lay ahead. Gregor stayed on board as the team disembarked. The orb followed them, once again displaying a countdown. It read six minutes and twenty-three seconds. It was allowing for other teams to reach their assigned locations.

'That is good,' Gregor said, pointing to the clock face, with his head poking out of the doors. 'Gives you time to get your bearings and plan a route.' He withdrew inside. 'Best of luck. Work as a team. As well as knowing each other's strengths, it is just as important to realise your individual weaknesses.'

The doors closed and the capsule sped off, back down the same route. They were alone now. Four eager competitors and one hovering orb.

Four minutes and ten seconds.

Moses and Kenta examined the map and correlated it with their compasses. Alisi and Bryn took a walk down either side of the track, searching for a clearer path. It was no use. The jungle was just as dense, whatever route they decided to set off on. They regrouped and faced forward looking for any hint of light beyond the trees. In the distance, as Bryn had imagined, they could hear the call of animals. Large and small, some sounds felt familiar and some Bryn had never heard. It was both wondrous and alarming.

Thirteen seconds left. They readied themselves on their marks. It was a race of speed but also endurance. For the first ten kilometres, they would be going straight ahead. Moses calculated that at that point they should reach a clearing, but with the map being so rudimentary, it was hard to tell.

The clock was on its final countdown. Bryn imagined the crowds back at the stadium going wild with anticipation. A bead of sweat slid down his forehead and dripped from his eyebrow onto his cheek. He hadn't noticed. He was fully focused and ready for anything.

CHAPTER 62

The starting horn sounded from the orb and they were off. They ran a steady sprint, leaping tree stumps and low-lying branches, simultaneously protecting their heads from protruding off-shoots. They moved in tandem, as they were trained to do. No one getting too far ahead, in case of an ambush, and nobody left behind. All four scanned the area for any possibility of an attack, as their first challenge could commence at any time.

Five kilometres in, Moses indicated that they should stop for a moment to evaluate their position. Kenta climbed the tallest tree in the vicinity. He leapt from branch to branch with the agility and nimbleness of a trained gymnast. Without pausing, Kenta disappeared in the bountiful leaves at the head of the tree in under a minute.

Moses consulted the map with Alisi, referring to the compass for direction. Bryn was instructed to keep watch. He couldn't help but notice the colourful lizard-like creatures scurrying through bushes and shrubs, or the butterflies, with all the shades of the spectrum – large and small alike – flying just overhead.

He only realised that Kenta was descending the tree when he was a few feet from its base. Moses was there to greet him, knowing that any information Kenta relayed would help determine the direction they took next. Alisi, meanwhile, explained to Bryn that there was a river up ahead but from the basic illustration on the map, there was no way of knowing how long or wide it was.

Kenta made it pretty clear with his gestures that the river was both wide and long. He signalled to continue forward and that they could assess the situation better at that point. Bryn was aware that this was a perfect position for their first strike. He thought the others felt that too.

Progressing at a slower pace, they focused on any foreboding threat. Weapons drawn, they moved forward with purpose. Before long Bryn could hear the fast flow of water up ahead. The trees were sparse as they approached the river. The foreground grew brighter and the terrain began to clear, the ground beneath them becoming stony and dry.

Emerging from the forest, the sun was momentarily blinding. The river was indeed wide and the current was strong. It appeared deep but there was no way of knowing how deep, from where they stood. There was a possibility that it may be easier to cross if they travelled farther along either side, but it was difficult to decide which direction to venture. The trees jutted out, blocking a clear view. Moses called his team together.

'It seems like we need to make a decision. We can try our luck and cross here or we can travel to where the river is more narrow or has a weaker current. Now, to do this we have to decide which direction to go. It's like a toss of a coin.'

'What if we split up?' Alisi suggested.

'Is that not the perfect opportunity to weaken the team? If we separate, we would become more vulnerable,' Bryn said, with concern.

Moses thought for a moment.

'I don't think we have a choice. We are under time constraints. If we keep it to a ten-minute scout, we won't be separated for long,' Moses decided.

'Bryn, with me. Kenta, Alisi, travel south. Be quick. Remember, five minutes and turn back,' he added.

The orb that had been travelling with them rose to the sky and out of sight – presumably to attain a better view as the team split into pairs. They separated quickly and ran with great speed. Time was certainly of the essence.

Moses regarded Bryn as fast. Not just because of his training. Bryn was travelling so effortlessly that Moses, even with his experience, was having difficulty keeping up. He didn't mind. He rarely came across a challenge he didn't relish. He even smiled to himself with the effort he was having to muster.

The river showed no evidence of narrowing, but in the distance there appeared to be a bend in its flow-path and it may be a hopeful sign. Moses checked the time. They had two minutes left before they had to turn around. Without losing pace they arrived at the turn in the river with a minute to spare.

'It looks hopeful,' Bryn mentioned as they assessed the risk.

The current had the same strength hitting the bend. Rocks protruded from the water's surface, giving the impression that it was shallow enough to cross. The surge ebbed slightly as the tide meandered along the curve, making this an ideal location to cross.

'This will do.' Moses was visibly relieved. 'Let's head back,' he instructed, checking the time, once again.

Bryn felt proud of their discovery and looked forward to informing Kenta and Alisi. Most of their journey back was downhill, so they should return ahead of schedule. Although the heat was evident, it didn't affect their stride. Tree branches protruded from the forest, blocking the view ahead but Bryn knew their meeting point was down just a little farther.

It was a welcome surprise to see their two teammates had arrived back before them. Because they were under time constraints, every second counted. Alisi was sitting on a rock, cleaning her rifle; Kenta was practising tai chi, by the edge of the water.

'Any luck?' Moses asked, certain that their assignment was a success due to their relaxed demeanour.

'Not so much,' Alisi replied, sounding genuinely disappointed. 'The river maintains a straight course, the water only getting deeper and the banks become wider farther down. You?'

Moses and Bryn explained their more successful discovery, and it was quickly decided that was the direction in which they should head.

Bryn reached for his flask of water. He didn't realise how

dehydrated he was. He then offered it to Moses, who accepted it graciously. Both Alisi and Kenta declined water. Bryn presumed that both must have drunk when they got back. However, looking at both of them now, he marvelled at how fresh they appeared in spite of the heat. It almost seemed like they hadn't moved at all. Was there a chance they disregarded Moses' instructions and just waited for them to return? It would be almost treasonous to do something so blatantly disrespectful. He tried to brush off the notion.

'Let's go,' Moses directed and turned in the direction they had just come from. Alisi dismounted the rock and Kenta retrieved his utility belt, which had been taken off while he was meditating.

That's odd, Bryn thought to himself. *It's not like Kenta to be so reckless.* They had been prepared to expect an attack at any time and Kenta was too experienced to commit such a simple error.

Moses paced slowly ahead, beckoning for the others to follow. Alisi and Kenta stood beside each other, looking directly at Bryn, waiting for him to move. Bryn started to turn, not dismissing his teammates' uncharacteristic behaviour, but thinking that it could be dealt with once they completed their first obstacle.

And then, in a flash it all made sense. Bryn's intuition had been correct. As he moved, the corner of his eye had caught something. It had taken just a fraction of a second, but it was there. It was the answer, but it certainly wasn't the one Bryn was hoping for.

CHAPTER 63

Bryn had spotted a glitch. It was just a glimmer of light at the tip of Kenta's little finger on his left hand. The flicker was enough for him to yell for Moses' attention at the top of his voice, grab his weapon, and turn to face his opponents.

Moses paused about fifty metres ahead, hearing Bryn calling for him. He wasn't expecting to see his blades pointed at their two teammates. He stood there for a moment, in disbelief.

'Bryn, what are you doing?' he shouted.

'Moses, I need you here, now.' Bryn's tone sounded nervous. Alisi and Kenta were standing, hands by their sides facing Bryn, seemingly unaware of Moses' presence in the distance.

Something is not right, Moses thought.

He started back towards Bryn, slow at first, but as he gathered speed he also reached behind his back for his sword. He had a feeling that the games had begun, not with a colony of oversized insects or a foreboding dragon or two. Whatever this was, it was more complicated.

Moses now stood alongside Bryn, not averting his eyes from Kenta or Alisi for even a second.

'His finger, Moses. Kenta's finger… it's glitching.' Bryn pointed at it with one of his blades, while the other was still directed at Alisi.

'Well done, Bryn,' Alisi congratulated him. 'You have indeed discovered your first task.' She spoke in a robotic monotone, no facial inflexions, no gestures with her hands. This wasn't the Alisi they knew. This was not Alisi. 'The games are indeed about teamwork,' she continued. 'You should have had ample time to realise your teammates' strengths, and more importantly, their weaknesses. It's time to put that to the test.'

With that, both Kenta and Alisi drew their weapons.

'Head for the trees,' Moses ordered. 'We need cover.'

As they ran back into the jungle they had emerged from half an hour before, Alisi fired her first shot. Moses caught the discharge from the corner of his eye and pounced on Bryn, knocking him to the ground. The bullet skimmed past Bryn's head, as if in slow motion. They scrambled back to their feet and carried on. They needed distance and somewhere to gather their thoughts and make a plan.

A kilometre in, they sheltered behind a large tree, wide enough that they could stand side by side and not be seen.

'This is going to be tricky, Bryn. But, what a first challenge eh?' Moses seemed rather impressed. 'Strengths and weakness...' he pondered. 'Both have the advantage of attacking from a distance, whether bullets or knives; it's going to be difficult to get close.'

'Also,' Bryn added, 'Alisi is an expert tracker. I don't think we have a lot of time.'

'Not to mention, Kenta is an expert hand-to-hand combat fighter,' Moses said.

Moses crouched down, covering his face and arms with mud, gesturing at Bryn to do the same.

He had a plan.

'We need to take out Alisi first. Hit them one by one. If we can do that, we may have a chance. We need to double-back, confuse our tracks a bit. Getting them to split up is key. I just haven't figured out how we are going to do that yet.'

They carefully and slowly made their way back. No point running away. It was a part of the tournament and they needed to defeat Alisi and Kenta to continue. It didn't matter if Alisi was tracking the general direction they were travelling in. What mattered now was the element of surprise. They needed to attack rather than defend. Continuing their cautious and steadfast journey, Bryn felt nervous. He expected Kenta to jump down from the branches above or Alisi to fire a shot, with a very high probability that it would hit her target, from any distance.

Moses and Bryn were careful, walking in the thickest of foliage, silent; they were listening out for any sign of approach. Within five minutes, Moses stopped in his tracks, gesturing with his hand that they should lie on the ground. As they lowered themselves to their stomachs, on the damp floor of the jungle, they kept watch, their heads barely lifted off the ground. Moses had heard the movement of branches being pushed aside. They were both aware that Kenta could move in absolute silence but Alisi wasn't so careful. This was a weakness – a minor one, but one that could offer an advantage.

A twig broke underfoot. It was from the same direction as before. There was no doubt now. Alisi and Kenta were approaching. They were close.

Bryn was trying to figure out how they could be split up. Considering that was the ruse to get them to battle each other, the reason they separated in the first place, he thought it was certainly not going to be easy.

They kept their position, hidden beneath the low-growing shrubbery, knowing that Alisi would discover their initial, previous tracks that led farther inland. That was the path they were now watching, and there was no doubt that Alisi and Kenta were destined to appear at any moment.

CHAPTER 64

Within thirty seconds, two sets of sandal-strapped feet emerged from a thicket of long grass. Their movements would not have been noticed if Bryn and Moses were not keeping such a close watch. The manufactured clones of their teammates moved quietly, with intent. Bryn could feel his heart beating, but that was the only sign of movement from where they had positioned themselves. He was waiting for a signal from Moses. It was to be imminent and inevitable. The seconds seemed to be passing like minutes and without a structured plan, there was no way of knowing how this exchange would play out.

When they were about to cross paths, when Bryn thought Moses may have changed tactics, Moses signalled with a flat outstretched hand, to attack low. He was gesturing at Alisi. They rose, but not fully. Hunched over, weapons again in hand, they moved forward, hoping to catch them by surprise. Kenta was the first to turn. It was too late for Alisi's clone. Bryn had dived and caught her by the tip of the blade, behind the ankle. She hobbled for a moment but didn't go down, holding her stance. Bryn, still in his position, used his legs to swipe behind Alisi's knees; this time she did fall. Meanwhile, Moses was sword-battling against Kenta's two long daggers. The fight was fast and furious. Both acutely skilled with their weapons, neither appearing that they would tire any time soon.

Alisi was striving to reach for her pistols. She was fast, but Bryn had predicted her movements, and knew he could, and needed, to be faster. If Alisi managed to retrieve her weapons, it was all over for him. He pounced, landing on her chest, pinning her arms to the ground.

Bryn made the mistake of leaving his weapons behind, so had no alternative but to punch her with a tightly closed fist. The surfacing sense of guilt didn't stop Bryn from reaching into Alisi's garment as she was recovering from the blow, and pulling out her pistols, throwing them as far away as he could muster. He could have used the guns against Alisi but in that second's decision, and in that proximity, all he could see was the face of a comrade, a friend.

With her larger rifle also metres from them, Alisi was now weaponless. So was Bryn.

The blow Bryn had delivered and the realisation that he was now without his cache, enraged Alisi. She started to fight back, thrashing about, attempting to free herself from Bryn's grasp. The top of her head collided with Bryn's forehead. It didn't hurt, oddly, but the force was enough to throw him backwards. It was a game, after all, Bryn reminded himself. The objective was not to injure the players.

He was dazed for a moment, but not long enough for Alisi to gain an advantage. Rising to his feet, he prepared himself for another impact, realising that to retrieve his blades, he needed to get past her. But, Alisi had other ideas.

Moses was so focused on his clash of blades with Kenta's clone, that he didn't notice Alisi diverting her attention towards him. Bryn did, however, and while Alisi threw her full body weight, side-swiping Moses, Bryn had no choice but to keep Kenta at bay. That was no easy task as Kenta still had his blades in hand. As quick as he could, Bryn recovered one of his own from beyond where Alisi had stood and fired one half in Kenta's direction.

Kenta was quick. Sensing the motion, he turned and blocked the assail, throwing the blade into the bush. But now Bryn had Kenta's attention and it gave Moses a chance.

As Kenta approached, Bryn backed away. Moses was right. To defeat them, they needed to be separated. He could see Moses and Alisi sparring in the background. Armed with only one of his blades, he edged backwards. Kenta smiled; Bryn thought it was the clone feeling confident, almost arrogant. That wasn't necessarily a bad thing. As he retreated, Bryn's pace quickened. When he thought he had gained Kenta's full attention, he turned and ran, knowing full well that Kenta would give chase.

A circular blade flew, nearly skimming his left ear. It was too close, Bryn thought, as it whistled past loudly. Another caught the edge of his sleeve, causing it to tear. He was not going to get very far at this rate. Kenta had an unfair advantage and Bryn needed to even the odds.

The enclosure of trees was tall and evenly packed. Bryn knew Kenta was adept at climbing but to do it he needed his hands, the very ones that were now wielding his weapons. Bryn was confident that he was fast on the ground but it was only a matter of time before one of the blades did significant damage.

There was no alternative but to go up. He leapt high and forward, but as he did, he could feel a numbness developing along his left, lower torso. He had been hit but had no idea how badly. He kept climbing but the tingling crept along his lower back. He feared that it might cause his exit from the game. An early end to his participation. He persevered. Kenta was only feet below him.

CHAPTER 65

Back at the farm, Bryn spent his youth climbing trees. There was one aspect he enjoyed most but if his parents had found out, he would have been in serious trouble.

When Bryn was about ten, he watched Greystoke: The Legend of Tarzan, a film made back in the eighties. It was shown in the small, local cinema. With a lot of persuasion, Bryn managed to convince his mother to take him. He was fascinated by Tarzan. Not only the idea of growing up being nurtured by the animal kingdom, which formed the base of the storyline, but what stood out was the idea of swinging from tree to tree. When Bryn saw this skill depicted on the television screen, and the ease with which the main character mastered it, he felt he could do it too. So, one day, when his parents were buying groceries in the village, he decided that he should give it a go.

Climbing the tree wasn't the issue, as he had been doing that since he was two. The main issue was, there were no vines for him to swing from. This caused a little frustration, but not enough to quell his ambition. He simply adapted the method. The first few attempts at what he later defined as tree-hopping, were a bit of a disaster. He slid. He fell. He cut himself pretty badly on two occasions. But it was nothing to deter him. He just needed to focus on his landing. It took close to a week to figure out, and he was lucky that all injuries were in places that he could easily cover up. He knew his parents would not approve. The trees were tall and the ground uneven. One bad fall could lead to a broken limb or two, maybe even significant damage to his neck or back.

His new hobby was fun, thrilling in fact. It was one that he practised and learned to perfect as he grew. The branches became higher. He rarely fell, bounding from one to another, occasionally using somersaults or twists in the air, resembling a gymnast on a high beam.

However, at that point, he hadn't been tree-hopping for at least two years. He now hoped that he hadn't lost the knack, as he was approaching the treetop and if he didn't act now, there would be nowhere else for him to go, but down.

Kenta was close to his heels. He was relieved to feel that, although his side and lower back had lost feeling completely, Kenta must have missed any major organ. He was still in the game.

Bryn paid attention to the neighbouring trees, calculating which would be the most suitable to transfer to. As he climbed, he veered in different directions, making it more difficult for Kenta to follow and giving him the opportunity needed to find an appropriate branch to launch from. Once he ascertained his destination and how he was going to get there, he simply went for it. He ran the length of the thickest branch he could find and leapt. This stumped Kenta for a moment. Bryn didn't dwell on Kenta's reaction but readied himself for his next tree-hop.

Figuring out his direction was easy once a plan formed in his head. The tree-hopping had slowed Kenta down. Bryn saw that some of his attempts had landed badly, scrapes and scratches appearing on his clothes and hands. He watched the terrain below as he moved along the treetops. If he veered too far away, he would get lost easily, and that would be disastrous.

He spotted Moses below. He was running in his direction. It seemed like he was neither chasing Alisi nor being chased by her. Bryn was conscious that Moses hadn't spotted him in the branches, so quickly descended the tree and landed only feet away.

'In the trees!' he shouted, as he positioned himself alongside. They both looked up, but Kenta was nowhere to be seen.

Bryn didn't need to tell him that Kenta was close. Moses knew Kenta's strengths well. He could silently approach them from any direction; he could also attack, with perfect aim, from afar. He was the most adept combatant Moses ever had the pleasure of fighting alongside. There was never a moment he could imagine in which he would have to battle against him, or even his replica.

There wasn't time for Bryn to ask Moses what happened with Alisi. He just had to assume that Moses had dealt with it. Plenty of time later for questions. Both of them wielded their weapons with purpose, Bryn feeling incomplete without the other half of his. They stood in silence, craning their necks, bracing themselves for impact.

Moses sensed movement and turned quickly. There was Kenta, with the same unnatural grin spread across his face. He had come from nowhere. It was as though he had been standing behind them the entire time, and it was only now they discovered he was there.

'Bryn, go wide!' Moses gestured that they should spread out. Bryn did as he was told, knowing that Moses' experience was guiding them now.

Kenta didn't express any sense of being under pressure or duress. He produced his blades, which had been hiding in his sleeves, and appeared to be relishing any form of nervousness he may be inflicting. Relaxed and confident, he motioned at them with his hand to approach. He was ready.

With one side glance, they both charged together. The initial clashing of blades disturbed a flock of birds nearby and they took flight, noisily cawing to express their objections. The fight was fast but infuriating, as Bryn thought Kenta was predicting every move they made. And, of course, he was. Kenta knew Bryn and Moses' strengths and weaknesses as well as them knowing his. It felt as though he was aiming to tire them out. If that was the case, it was only a matter of time before he succeeded. They needed to change tack. Bryn backed away. This move surprised Moses as he battled on.

'What are you doing, Bryn?' Moses asked, sounding very unimpressed.

'Give me a mo—' As he spoke Kenta launched a circular blade in his direction, missing him by less than a centimetre. Bryn smiled.

Kenta missed and he hadn't even tried to dodge the blade. It was almost effortless for Kenta to take on both of them at close proximity, but one close and the other farther away was proving a little more challenging. He had an idea. It seemed very simplistic and Bryn had no idea if it would work but there was no harm in trying. They had nothing to lose.

He began running in circles and a zig-zag motion around Moses and Kenta as they fought. Kenta was focusing his attention on Moses. Bryn was distracting him. Once Bryn had done three circuits, and when Kenta felt that a distraction was all he was offering, he came up close to him, catching his forearm with his blade. He never stopped moving, gaining speed and rhythm. Kenta's expression changed suddenly. He didn't seem so confident now. Moses' attack intensified as Kenta reached for more blades to hurl at Bryn. He dropped one. Moses caught Bryn's eye and he ran past. He was smiling. Kenta had never dropped a blade or missed a target. Moses was beginning to believe that Kenta didn't bear any weaknesses, that he was infallible. He was wrong.

Bryn continued to inflict cuts and nicks on any accessible body part as he ran past Kenta. Sometimes, he didn't even bother. The idea of it was all that was needed to throw him off his game. Moses needed to finish this. It felt like they had been fighting for hours.

But, with time, the clone began to regain focus. He realised that Bryn was barely grazing him, not doing any conceivable damage. Moses appeared under pressure once again. That's what Bryn was hoping for. With Kenta's focus off him, he circled them one last time, but instead of finishing his lap, he stopped dead behind where Kenta was standing and drew his blade deep into his spine.

Kenta let out a low growling moan and vanished in an instant.

Moses dropped his sword, reaching down to put his hands on his knees. He was breathing heavily. A moment later, he rose again and started laughing aloud.

'He certainly wasn't expecting that!' he managed to utter.

Bryn was laughing now. It was mainly due to relief.

Moses put his hand on Bryn's shoulder and smiled in approval.

'We better get back. Let's hope the other two had as much luck killing us as we had in killing them.'

CHAPTER 66

When they got back to the beach, after stopping for a short time to find the other half of Bryn's weapon, there was no sign of the others. They decided to head downstream, in case they may need their assistance. Two kilometres into their journey, they spotted both Kenta and Alisi emerging from the trees. They appeared tired and on closer inspection, Bryn could see blood oozing from a cut on the side of Alisi's head.

'You two okay?' Moses asked, concerned.

'We'll survive,' Alisi answered, as she approached.

'How did you cut your head?' Bryn inquired.

'Tripped on a branch. Looks worse than it is,' Alisi answered reassuringly.

They sat in silence, recovering. Moses suggested they took the opportunity to eat something before they crossed the river. They ate in relative silence. They had some water but didn't waste too much time. On the way back upstream, they spoke about the challenge and what they had learned from it. Alisi told Bryn and Moses how their predictable fighting methods led to their defeat. That was when Moses told them about Bryn's strategy that led to the demise of Kenta's clone.

'Aren't you full of surprises!' Alisi remarked, while she giggled at the imagery as it played out in her head.

Once they arrived at the bend in the river, they didn't delay their crossing. It was almost effortless, and it was no time before they arrived at the other side. At that stage it was beginning to get dark, so they decided to set up camp and retire for the evening. Before settling down they consulted the map, calculated their next day's journey and configured their compasses. Moses spoke of how they had, without doubt, discovered each other's weaknesses and it was up to each team member to be aware of them going forward. Kenta wasn't impressed to hear that he wasn't as adept fighting two people at different distances, and Bryn could see him pondering the notion for some time after the talk.

They sat together, firmly as a team. If Bryn had any doubts that he wasn't worthy to be amongst them, those were quashed now. They spoke about nothing and everything. They had all forgotten about the orb, which they hadn't seen since that afternoon. Without question it was still there, somewhere.

CHAPTER 67

The dawn was on the cusp of breaking when Bryn woke. The others were still asleep. He went to the river's edge and splashed his face with water. Returning to the camp, he noticed that there were still embers glowing from the fire they had lit, the night before. Although it wasn't cold, Bryn still held his hands up to it, drawing from its warmth.

Alisi was the next to wake. She went behind a nearby bush to relieve herself before she too decided to wash down by the river. Once cleansed, she sat by the fire with Bryn.

'You know, we both underestimated you yesterday, Bryn,' Alisi admitted. 'Kenta had been fighting with Moses for years, and it took time, but we managed to knock him out. But you were different. I know I said we had predicted how we could defeat your clones… or whatever they're called… but you weren't that predictable. It was as if your strength was just that. You are unpredictable, Bryn. I can see how it can be a weakness, though I have to say, yesterday, unpredictability was your biggest strength. That… and… you're fast. We couldn't keep up…'

Moses and Kenta stirred. It interrupted Alisi's words of encouragement, but Bryn felt that was all he needed to hear. He was grateful for it.

Within ten minutes, they were up and resuming their journey once again.

The sun had broken the day and though still early, Bryn knew it was going to be a hot one. They had chosen a route on the map, through a gap, where two mountains met. The range was visible from the camp, the distance difficult to fathom. They were expecting hilly, rocky terrain but it would be relatively clear of trees and rivers.

Although chances of being separated for another task were slim, a decision was made that today they would stick together, whatever the risk.

As they travelled, the ground beneath them became sandy, awash with small stones. Their pace was steady, taking long strides, avoiding tiring too early in the day. They were prepared for an ambush, one that could happen at any moment. Travelling without shelter to be availed of nearby, left them vulnerable. Moses wanted to get to the range quickly but realised that it would also be a perfect position for a trap, another challenge. No point trying to avoid it. It was either travel through the gap or they would be forced to climb. Some of the mountains were so tall that they breached the skyline. That was not going to be an option for them. It would also seem cowardly. Avoiding chances of conflict would appear fearful. The audience wouldn't react well, he thought.

Arriving at the entrance to the passage, the gap between the two foreboding mountains was relatively narrow and the pathway meandered around large boulders, hindering their long-range view. They had two choices. Either continue along the route, as planned, or gain a bit of height by climbing a section of one of the mountainsides, thus obtaining a more measured perspective.

It was almost midday. The sun was directly overhead, but a gentle breeze protected them from getting overheated.

A sudden buzzing noise emanated from somewhere, and discussions about their planned approach abruptly ceased. It sounded like a muffled voice drowned in static. The pitch was low and barely audible. If it was not for the desolated terrain, the lack of rolling river and the absence of animal calls, they may not have heard it at all. The sound came from everywhere, but nowhere. It wasn't until Moses reached into his satchel and dug out the earpiece he used at the arena, that they realised someone was trying to make contact. This was highly irregular. They could easily have left their earpieces in the travelling capsule. It was rare that they were ever needed to be used in competition. Kenta, ignoring proper procedure, had left his behind.

Moses had his earpiece on by the time Bryn and Alisi found their own. He looked concerned. The colour began to drain from his face.

Alisi held her earpiece so that Kenta could also hear what was being said. Bryn secured his to his ear. It was difficult to understand what was being relayed at first. He realised it was a message played on a loop. The message was from Gregor.

'The games have been sabotaged... The Goyteks... Get to the source... They want the power... We are losing transmission and the travel line is down... Will get to you when we can... Be safe!'

CHAPTER 68

Bryn was flummoxed. What did this mean? Where was the source and what was its power?

Moses was reading the map. His hands were shaking. Kenta joined him and soon had a destination in mind. He pointed to it with his finger.

'You are right, Kenta. That's where we need to go,' Moses agreed. 'We are going through the gap and changing course.' He addressed Bryn and Alisi. 'Heading north. Keep your wits about you. With the technology the Goyteks possess, we can expect to encounter the full force of it.'

'Could this be just a ruse, part of the game?' asked Bryn.

'Never,' responded Moses. 'The only reason communication would be used through the earpiece, is if there was a genuine distress call. Otherwise, it would be a flagrant disregard of the situation. The committee would not approve such contempt.'

Bryn didn't fully understand what was going on. All he knew was that the Goyteks were now considered a threat. There wasn't even a moment to ask another question as Moses and Kenta had sprinted off without saying another word. Bryn looked at Alisi – who appeared just as perplexed – long enough to acknowledge each other's concern, before they followed suit.

Winding their way through the mountains, weapons were drawn. Any large boulders or possible enemy vantage areas were carefully approached, but their focus now was on speed. The end of the passage was in sight. Bryn felt a tinge of relief, but it was short-lived. They had no idea what was waiting for them at the other end.

He was about to offer to scout ahead but Moses had made it clear that they couldn't split up. Instead, as they neared the opening,

Moses slowed, and the others followed suit.

The map was placed on the ground. They crouched so that all four could see its markings. Moses indicated their current position on it, with his index finger.

'This is where we now stand. We need to travel north,' he pointed nearer to the top of the page, 'because that is where the source Gregor was referring to is positioned.'

Bryn was visibly bewildered. Alisi seemed a little less so.

'This planet is a relatively young phenomenon,' Alisi explained to Bryn. 'It's still in the process of being established. The source is seen as an access point that leads to the power core of the entire celestial body. It's a series of caverns and tunnels and has been explored many times. At its farthest point, it has been said that you can cook an egg on the floor's surface. Nobody has ever made any attempt to dig in too deep as it could destabilise the entire structure and lead to irreparable destruction. It was declared that it should be left alone to evolve at its own speed. The people of Zhivrah are banned from going near it. No attempt has been made since to defy that order. We all know what's at stake.'

'I have recently heard rumours,' Moses continued, 'that the Goyteks' home planet, Goya, is in trouble. It is one of the oldest planets in their solar system and it is starting to die. I have been thinking, just now. I believe they may have developed technology that could transfer the energy from the source back through the gateway. It may seem inconceivable to us, but they are an advanced race, far more than we can begin to realise.'

They let Moses' words sink in. This was beyond anything Bryn could ever have imagined. 'How far away from the source are we?' he asked.

'About a day's trek, but that's if we're fast and we don't encounter any resistance,' Moses answered.

'If that's the case, won't they have predicted the path we will take? Won't they know to prepare for that?'

Moses thought for a moment.

'I don't think they will see us as much of a threat. They have disabled the communications and mobility network in the city; but I can guarantee, it won't be out for long. Gregor, and the others, will find a way. They have to,' he said. 'Meanwhile, we must move forward. The Goyteks will be armed with sophisticated weaponry. They also have the nanotech and holographic imagery to add to their arsenal and they have probably weaponised it.'

Moses turned to go, but Bryn had one more question.

'But why now? They must have known that Zhivrah would be full of warriors ready to fight back.'

'Did you see the crowds at the stadium, Bryn? Hundreds, maybe thousands of Goyteks ready to fight for their cause. They would have needed their people to destabilise the city, launch the artillery, operate the machinery at the source. What better time to do it when everyone else is distracted by the Games? It would never have gone unnoticed otherwise. Now, we need to move!'

CHAPTER 69

They ran to the end of the passage. Moses signalled for them to stop as he moved slowly forward to see what lay ahead, beyond the mountain pass. Once surveyed, he motioned for them to move forward.

The passage led to a clearing, much like the one behind them. Not many trees. Sparse vegetation and dry ground. Again, nowhere for them to hide. Instead of following their original coordinates, which would have led them straight ahead, they veered left. Continuing their journey north, they kept close to the mountain ridge. The terrain was becoming darker, browner. The foliage appeared blackened, possibly due to lack of nutrients. In the distance pockets of noxious gas emitted from the soil, giving the sky, just above, a foggy appearance. The air had a slight odour of rotten eggs. All of this did little to deter the four teammates from their ultimate goal.

Farther ahead, they found they had to meander around larger pools of black tar that blistered at the surface. The fog became thicker and the stench more apparent. This time, Kenta was the first to stop and motion for the others to do the same. He reached for his bag and pulled out a spare tunic, which he wasted no time ripping into four pieces. He wrapped one over his nose and mouth, tying it at the back of his head. He tossed the other three to his teammates and they did the same.

'I have heard of this place,' Alisi said. 'I have never had the urge to visit, for obvious reasons.'

'The Black Pit,' added Moses. 'It has never had the reputation of being a holiday destination. People have been warned to stay away. I have heard that if you fall into one of these tar pools, it drags you down like quicksand, and it will not let you go. We could look for a way around it, but the air being so dense, I would have no idea which way to go or how far it stretches out at either side.'

He pulled out the map for reference. 'It's not even on here. Who would have thought we'd need it? I know they wanted the map to appear rudimentary, but this is ridiculous.'

Moses was demonstrating the frustration they all now felt. He scrunched up the map as though it was just a worthless piece of paper and returned it to his satchel.

'I think we should keep moving forward,' he said. 'I can't see that we have much choice.'

As they continued their journey, the pool of tar became larger, the air denser. The odour was so putrid that Bryn was trying not to gag. The mountain protecting them had dissipated to a rocky base, barely two feet from the ground. Tar spat and oozed from its entire surface, spilling into a stream, which slowly ebbed forward in the direction they were going.

They started taking slower, more deliberate steps. Apart from the tar, the surface had become mostly rock. The landscape seemed to slowly descend ahead of them, as though they were travelling down a slight incline or hillside. The tar moved forward, spreading like spilt treacle. They needed to be very careful with their footing as there was very little space to tread. Visibility was becoming so poor that they were having difficulty keeping each other in sight. They walked in silence, concentrating on every movement.

Bryn spotted something just ahead. It was in his eyeline, but he couldn't quite make out what it could be. It was like a black hole, only it was the size of a tennis ball. It appeared to be floating. Suddenly it popped, startling Bryn to the point that he almost lost his balance.

'Damn it!' he uttered under his breath. 'Careful, the tar is now floating in bubbles above the ground,' he announced, hoping that his teammates were still nearby.

'That's all we need,' Moses said from behind.

Bryn carefully meandered around more globules of blackened tar, silently praying not to get sprayed by its contents. He was panicking slightly as the ground was running out of rocky space. The piece of tunic wrapped around his face was soaked in sweat; he was not sure if it was caused by the heat or his frayed nerves.

He was so focused on his immediate surroundings that he almost missed the light that filtered through the dense cloud up ahead. It was the relief he so desperately needed as he wasn't sure how far he could keep going like this.

'I think it's starting to clear,' he shouted, the relief in his voice apparent.

He heard Moses and Alisi reply, but their voices were muffled. They were farther behind than Bryn had thought.

With every step came more light. He could almost make out the shape of the sun. The ground was also becoming more visible, though the amount of flowing tar stayed the same. Luckily, he spotted a raised rock platform on his right, about a foot off the ground. It was at least two feet wide. He stepped up and looked behind, hoping to catch a glimpse of the others. Visibility was still a little poor, but he thought he could make out one, maybe two figures in the distance. He sidestepped along the rock to get a better view. One step, then two. As he went for the third step, he quickly found out that there wasn't one there. It was an empty space. He tried to regain his balance but failed. All he had managed was to drop to the ground as he fell.

It all happened to Bryn in slow motion. He could see Moses' hand reaching out for him, but he was too far away. He saw the flowing tar edge over the surface and drop below, like a waterfall in slow motion. And then he looked down. There was nothing but a black, darkened void. It appeared to be bottomless, though it was difficult to be sure. He slid, slow at first. He was clinging to the rock as best he could, but the surface was smooth. There were no cracks or crevices he could grip on to. Moments before he fell from the edge, he knew it was inevitable. He had never been so fearful in his life. There was nothing he could do. Within moments, he lost his handhold of the rock and started free falling.

CHAPTER 70

Moses could see just the top of Bryn's head stretching from side to side desperately searching for him, or anyone. He knew that Bryn was in trouble. He ran and called out but didn't think Bryn was able to decipher what he said. As he hastily approached, he called out to him again. This time with a sense of urgency. He saw Bryn's hands slide off the rock as he climbed onto it. It was too late.

Moses called for Alisi and Kenta to join him, and to be careful not to fall off the edge. He then lay on the rock face, head over the side, hoping to catch sight of Bryn. The pungent fog hadn't dissipated completely but a breeze funnelled by fresh air hitting the crevice below had created significant more visibility. He roared down to Bryn for a third time, hoping for any signs of life below. The response was silence. Alisi and Kenta joined him now, all three looking over the edge, watching for any sign of movement.

Moses was on the verge of giving up. He had beckoned for Bryn several times and was about to get up when he spotted movement on the crevice wall below. Alisi had seen it too. In places, wisps of fog moved beneath, occasionally blocking their view. Kenta moved his head from left to right, trying to get a better look at what they had stumbled upon. It appeared that the ground had split. The fissure seemed endless at both sides.

More movement. Alisi was the first to witness Bryn's hand reaching upwards, the rest of his body hidden behind a jutting rock. In Bryn's hand was a blade, which he drove into the rock face as he climbed. Up came another hand and another blade, again it was wedged into the rock face. Moses called to Bryn again. This time Bryn called back to say that he was okay. His head was the next to appear. He had lost the piece of cloth protecting his face; the almost two-day hair growth underneath gave the impression that he was older than his years. Inches from the top, Alisi and Kenta reached for him, pulling him back over the upper surface, where he lay, catching his breath, grateful to be still alive.

Fifteen feet, Kenta reckoned the crevice measured. It was a substantial gap. As the tar flowed into the crevice, it didn't appear that there was any at the other side. The terrain was barren but nothing like the ground they were now on. There were a few fallen trees and darkened foliage. It was inviting by comparison. Bryn had recovered quicker than expected. It was time to form a plan. Kenta had an idea to what they should do. But it was risky and he needed the help of his teammates for it to be accomplished.

'Kenta, you've thought of something, haven't you?' Moses asked.

Kenta described his plan with hand gestures. Moses was the most familiar with Kenta's sign language. He had trained with him for a long time and by now they conversed effortlessly, mostly without words.

'I'm not sure, Kenta,' Moses responded.

'What's he saying?' Alisi asked.

'He figures he can make the jump,' said Moses. 'He thinks if we can give him a boost, he can get to the other side. There's a fallen tree he thinks he can move across to us.'

'Hmmm... I dunno.' Alisi thought for a moment. 'That's a significant leap of faith, and that's a pretty big tree.'

Bryn couldn't help but agree with Alisi. Even if Kenta made the jump, that tree looked massive. There was no way he could move it on his own.

Kenta gestured, with a simple shrug, that he didn't think they had many choices. He busied himself trying to ascertain where would be the best position to launch from. He needed a bit of running space and he also needed to figure out where was the best place for him to land, on the other side.

Bryn relayed his thoughts about Kenta's idea to Moses. It was risky and if he fell, it wasn't a matter that he'd be out of the games.

He could die.

'Kenta would never volunteer for anything unless he had a positive feeling about it.' Moses did his best to reassure Bryn.

At the edge of the crevice, in a position Kenta directed them to, Alisi and Moses stretched both of their arms forward and linked fingers. The plan was that Kenta would use the boost to propel him forward. There was nothing for Bryn to do but watch. Kenta took five steps backwards. This was as much as he could afford. He didn't waste any time. Moses and Alisi's hands were almost touching the ground when Kenta landed on them. They raised their arms to the height of their shoulders when he leapt forward. Bryn could barely watch.

Kenta somersaulted in the air before he started to descend. He hadn't quite reached halfway at that stage, but it was still hopeful. After seeing Bryn using his blades to climb the rock face, Kenta thought he would use his to aid his landing. He was relieved that he did. With out-reaching arms, he stretched forward, knowing he was going to slightly fall short on his landing. The blades scraped the ground at the far side, his legs still dangling over the edge. Before he started to slide, he scrambled to his feet. He had made it and the relief all round was evident.

Making his way over to the fallen tree, he realised that it was a lot larger than he had initially thought. He scanned the area for anything else he could use as a bridge. There were other fallen trees. They were either too short or too brittle. There wasn't a choice. He would have to move it, or at least try. There was no way the others were going to be able to make that leap. None of them, apart from…

Bryn watched Kenta struggle to move the tree trunk. It wasn't shifting. The moment of hope they all felt was fast beginning to fade. All three of them stood side by side watching his efforts. There was nothing they could do to help.

In spite of Kenta's persistence, he knew that it was a hopeless endeavour. He suddenly stopped what he was doing and approached the edge. Looking at Moses, he made a slight gesture before pointing at Bryn. Moses then looked at Bryn and gestured back, with what looked like a solid no. Kenta signed again at Moses, who pondered his suggestion for a moment.

Bryn wanted to know what was being said and that feeling was apparent when Moses looked at him.

'Kenta reckons you'd make the jump,' Moses told him.

Bryn was more than surprised to hear this. Kenta was known as the agile one. Bryn was a little clumsy in comparison.

'I'm not going to make you do it, Bryn. It's your choice. It is wider in distance than it looks, and you know how deep that drop is.' Moses seemed concerned.

It only took Bryn a moment to realise that there wasn't much of a choice. They were held up by the tar-pit and they couldn't afford to waste any more time.

Moses and Alisi stretched their arms out as they had before. Bryn replicated Kenta's moves and took five steps backwards. He, too, held his blades in his hands. The air was clearer than it was when Kenta had vaulted. There was nothing to hinder his vision. He kept his eyes on where he was aiming to land. It was better for him not to think about it.

Alisi shouted words of encouragement. Moses kept silent. Bryn was starting to second guess whether this was the best solution they could come up with. It was too late. With two long strides, Bryn was boosted into the air. There was nothing more any of them could do.

CHAPTER 71

Bryn had gained more height than Kenta had, in spite of their weight difference. He hadn't expected that. His leap lacked the finesse, the somersault and was clumsily executed, but he was still in the air. The world went by in slow motion. He kept his eyes on where he was hoping to land, glimpsing towards Kenta once or twice to make sure he was close by, in case he needed a hand.

As he descended, he felt hopeful. He had travelled a longer distance than he had ever expected. Landing effortlessly in a crouched position, he could barely believe it. As he rose to his feet, he saw that Kenta was smiling at him with approval. He could hear Alisi and Moses cheering from behind.

Sliding the tree across the ravine, it only took moments for the others to join them. There was such a great sense of relief, they momentarily forgot the serious predicament they were in. However, it didn't delay them for long. Within minutes they were sprinting again northwards, hoping to catch up on lost time. The dead terrain began to gain life, the greenery a welcome sight. The sky had cleared, and the sun regained its glory.

Without the mountain range, they were fully exposed to any enemy attack. They remained wary as they travelled, watching for movement on the horizon. Several miles along they came across a dirt road. It was trailing along the direction they were heading so Moses decided they should follow it. Beyond a small cluster of trees, they saw it led to a hamlet, a seemingly deserted one. There was only a scattering of old, clay-built structures; most likely abandoned homesteads. It was apparent that they hadn't been lived in for some time.

Spreading out, keeping in each other's sights, they surveyed the area. The sound of wind chimes hanging from a porch broke the eerie silence. There was a total of seven houses and three outhouses, all of them devoid of life. If they had time to rest, this would be the perfect place to shelter. Unfortunately, they couldn't afford the luxury of sleep. They needed to keep moving.

At the far end of the hamlet, another road led away from it. It was on course, so they followed it, wasting no time exploring. It led uphill and from where they were, they couldn't see over the crest. Westward, the sun was beginning to make its slow descent. Moses initially thought they might reach their destination by nightfall, but at this rate, they would be lucky to get there by midnight. Their only hope was that the Goyteks' efforts to break through to the source would take time, and they would make it there to stop them before any permanent damage could be achieved.

Lost in his thoughts, Moses almost missed movement up ahead. Something, it was difficult to see what from their distance, rose from the hilltop and entered the sky above.

'On your guard,' he commanded. They all stopped dead in their tracks. 'Can you see what it is, Kenta?'

From Kenta's satchel, he produced a miniature mono-scope. Peering through, there was a sense of relief when he realised what, or more importantly who, was in his sights.

When he showed Moses, his reaction was one of surprise.

'It's Lars,' he exclaimed. 'Someone is riding behind.'

He unwound the mono-scope to get a better view.

Regardless of whoever rode with Lars, both were travelling on a bird, large enough to carry them both on its back. Bryn's eyes were transfixed by the sight of it. What was his father doing here? As it neared, Bryn thought the bird resembled a falcon, apart from significantly longer tail feathers.

Lars had spotted them from above and the bird began its swoop towards the ground, its approach both graceful and intimidating. It was still metres above their heads when Lars and his co-rider dismounted, landing directly in their path. He wasted no time with pleasantries.

'Move!' He started running towards back towards the hamlet. Sprinting alongside was Kyra. Bryn was not expecting to see her. She never even looked at him. Moses knew better than to ask questions and signalled for the others to follow. They did, except for Bryn. He just stood and watched Kyra and his father run away from him, unable to believe they were here.

Lost in his thoughts, he barely noticed a rumbling sound coming from behind. It sounded like a herd of horses, or possibly elephants, approaching from beyond the horizon. He turned. There was something or someone at the crest of the hill. It appeared as a silhouette, so Bryn couldn't make out any features. Two more figures came over the hillside and all three stood together, just as another four came into view. Bryn's focus was distracted by something breaking the skyline, as Lars had done before. Again, it was only a silhouette against the sun – the dark outline was different from that of the bird. The wings were long, narrow but shaped like they belonged to a bat. Its core, from what Bryn could see, was part-human in shape, possibly bulkier, but Bryn couldn't quite make it out from his position.

He had to move. He turned to follow the others and as he did, from the corner of his eye he could see wings unfurling from behind some of the small army of about twenty bizarre forms congregating on the hillside. They, too, started to take to flight. Bryn ran. He did so at a speed he had never reached before. He needed to catch up with his comrades, and fast.

At the entrance to the hamlet, Lars instructed that they split up in pairs. Moses and Kyra found shelter in an outhouse, adjacent to one of the larger houses. Kenta and Alisi disappeared into a building close by. Lars led Bryn into another house a little farther along. There, he immediately checked the satchel hanging from his back and pulled out several bundles of small arrows, each tied with cord. He undid the knot on some of them, leaving them to spill onto the ground, forming a pile. Over his shoulder hung a crossbow.

Bryn was keeping watch through a window facing the direction they were expecting to be attacked from. He was terrified but doing his best not to show it.

'They're called Borks! A somewhat less desirable species from Goya. Mostly wiped from their planet by now,' Bryn's father explained as he worked. 'Tough, scaly exterior; large teeth and claws. They fly, but only for small stretches. Their bodies are too large and cumbersome to last in the air for long.'

Bryn didn't move from his position while Lars spoke, taking in every word. He had never seen him like this, speaking like an army commander.

'They like to pick their prey up with their clawed toes, fly high and drop them. Instant kill. Don't let that happen, Bryn.' He paused to load five arrows in his crossbow. 'Remember, we have to presume that every strike will hurt. I'm guessing the Goyteks have modified their software. You need to know they will probably kill you if you don't pay attention. This isn't a game anymore. This is war.'

Bryn had never seen his father like this. He was afraid. And, although he was trying to hide it, Bryn could hear it in his voice.

'Where's Mum?' Bryn asked. 'Is she okay?'

Lars was now keeping watch from a gap in the doorway. 'Last I saw, she was with Gregor heading to the control centre, trying to restore communications and transport.' He saw the concern on Bryn's face. 'Don't worry!' He tried to sound reassuring. 'Knowing those two, they'll have everything up and running in no time.'

There was a loud screeching sound from overhead. The Borks had caught up with them and were now searching the village.

Lars re-closed the door and gestured to Bryn to keep quiet.

CHAPTER 72

Most of the Borks had landed back on their feet. A few hovered just above, keeping watch for any sign of movement. Bryn had so far counted six scouts. They were bigger in stature than he had expected, about the size and a half of an average human, he reckoned. Their heads were large and bulbous, their eyes seemed small and beady. Their mouths were massive, with sharp, oversized teeth. Every feature seemed to be completely out of proportion. With their grey, scaly complexion, it was as if they were all originally cast in stone, somehow.

After monitoring the periphery, the remaining Bork infantry entered the hamlet, spread out to join the scouting party, and slowly advanced towards each structure. They appeared organised and determined. Hiding seemed pointless. They were going to be boxed in, with nowhere to go.

'I counted eighteen of them.' Lars was trying to formulate a plan.

'You need to cover me,' Bryn said. 'I'm useless, cooped up here with blades. By the time they get through the door, there will be too many of them for us to handle.'

'Bryn, it's too dangerous. You haven't enough experience in the field. It's a suicide mission.'

Before Bryn had a chance to respond, they both watched through the window, as Kyra dismounted the roof of the building she had been hiding in. In one hand, she held a spear and in the other, a poleaxe. Bryn hadn't noticed earlier that on her back, she wore a brightly coloured shield. He thought her magnificent and there was no chance he was going to leave her out there, battling alone.

'Cover me.' He repeated his instruction to his father as he withdrew both blades from the wooden sheath. Bryn took Lars' nod of hesitant agreement as a blessing and didn't waste time discussing it further. He disappeared through the door quickly and quietly. His sole aim was to get to Kyra. She was tougher and possibly more determined than Bryn, but there was no way she could defeat them on her own.

Bryn moved swiftly but it wasn't fast enough to go unnoticed. Hearing heavy stomping from behind, he turned to see two Borks giving chase. Lars released several arrows from his position, but none except one burrowed through their tough exterior. The one that did, hit the Bork coming up on Bryn's left, in the leg. It barely flinched. Lars' weapon was proving useless against these creatures, Bryn thought. What if all of the weapons were? It didn't bear thinking about.

He could hear, from behind, his father releasing more arrows. This time they all hit the base of one of the Borks' necks. Down it fell with a thud. With a newfound sense of encouragement, Bryn moved on. Kyra was only metres ahead when, from behind one of the outhouses, appeared another Bork. It was as startled as Bryn was by their sudden encounter. It hissed, and then howled; probably alerting the others of its discovery. Drool dripped from the corners of its open mouth, teeth on full display to show its readiness for battle. From behind, the remaining half of the pair that chased Bryn from his shelter, had caught up. Three feathered ends of another rally from Lars' crossbow, were lodged in its neck, this time just below this one's heavy jawline. Charcoal-coloured liquid oozed from the wounds, dripping down the chest cavity, resting on the protruding belly below. It limped forward, still full of purpose.

Bryn's blade clashed with the sharp claws of the Bork that faced him. He wasn't surprised it left no impression. The Bork swiped at him with his other hand. Bryn swerved in time to avoid contact. There was no fear in the eyes of the Bork, just sheer determination. He battled on, aware that at any moment, the injured Bork advancing from behind would be joining the fight.

Both blades were in full motion, Bryn scrutinising its body for any vulnerability. Striking the chest and back proved pointless. His blades just bounced off its thick scales. Several cuts were visible on its limbs, but after seeing the damage done by his father's arrows, the ideal target area seemed to be around the neck. That's where Bryn needed to focus.

The Bork lunged and snapped its toothy jaw. Without thinking, Bryn leapt onto its shoulders, turned and plunged both blades into the soft tissue under its neckline. It attempted to screech in pain, but no sound came out. It was dead before it collapsed onto the ground. As Bryn dismounted, the Bork who had struggled to catch up, was now upon him. Wasting no time, he retracted both blades and plunged one under its chin, with such force that it penetrated the skull and protruded through the top of its head. The Bork instantly fell and before it landed on top of him, a hand grabbed Bryn by the elbow and pulled him out of the way. It was Lars.

'Time to move, Bryn.' Lars offered an arm and pulled him to his feet. Moses was with him. Both men relieved to see Bryn unhurt. Lars was now brandishing a mace. It had a thick wooden handle, the spiked head shaped like a skull. Bryn realised he must have raided the armoury before he left. Darkness was setting in and Kyra had disappeared, nowhere to be seen. Bryn had lost sight of her and felt a little panicked, worried that she may have been hurt. There was no sign of Kenta or Alisi either, although Bryn was sure he had heard Alisi's gun being fired only moments before.

'Keep quiet and keep low,' Lars instructed as they ran to seek shelter behind one of the outhouses.

Somewhere in the distance, a Bork howled. It was summoning support, they figured. It gave them an idea of where the others were. They needed to move fast. With only the light from the moon to guide them, it wouldn't be long before they were fighting blind.

CHAPTER 73

Alisi kept enough ammunition to last as long as she estimated was needed for any battle. She had to consider the weight of it and whether it would be cumbersome. So far, she managed to take down five Borks, but her artillery stock suffered as a consequence. There could be a long battle ahead and she had to keep a healthy reserve. Every shot from then on needed to be aimed at their eyes. It was proving most effective to neutralise the targets and only required one cartridge. It was more difficult as the night was upon them; the creatures were almost camouflaged by the stone structures as they scurried past. She was alone on a rooftop, providing cover for Kenta and Kyra, as they went to search for the others. They had caught sight of them less than twenty minutes before but a herd of eight Borks drove them away.

Not too far from where she lay, she heard a Bork howl. She shifted the rifle in the direction of the cry. Looking down the eyepiece, she scanned the area. Nothing. Silence.

Suddenly, from behind, Alisi heard a scratching sound and before she turned, she realised she wasn't alone on the rooftop anymore.

Moses had a fairly good idea where the howling originated from. He motioned for Lars and Bryn to follow. Using the stone dwellings as cover, they quickly moved forward. They couldn't afford to be overly cautious as they were running out of time. They needed to end this battle quickly and move on. Passing three dead Borks, Bryn's thoughts were with the others, hoping they were not hurt.

It was eerily quiet. As they made their way around what was probably the largest dwelling, Moses caught sight of a shadow in the distance. The three of them ducked through the front door. With their backs against a wall, Moses peered around the corner. He then whistled like a songbird toward the dark void. Within seconds, Kenta and Kyra appeared, joining them in the hallway of the building, which gave them temporary cover.

'Where's Alisi?' Moses asked.

Kenta pointed south.

'She's on a rooftop. She was covering us while we searched for you,' Kyra explained.

'We need to get to her. Best if we finish this off as a team… Cleanse this place of their filth,' said Moses. 'Kenta, you lead. Let's go!'

When they arrived, it took Kenta seconds to clamber up onto the roof. He peered from over the edge and shrugged. There was no sign of Alisi.

'Okay,' said Moses. 'We need to sweep the area. Hopefully, Alisi is not hurt and we can pick her up along the way. Fan out, keeping each other in sight at all times. We will start from behind that outhouse,' he pointed to the building that edged the hamlet, 'and we will work our way to the other side.'

They were now the ones hunting and Bryn felt they had gained some element of control. It was both reassuring and empowering. Wasting no time, they took their positions and started to move forward, scouring every aspect of the landscape, inside and out.

He estimated that there were possibly eight Borks left, maybe nine. All was quiet. No howling, no sound of movement. They had made it halfway across the hamlet and had yet to encounter movement of any kind, with no sight of Alisi either. Bryn was beginning to wonder if the Borks had fled. It was possible but unlikely.

The deathly silence was suddenly broken by the sound of a gunshot, quickly followed by the guttural cry of one of the beasts they were tracking. The sound resonated through the vacant buildings. Everyone stopped for a moment to ascertain where the gunshot came from. It seemed to emanate ahead of where Lars was scouting. With a sense of urgency, they launched their pursuit.

Bryn clambered onto a rooftop and leapt from one building to the next with ease and speed. His father could see his shadow passing by him from above. His agility and pace were remarkable.

Another gunshot. Bryn knew Alisi wasn't far and prepared to dismount into a foray. Apart from the dark outlines of the rooftops, there was no other visibility. The only light came from the moon above, which was partly cloud-covered. Another howl. This time it came from the pack. It was so loud that Bryn nearly lost his footing with fright. They were right below him.

Leaning over the edge, Bryn was hoping to catch sight of Alisi. The pack of Borks seemed undecided in which direction they were heading. It appeared as though they knew their prey was near, but had no idea where. This was good. It meant that Alisi was hiding somewhere and she must have lost them. Bryn would leap down straight away but he knew he was no match for that number. As long as Alisi kept still for a few more seconds, the others would catch up and they could defeat them together.

It was too late. Alisi released another cartridge from her rifle. One of the Borks slumped, hitting the ground with a thump. The remaining Borks howled again, in pain and triumph. They found Alisi's hideout and they hissed and wheezed as they cautiously approached. It was only then that Bryn realised there were only five left. Alisi must have taken out at least three, possibly four or even five.

Bryn spotted Kenta and Kyra below, emerging into the moonlight on his left, followed by Lars and Moses on his right. To add a distraction, Lars whistled, followed by Kyra, Moses, even Kenta, and finally Bryn. Alisi was no longer the Borks' intended target as they quickly determined that they had become targets themselves. Four of them stayed on the ground to face their challengers, while one took to flight. It was slow to take off, lifting its heavy bodyweight, slow enough for Bryn to thrust himself from the rooftop and land on its back. It tried to fight him off, throwing its large muscular arms behind, with its claws outstretched. Bryn climbed up to its shoulders and tried to fend off the claws with his blades. He just needed one clear stab at the neck or face.

Down below, Bryn caught sight of the others in full fighting mode. His father and Moses had separated so they were fighting a Bork each, but Kyra and Kenta had paired up and fought the remaining two together.

Bryn managed to embed one of the tips of his blades into the base of the neck. The Bork cried out but its wings kept it in flight, slowly gaining elevation. Bryn was beginning to worry that if he didn't defeat it soon, the drop could kill him. As he did his best to avoid an assault, he also managed inflict two more stabs, but they were not deep enough to bring it down. Reassessing his target area, he came up with an idea. Reaching out, he used the blade in his right hand to slice through one of the wings. The Bork suddenly slanted to his left side, the wing almost too damaged to sustain him. Bryn nearly fell off, sliding down its arm. With Bryn's weight added to the side of the damaged wing, the Bork started to spin, slowly. This was causing Bryn added difficulty, but he did notice that they were descending. The Bork began to panic, flapping vigorously, causing them to rotate with greater speed. All Bryn could do was hold on.

CHAPTER 74

With a thud, the Bork landed on a rooftop. Bryn let go just before they landed, but the disorientation from the circular motion nearly caused him to fall to the ground. He held on to the roof edge and pulled himself back up. Only then did he notice that his arm had been cut. It wasn't deep but it did cause his sleeve to become blood-stained. The Bork was standing above him as he tried to get back on his feet, shrieking in anger and pain. It bore its claws, lashing down at where Bryn was hunched, but luckily, he managed to roll quickly out from under its footing.

Standing up, blades in his hands, he stared into the deep-pitted eyes of his foe. They paced from side to side, both waiting for an opportunity to strike. The Bork was beastly, withdrawing from its organised military stance to a more animalistic nature. Earlier that evening this creature stood tall, on two legs, scouring the area for the chance of battle, not on all fours waiting to pounce.

Bryn could still hear the clashing of swords and claws from below. His friends were close, but still battling for victory. Both he and the Bork had positioned themselves on the apex of the roof. The red-slate tiles were slippery underfoot and proving difficult to grip. There was no point delaying any longer. Bryn started his advance, slow at first but quickly built up speed. He leapt, intending to aim high, but his foot slipped, and he fell. The Bork knew that it wasn't going to be beaten today, savouring the fortuitous stance it now held above Bryn. Bryn could do nothing more than lay on his stomach as the Bork pounced, and caged his body in with its four limbs. Its head was positioned above the back of his, drool dripping onto the back of his neck. Bryn was pinned to the ground and there was nothing more he could do. He closed his eyes, awaiting his inevitable demise, thoughts drifting to his parents and his youth, his dog, the farm, and then to the geyser. Did he have regrets? Not for one second.

Another gunshot. This time, much closer than before. There was a splattering of blackened blood and then the Bork fell. It was heavy and although Bryn felt suffocated, he was so overcome with relief, he barely noticed. The seconds went past slowly before he felt a strong tug on his arm. Bryn used his other arm and his legs to aid with his dislodgement from under the beast. Bryn couldn't be happier to see Alisi's face. She had saved him, and he was equally pleased to see her unscathed after her disappearance.

'You're hurt.' Alisi had seen the blood on Bryn's sleeve.

'Just a graze, Alisi. Looks worse than it is.' Bryn retracted his blades and slapped her on the shoulder as a gesture of gratitude.

They both jumped down from the roof intending help others in the group. There was no need. Bryn and Alisi were greeted with relief by the other four, who had come together, possibly organising a search party. Bryn noticed that even Kyra appeared glad to see him. They managed to maintain eye contact for a short moment before she appeared uncomfortable and averted her gaze.

'Right, although we don't have much time to waste, we need rest or we won't be much good to anyone,' Lars advised. 'The Shiakana and the Hazuru teams had been radioed the coordinates I gave to you, by their team leaders, so hopefully they will be there before us. Experienced warriors were also dispatched. We were lucky to find a farm that still breeds working animals. There were about half a dozen birds, maybe a few horses. We took what we could.'

He then addressed Bryn.

'I'm hoping your mother and Gregor get the transport and comms up and running soon, Bryn. It would offer us a bit more than the miracle we are hoping for.' He turned again to the group. 'Until then, we will be fighting blind. We need our wits about us. I cannot think of better company to see this through.'

Moses lit a small fire in the front room of the building they now shared. They had two hours before they needed to move on. Lars insisted on keeping watch. Alisi offered to relieve him after an hour but he was insistent. He would rather stay up, formulate a plan.

Bryn sat close to the fire, hands reaching out for heat. Kyra joined him.

'Your fighting has improved since training.' Her voice soft and encouraging.

Bryn was taken aback by her polite tone and even her willingness to sit beside him. He looked at her for a moment. She was beautiful; the warm, orange flames reflected on her cheeks, causing them to glow.

'Well, thanks for helping out today,' he said coyly. He moved his attention back to the fire as he realised he was staring at her.

'Get some sleep. We have a long day tomorrow,' Kyra added as she rose to her feet. She smiled down at him before she went to find a corner to lie down, farther away from Bryn than he would have liked.

Bryn couldn't help but wonder why Kyra had softened towards him. Had he finally proved himself worthy or was it because it was just what the situation called for, a bit of encouragement? He didn't care too much; he was only glad that it seemed they were now on better terms. Suddenly overcome with tiredness, he lay down and drifted into a heavy sleep.

CHAPTER 75

Bryn was rustled from his deep slumber by a foot nestling into his ribcage. He had momentarily forgotten where he was.

'You sleep like the dead,' Alisi commented, looking down at him.

Everyone else was up, busying themselves with snacks from their satchels or stretching their legs, getting ready for the journey ahead. Kyra glanced at him as she conversed with Moses. Was that a flirtatious gesture? Living his life in relative isolation didn't give him much experience in the matter of the heart. And after the fiery temperament he experienced at the training arena, he was fearful of being presumptuous.

Bryn's musing was interrupted by his father, as he entered through the front door.

'The sun is breaching the skyline. It's time to move,' Lars ordered.

Without delay, they left the hamlet and made their way towards the hill the Borks had crested the night before, where Lars and Kyra had joined them. Bryn walked with Alisi and Kenta. Moses walked ahead with Kyra and Lars.

Kenta sharpened throwing blades with a stone as he listened to Alisi regaling the story of how she managed to avoid detection from the Borks for such a duration. Bryn was listening but also watched Moses, who was seemingly hatching an attack plan with Lars and Kyra. He wanted to be walking with them, planning, contributing. He wanted time to talk to his father, but realised it wasn't the time.

'…and now my stock is depleted. Am I worried that I'll run out? If I'm careful, kill shots only, I'll be fine. I do have an emergency stash in my satchel, if it comes to it,' Alisi said. Bryn hadn't paid attention to everything she had said but did hear her concern.

Kenta reached into one of his inside pockets and produced a long-blade dagger. He proceeded to hand it to Alisi.

'Kenta, that is very kind of you,' Alisi said, accepting it gratefully.

Bryn wondered how Kenta carried the weight of his artillery. It surely must be cumbersome, but he seemed to manage effortlessly.

From the top of the hill, the landscape stretched for miles. The pasture seemed viridescent in the distance, with uneven high ground touching the horizon.

'The light source is buried on the far side of those hills,' Lars explained to the group. 'We will have to move fast through the flat land to avoid detection. Keep your eyes open for enemy activity.'

He then turned to Bryn.

'I need you to scout ahead. I know this isn't protocol. But we need to know what may be facing us and if any of our allies made there already.'

Moses looked at Lars, giving the impression he didn't think it was a good idea. But he said nothing. Bryn couldn't believe his father was giving him such responsibility, but he was pleased and grateful for the chance to prove himself. At this stage, he fully realised he was faster than his teammates, much faster. He didn't understand why or how, but the was time to question that when this was all over.

'Kyra, go with him.'

Bryn thought this wasn't the best idea. She would hold him back. He was hoping for the opportunity to see what speed he could possibly achieve and show his father how strong he had become. Since he began training, he had become much tougher and more fast-paced than before. It was a noticeable difference, and considering he was deemed abnormally athletic back home – to the point where he was prohibited from displaying any degree of strength or resilience, in case it was noticed – this development was significant.

Moses wasn't given time to argue and Bryn didn't want him to. The group of six began descending the hill, side by side, sprinting towards the base. Bryn's speed started to increase once they reached the plateau. He carried a steady pace at first, trying his best not to overexert his muscles. For all he knew he could collapse with exhaustion halfway through crossing the flatland; that, to him, was not an option.

He began to increase his speed. There was no sign of Kyra. That didn't surprise him. It wasn't his fault she couldn't keep up. The faster he travelled, the more liberated he felt. His eyes targeted his destination, the ground beneath became dotted with mounds of grass. He had to be careful not to trip up. As he was concentrating on his footing, he didn't notice a presence beside him. He glanced across and almost tripped up. It was Kyra. She was running alongside with ease. She looked at him and smiled. Then she passed him. He couldn't believe what he was seeing. Several metres ahead, taking two long strides, she launched herself into the air and landed about thirty metres farther along. What Bryn was seeing was incredible. He was like her; but how? It made no sense.

CHAPTER 76

Bryn was finding it difficult to keep up. He had never run so fast, but there was no fathomable way to match Kyra's speed. All he could see was the dust trail behind her and occasional clarity when she leapt into the air. Sweat trickled down his temples, which he wiped away with the back of his hand.

He needed to slow down. He was tiring from the effort. Stopping for a moment, bending over with his hands on his knees, he took several deep breaths. Lifting his head, Bryn was momentarily taken aback by Kyra, who now stood facing him, smiling broadly.

'Bet you thought you were the only one who could run fast,' she said, smiling.

'I didn't think I could do that, not really anyway,' Bryn responded, still gasping for air.

'You should try jumping. It takes less effort, and you travel quicker.'

'I don't know if I can do what you do, Kyra.'

'You'll never know unless you try. Come on. Are you ready?'

Bryn wasn't given much of a choice. They needed to get where they were going fast. They were only about halfway there. If he didn't take her advice, he would be completely wiped out when they reached the hillside. She stood to the left of him, with her right foot forward. He mimicked her stance.

'If you fall, get up and try again. It'll take a couple of attempts to get it right. Let's go.'

As they ran, they kept side by side, accelerating quickly. Kyra was the first to leap. Bryn followed, nowhere near achieving the same distance. As predicted, he took a tumble as he landed. Kyra came back for him.

'You okay?' She seemed concerned.

Bryn was trying to ascertain the distance he travelled. That was the most amazing experience he had ever felt. Before he got back on his feet, he smiled at Kyra. 'That was incredible,' he told her.

The second attempt at vaulting while running was better. A little stumble but this time, he didn't fall. Kyra didn't travel as far as she did before as she wanted to stay near him. Once he got used to it, he managed to keep moving when he landed. It was exhilarating. He knew he wasn't as fast as Kyra, and may never be, but that didn't matter. They were covering ground significantly faster than before and that was what was important.

Closing in on their destination, Bryn noticed that the hills were far taller than he had estimated from afar. It was a mountain range, though not as large as the one they encountered the day before. It seemed to span for miles at either side. Looking back, Bryn could barely make out Lars and the others; he then wondered if his father was impressed. They appeared as specks in the distance. The terrain had become grassland, devoid of a pathway. The greenery rose to their knees, though it wasn't too difficult to negotiate. They walked while watching for any sign of enemy presence or allied friends. Kyra asked how Bryn managed with the game's challenges and Bryn told her everything that had happened from when they left the arena.

'You must have been wondering why?' Kyra asked.

'Wondering about what?' Bryn had a fair idea what she was asking but didn't want to assume.

'You must be wondering why you run as fast as you do and leap long distances?' Kyra clarified.

'I didn't realise I did until now, if I'm honest,' Bryn responded.

'Has your mother ever told you why she didn't compete after her first year?'

'What has my mother got to do with this?' Bryn was genuinely confused.

'You really don't know, do you?' The question seemed rhetorical.

Neither of them spoke for a moment. Bryn was unsure of what to say next. Where was Kyra going with this? He was beginning to get what she was trying to say, but was unsure if he wanted to hear her say it.

'Your mother is fourth-generation Hazuru. She had to stop competing because it was seen as cheating,' Kyra explained.

Bryn didn't believe it. He knew there had to be an explanation for the way he was. He just hadn't the time to digest why, or how, he was so different from the others. His thoughts were marred with confusion. He needed time to digest what Kyra said. Time, he didn't have. It made sense, he guessed. There were so many questions, but he thought he'd start with the most relevant.

'So, why was I allowed to compete?' he asked.

'The council made a special dispensation because of your father. The games were adjusted accordingly.'

'Adjusted in what way?'

Kyra continued.

'Each team's journey to the Zhavia Shield differs, depending on the strengths and weaknesses of the tribe. This, you know. The Hazuru team have a more complex course, with trickier obstacles. Different challenges and hurdles reflect tribal advantages or disadvantages. Are you following me so far?'

Bryn nodded.

'What this does conveys fairness. We are all different, Bryn. It would be impossible to create a competition in which all teams could compete together on the same field.'

He understood but he found the idea of being part Hazuru incredible.

'For you to partake in this year's competition, they had to make the challenges more difficult for the tribe. It was up to Gregor to decide if that was a risk worth taking. He obviously thought it was,' Kyra added. 'My mother competed in your tribe and if my father wasn't half Hazuru, she would have passed the opportunity to compete to me.'

Bryn now understood Kyra's hostility towards him. He was able to compete and she wasn't. It was all circumstantial.

'If I wasn't able to compete, then I felt you couldn't either. I have to admit, Bryn, I still feel the same way.'

Bryn was surprised her feelings hadn't changed, especially as she was now being so nice to him.

'But why the change of attitude? You've become… friendly.' Bryn was curious.

'I guess I realised this is not your fault. You arrived at Zhivrah with no idea what to expect. Other competitors have been training all their lives, fully aware of their family history and how importantly this competition is regarded. You would never have known about your family heritage if your father hadn't pushed the council, to the point where they probably felt that they didn't have a choice.'

Bryn was getting annoyed. He understood Kyra's perspective but she sounded so bitter about Bryn's father and the effort he had made. This wasn't about her. It was about family legacy and the right to participate. His excitement about the notion that Kyra may have been interested in him started to wane. How could he possibly entertain the sentiment that he could be with someone who thought he was chosen solely on his father's merit and pressure tactics?

'Kyra, I am sorry you cannot participate in the games. I truly am. But if you have a problem with it, I suggest you take it up with the council. Leave me and my family out of it,' he said, walking away, leaving her with her thoughts.

CHAPTER 77

Moses was watching Bryn bound into the sky and run faster than he had seen any human ever achieve. He was truly astounded.

'Do you think that was wise?' he asked Lars when they slowed, entering the grassland.

'What harm could it do?' was Lars' response.

'I thought we agreed to not encourage him. It's too much pressure for his first competition. The level of difficulty was based on the skills he brought to the table this year. The last thing I need is a teenager thinking that he is invincible. That's when mistakes happen.' Moses aired his frustration.

'But the competition is over, Moses. The more skills we can bring to the battle the better. Bryn's fine. Kyra is with him. We don't have time for him to get used to being different.'

Lars' patience was running thin.

Moses didn't agree, but there was nothing more to say. Lars was still his superior, though he wasn't competing anymore, and he respected him. He knew better than to push the matter.

There was no sign of Bryn and Kyra when they arrived. The last sighting of them was when they had disappeared behind one of the mounds. Climbing the first hill wasn't too taxing but, because the hills behind were higher, they didn't get much of a view. Moments later they caught sight of Bryn running towards them. Moses was anxious to hear of any news he might bring.

CHAPTER 78

'We didn't find anything,' Bryn told them. 'Kyra is still searching the area but there is no indication of a cave opening or that anyone else has arrived.'

Moses was dismayed. He was sure the coordinates led here. According to his calculations, the opening was within a hundred-metre perimeter.

Lars reached into his pocket and retrieved a small headset. He was hoping communications might be restored, at least to some degree, but there was no suggestion from his repetitive attempts that it was.

Slowly and cautiously making their way forward, they searched for any possible aperture or gap in the rock base that may lead them to where they needed to be, each of them becoming more frustrated as they journeyed.

'This makes no sense.' Moses was the first to air his annoyance.

'Would it be possible that the coordinates were wrong?' Alisi queried.

Kenta shook his head. He had worked out the positions on the map with Moses. They were in the right place.

'No,' Moses replied.

'How much time do we have?' he asked Lars.

'The cave is highly reinforced,' Lars responded. 'They would also have many miles to travel to get close enough to extract the source's energy. Their technology is highly advanced. But, I am guessing we may still have a couple of hours.'

Bryn moved to higher ground, but he was having no better luck than his teammates below. It wasn't long before Kyra joined him.

'None of this makes any sense,' he told her. 'Dad said reinforcements were on the way. Where are the Hazuru and Shiakana teams? Surely they would have received some form of communication before the blackout,'

'I agree,' Kyra said. 'It is too quiet. I was also expecting, by now, we would be set upon by whatever they considered necessary to keep us from getting any closer.'

They stood near the apex, looking down at miles of mountainous landscape, forests in the distance and undisturbed greenery all around.

'If it wasn't for the circumstances, this would truly be a romantic setting,' said Kyra. Her eyes were wide and radiant with the reflection of the sun.

Her comment took Bryn by complete surprise but as he looked at her, before he considered how to react, he noticed something. It took a moment for him to realise what it was. He couldn't believe he hadn't seen it before.

'We need to get back to the others,' he told Kyra before bolting away from her.

Lars was still attempting to connect with the base as the rest of the group searched the area below. Moses donned his earpiece and could hear intermittent segments of words between crackling, static noise. It was an improvement to the hour before when there was nothing. At this stage, he was becoming impatient. They needed reinforcements and they were running out of time.

He could see Bryn approaching, fast. Kyra was following behind. Although they were desperate for a development, he wasn't hopeful.

Bryn was shouting at Moses as he neared.

Moses couldn't hear what he was saying.

'It's a ruse,' Bryn repeated as he arrived. 'It's not very obvious, and I have no idea how they did it, but they tricked us.'

Moses looked at Lars who was several metres away on his headpiece, hardly noticing Bryn's approach. Kenta and Alisi were scouting farther on, so were not in sight. Moses ushered Bryn to one side, asking Kyra to give them privacy.

'What are you saying, Bryn?' he asked once they were alone.

'The mountain range has a sequence. It's not obvious unless you are looking at it for a while. The peaks have different heights and widths. It appears that some of them are identical, like looking at the same mountain from several angles,' Bryn explained. 'I believe that the landscape has been modified in some way. They are making us see what they want us to see. It is all a ruse.'

Bryn was finding it difficult to contain the excitement of his discovery, but Moses insisted that he stay calm and not tell the others. He would handle it. This made no sense to Bryn but he knew better than to argue.

'What will I tell Kyra?' he asked Moses. She would be just as curious to know what he had to say. Moses told him to think of something but not let her know what he had figured out. As Moses left to find Alisi and Kenta, Bryn was left with Kyra looking at him, wanting answers.

'What about Dad? Are you going to fill him in?' Bryn asked.

'Just give me a little time, Bryn. I will gather everyone and we will figure this out together,' Moses said. Bryn wasn't sure. He knew better than to go over Moses' head, but his father should be made aware of this new information.

'I thought I saw smoke in the distance,' Bryn lied. Kyra had approached and it was obvious she wanted to know what made him rush away. 'Moses reckons it was too far off to be significant but has gone to check it out.'

He felt awful hiding the truth from Kyra. He wasn't sure why he had to do it. Moses must have had a good reason. Could it be possible that Kyra wasn't to be trusted? It took Bryn time to realise, and although he was hoping that Moses was being paranoid, it would be far worse if his suspicions were true. It meant that somehow, the Goyteks had created another deception. One part of its plot may now be standing in front of him and he was willing her to believe his blatant lie. The other part of the ruse could be his father. It was difficult to tell. With Lars not too far away, if they became suspicious and if indeed they were created as a decoy, there was no way he could take them both on. And how could he even consider it? Bryn's only hope was that Moses would return to tell him his theory was wrong. Unfortunately, the more Bryn got to know Moses, the more he realised he was rarely mistaken in his judgement.

CHAPTER 79

Moses found Alisi and Kenta. He informed them of Bryn's observation and his suspicions. Alisi was the first to react.

'If this is what you say it is, it will be almost impossible to uncloak the entrance if Lars is indeed a clone and is helping hide it.'

Moses agreed. The Goyteks may have infiltrated their party. It was a clear ploy if it was true. Lars and Kyra had gained their trust back at the hamlet. It was only natural to assume they were indeed themselves. It was difficult to know for sure. If it was not a ploy, it would not only be embarrassing but could also hinder their progress. The best he could suggest was for them to return to where he had left Bryn and cautiously investigate.

Meanwhile, Bryn waited in silence with Kyra. It felt awkward but he was afraid to say much in case what Moses said was true. Instead, he put in his earpiece and listened in to his father's transmission.

'Lars to base, can you hear me?' he said over and over.

There was a static sound wave, a crackling, followed by, '….lies… key… and…' It made no sense. Bryn was trying to deduce the message.

There must be a key or power bank they needed to use. It 'lies' where? He needed to hear more. But the same message was repeated over and over again.

When Moses, Alisi and Kenta returned, Moses went to Lars for any updates. Kenta and Alisi sat close to Bryn and Kyra. It was as though Moses hadn't mentioned a word until Alisi threw Bryn a knowing look.

'I'm guessing you two had no luck from above?' Alisi asked Kyra, trying to avoid suspicion.

'I would have thought that was obvious,' she remarked snidely.

Bryn thought that was a pretty inane question to ask but it confirmed that Alisi was nervous about the situation. He replayed the words projected into his earpiece and listened again in case there was anything else he could pick up on. If Lars was his father and not a Goytek imposter, he was being highly resolute with his efforts to get a response from the base. Most people would have given up by now, or at least passed the headphones for someone else to try. His father was certainly determined. Bryn knew him to be resourceful but thought he would have been focused on planning alternative strategies with Moses, instead of his repeated efforts to contact the base. At least if Bryn listened in, he could help indirectly.

Between them, they had scoured the entire area. There was nowhere else for them to look. It seemed like they were doing it for hours and if the entrance was hidden by contrived imagery, there was no telling what they were looking for. Maybe Lars was right. It seemed the only chance they had was to decipher the message relayed. Bryn listened to it over and over. 'Lies', 'key', 'and'; those were the only words said with clarity.

He then had an idea. Taking his earpiece out, he searched it for a volume control. Playing the message again, this time as loud as he could bear it, he listened. He couldn't pick up on anything new. He did hear his father tell Moses that they needed to wait until they heard instructions from base before deciding what they should do next. Moses then suggested they must formulate a plan if they didn't hear back. They were running out of time and had to do something soon. There was frustration in his voice. Lars resumed his effort to gain contact through his headset. Bryn presumed Moses had been dismissed.

Before now, Bryn would have relished the idea of being in Kyra's company, but now all he wanted was for her to leave them so that they could talk. He could sense his teammates were as restless and uncomfortable as he was. Alisi was talking about random subjects. Bryn thought she may have been trying to maintain a status quo, but all it was doing was heightening the discomfort and distracting him from listening through his earpiece. Kenta went to join Moses and Bryn decided to go somewhere quiet, abandoning Kyra with Alisi and her ramblings.

'…lies… key… and…' Bryn listened to the words as the message repeated itself over and over. Now that he had increased the volume, he hoped to pick up another word or two. The crackling and static noise reverberated through his eardrum, causing mild irritation, though it wasn't discouraging his efforts and he kept the volume to its maximum. Once out of sight of the others, he sat on a rock, closed his eyes and concentrated.

Lars' voice boomed, 'Lars to base, do you read me?'

Scratching, hissing, crackling, and then there was something before 'lies'. What was that? Bryn felt a tiny glimmer of hope. There was nothing else through the rest of the message. He had to listen again. He was more confident the second time. It sounded like 'no' or 'new'.

Third time round he was confident the word was 'new'.

'…new… lies… key… and…' What could that possibly mean?

Bryn felt a tap on his shoulder, startling him and disrupting his train of thought. It was Moses and Kenta. They looked concerned.

'Bryn, we can't get to Alisi. She's with Kyra. We need to make a plan. I'm sorry but it has to be one that won't involve your father or Kyra.' Moses indicated to Kenta. 'I… we believe that the Goyteks created their version of Lars and Kyra, as a weapon. Very clever when you think about it. They gained our trust back in the hamlet so we wouldn't suspect a thing. We have to do something and we don't have much time. We're thinking if we lose them, we may have a chance.'

Bryn felt conflicted. What if they were wrong? He didn't know Kyra very well, so couldn't be sure, but his father? He hadn't witnessed any significant behavioural abnormalities. However, their relationship wasn't a close one, and he never had seen this side to his father, so it was difficult to tell. He realised, as he thought about it, they may not have much of a choice. They needed answers, fast. Bryn told them of his discovery of the word 'new' in the recorded message and hoped it might bear some significance.

'Give me the message again, Bryn,' Moses requested.

'New… lies… key…and…'

Moses paced as he pondered the added element, attempting to make sense of it, reciting the message aloud. He paused for a moment, was about to say something, but dismissed his thought almost immediately. He resumed pacing. Within moments, he stopped again, this time appearing more certain but also concerned, as though his findings led to an answer that he didn't want to accept.

'I don't believe it,' he said. His voice was quiet, as though he was addressing himself. 'This is not good,' he told Bryn and Kenta. 'We need to get to Alisi, fast.'

CHAPTER 80

'Neutralise Kyra and Lars.'

When Moses revealed the entire message, Bryn couldn't believe what he was hearing. Although they had their suspicions, he hoped they were wrong about them. The idea of fighting against Kyra and his father – understanding they were mechanically fabricated imposters – was a devastating development. The idea of facing them in battle and then fighting on without them was almost tragic.

Alisi was their focus now. They needed to separate her from Kyra's side. From there, the plan was to make a quick and unnoticed getaway. Heading back to their previous position, they walked in silence. Bryn knew the plan might be too simple and a fight may ensue. He just couldn't imagine it. All evidence pointed to the inevitable, but he still had doubts. He needed to know for sure.

Because they hadn't ventured too far away, it took just moments to return. What they were expecting was to see Lars still feigning his efforts to contact base, and Alisi achieving little from her efforts of small-talk with Kyra. What they actually saw was nothing, nobody. In the relatively short time of their absence, Lars and Kyra left, presumably taking Alisi with them. They must have figured out that Moses had become suspicious and decided to disappear. This was worse than Bryn could have imagined.

'Bryn, get to high ground. See if you can spot them. Be quick about it and whatever you do, do not engage,' Moses instructed. Kenta gave him his mono-scope to aid his task.

Bryn didn't waste any time. It took about three minutes to reach the summit of the nearest peak. It was high enough but not so lofty that he couldn't see what was happening down below. He saw Kenta and Moses watching his movements from where he left them. Mono-scope in hand, he surveyed the area. Within moments he caught sight of Lars, Kyra and Alisi. They were heading back the way they came, back to the flat land, away from where they needed to be. Alisi appeared to be unhurt, her hands bound and head lowered as she walked. Kyra pushed her along, trying to quicken the pace. Bryn estimated that they were less than a kilometre from their previous position. It wouldn't take long to catch up.

He hurried back to Moses and Kenta with his findings.

'We need to stick together, Bryn. Don't run off. Both Lars and Kyra are formidable opponents, so assume their clones are the same. Do not underestimate their capabilities. It will take all four of us to defeat them. They cannot get away. We have no choice. They must die. It's the only way forward,' Moses told them, resting his eyes on Bryn for a reaction.

Bryn knew Moses was suggesting the killing of the clones might be a key to unlocking the ruse, the cloaking device that prevented them from seeing what was really there. It was an unfortunate but inevitable mission.

'We must do our utmost to rescue Alisi, but our primary aim is neutralising the fake Lars and Kyra,' he continued. It took a moment for Bryn to realise that Alisi may not make it. It was an impossible situation and although he felt the need to protest, he knew Moses was right. They had little to no time left and the fate of Zhivrah rested on them fulfilling this mission.

'We need to go,' Moses said. He led the way, running fast, with Kenta and Bryn keeping pace alongside.

They thought it wise to attack from the lower ground so that they could achieve a closer proximity. From the hills, they could easily be seen. Though Bryn could have travelled quicker, they were by no means slow and it wasn't long before they had caught up. Ducking behind a large rock, for fear of being seen, they devised a plan. It was risky and bold. It may not work but it was the best they could come up in the short time they had.

CHAPTER 81

Alisi was finding it difficult to believe the predicament she was in. She never really had a chance to get to know Kyra very well, but it was becoming apparent Moses' theory was viable. Kyra's desire to compete wasn't a secret, and it was understandable if she felt resentful that she couldn't, but Gregor would never have enlisted her as a trainer if he thought she couldn't put her feelings aside.

Alisi had given up initiating conversation once Bryn left and they just sat in silence, Kyra appearing restless or distracted as if something was wrong. When Moses and Kenta decided to leave them to follow Bryn, Kyra rose to her feet and went to Lars, whispering to him in between transmissions. When Alisi glanced at her, she turned her head, trying to avoid suspicion but feared it may be too late.

Where were the others? She was becoming apprehensive, sweat forming on her brow, nervousness setting in. Should she wait for her teammates to return or act now? Before Alisi had the chance to make a decision, a blade curved around her neckline and a hand grabbed a clump of her hair. Kyra stood above her, eyes cold and vacant, her upper lip curled with disdain. The imposter that was disguised as Lars, approached from behind. He hunched down and rifled through Alisi's pockets, taking guns and ammunition, grabbing the satchel beside her as he got up.

They bound Alisi's hands with rope and marched her back the way they came, this time walking around the base of the hill they had previously climbed over. There was nothing she could do. She should have acted sooner. It was too late now. Her only hope was to be rescued, but how long would it be before the others realised that she was missing?

She walked slowly, Kyra pushing her occasionally to hurry them along. It had little effect. Lars walked ahead, not saying a word. It was incredible to think that there was technology so advanced they could create forms that would mimic others, just like when they were back at the river. Alisi had to keep reminding herself that this was not Lars and Kyra sabotaging the mission, but the Goyteks. Hard to believe, especially when there hadn't been a Goytek to be seen since the start of the mission.

Alisi was deep in thought when Bryn appeared on the hillside. He was approaching fast but not bearing arms as Alisi had expected. Fake Lars and Kyra were about to produce their own but realised Bryn had not come to fight. He appeared confused, possibly perplexed as he neared. Hardly surprising. They relaxed their stance. He was young and clueless. Best to see what he had to say before reacting.

'What are you doing?' Bryn asked. 'Why is Alisi bound like that? Where are the others?'

Lars' clone paused for a moment, watching Bryn's expressions, gauging whether he was being sincere with his questions.

'We believe Kenta and Moses have abandoned the mission,' he lied. 'We also believe they were conspiring to have us fail in our quest. I know this is difficult for you to hear, son. They betrayed us. Must be working with the Goyteks. This is a sad day for Zhivrah.'

His voice sounded robotic and insincere. Bryn seemed gullible enough to be convinced. Alisi was about to protest but could feel a blade tip at the small of her back, from Kyra's clone, who was right behind him.

'I don't believe it,' Bryn said. 'What about Alisi? Why have you tied her hands and where are you going?'

Kyra's forged demeanour was quite enjoying this. *What a simple boy he is. A fool.*

'She was in on the conspiracy, Bryn,' she told him. 'These are obviously the wrong coordinates. We need to go south.'

Bryn approached Alisi. She had a look of contempt that gave the impression she believed every word Bryn said, his blatant naivety.

Alisi looked crushingly disappointed.

'Is this true, Alisi?' Bryn screamed at her. His reaction even caught Kyra by surprise. It was beautiful. She couldn't have hoped for better.

Without warning, Bryn back-handed Alisi on the face so hard that she fell to the ground. Bryn landed on her, and instead of hitting her a second time, he simply bent over her and whispered in her ear.

'Stay down, don't move.'

Within seconds, Bryn heard blades swishing past from above. Kenta, who had been hiding behind a rock close by with Moses, had launched several throwing blades aimed at Lars and Kyra. Three had been thrown, and hit each target's extremities. It didn't deter them and was as though they had never been launched. However, it was enough to distract them. Bryn cut Alisi's bonds and they both got back onto their feet. Realising Alisi was without weapons, Bryn pushed her behind to try and protect her, and pointed both of his blades at Kyra. Moses and Kenta had emerged from behind the rock and approached, ready to fight.

Kyra pulled out the blades protruding from her leg as if they were pine needles. She smiled at Bryn and then at the others. It was like she was possessed by evil, finding this predicament amusing.

'Tick-tock, tick-tock. I think we are running out of time. For all you know, we have drained this wasteland already and what you are seeing is imagery we have created to keep you distracted,' she exclaimed.

Moses was disgusted with this possibility but unconvinced. They would certainly have not put so much effort into this charade if there was just a fraction of hope left.

'It's time for you both to put your weapons down,' Moses said, careful to not use their names. He wasn't going to associate these imposters with people he admired greatly. 'You two have played us for long enough.'

Kyra laughed hysterically. Lars remained calm and collected.

'You have finally figured it out, Moses. We are not the friends you thought we were. They are weak, like you. We are strong, like you wouldn't believe,' Kyra told him. 'We will give you a chance though, an opportunity to escape death. Simply, lower your weapons and come with us to the hamlet, where we can just wait this out. As you said, it won't be long now. And, you may even have time to return to Earth before this world decomposes completely.'

'But what about Zhivrah?' Bryn asked.

Kyra turned and faced him.

'You don't need Zhivrah, Bryn. You have a planet to return to. We need Zhivrah for ours to survive.' She spoke softer now.

'But what about the real Kyra, and other Panaks like her? Where are they expected to live?' Bryn was trying to promote an element of compassion. 'They cannot travel to worlds they have never seen. They would never be accepted. You are giving them a death sentence.'

'They'll just have to figure it out, Bryn. We have to put our planet first. There is nothing you can say to convince us otherwise.' She was becoming irritated by Bryn's line of questioning.

'You want to fight?' She was impatient. 'Let's get this over with.'

CHAPTER 82

Kyra's imposter held her spear in her right hand while using her left to protect her torso with her shield. The poleaxe was strapped to her back, ready for use if needed. Lars' imposter kept his crossbow in arm's reach. He was brandishing his mace, swinging it in a circular motion, readying himself for battle.

Moses, Kenta and Bryn also had their weapons drawn. Alisi emerged from behind Bryn with the dagger Kenta had given her, grateful Lars hadn't thought to search for one. The four team members stood side by side, without fear or doubt. They were no longer staring at the faces of friends but at the faces of their enemy. Their gestures, posture, manner of speaking altered them into people they couldn't recognise, mere strangers.

Lars laughed out loud. It was odd as he had barely uttered a word or expressed an emotion since he put his earpiece in, hoping he'd appear productive.

'What's so funny?' asked Moses.

'You have to admit, we nearly had you. Look!' He pointed at Bryn. 'That's my son, little Bryn. You made your daddy really proud. Is that what you want to hear?'

Bryn glared at the imposter.

'You know your father wouldn't talk to you like this. He's devoid of any humour or personality. Always... so... serious. Must have been a difficult man to grow up with, eh?' The imposter was mocking Bryn's father.

Bryn felt anger rise from within. He was about to pounce when Kenta put his arm out to stop him moving forward. Moses was the first to attack. Lars stared at him, willing him to make the first move. He wasn't going to disappoint. His blade clashed against one of the mace's spikes on the first swing of his sword. He aimed the second swing lower. Lars was quick to defend himself. Kenta, being the second most experienced fighter, dispersed throwing blades at Kyra as he approached her. This time, she was prepared so waved several of them off with her spear, the rest lodged into her raised shield.

Bryn had no hesitation when Kenta urged him away from Moses and to battle with Kyra instead. He had practised fighting techniques with his real father all his life, but he couldn't bring himself to fight the fake one now. He was relieved to see Moses take him on. Besides, chances were that if Kyra ran, he would be the only one with any hope of keeping up with her. Alisi, aware of her lack of weaponry, was cautiously approaching Lars from behind. She was hoping she could either inflict injury or use Moses as a distraction to get hold of her gun sling, which was hanging from Lars' shoulder. Ideally, she'd like to accomplish both.

A full-on battle had now begun. It was fast and furious. Blade clashed with blade. Kenta's mastery of martial arts meant he was matching Kyra's speed. They spun and somersaulted, their motion was fluid and calculated, using every bit of acrobatic and athletic training they had each developed. It was as skilled as it was beautiful to watch. Bryn felt his contribution to the fight was clumsy and methodical by comparison. Kenta's fists bore two small blades and he was doing his utmost to use them to inflict damage. Kyra's spear kept him at bay but Bryn thought if he could draw the spear away, Kenta might have a better chance.

Moses showed no signs of tiring as he battled Lars. Alisi fought beside him. They kept a bit of distance between them so that they could attack from different angles. Moses was also aware that Alisi was trying to recover her arsenal and the shotgun hanging from Lars' shoulder, and although she was doing the best she could with the dagger, they would both benefit greatly if she had her shotgun back.

When Moses finally managed to strike Lars with his sword, across the thigh of his right leg, he bled as any human would. Lars barely flinched, but it did anger him. Dropping his mace, he reached for his crossbow, releasing a cluster of arrows. Moses and Alisi ran behind a rock for cover, narrowly escaping the barrage.

Kenta's blades had inflicted only minor cuts and Bryn had barely gotten close enough to Kyra to make any impact. She was watching them both too closely. He paced, circling both her and Kenta, hoping he could catch her off-guard. He could see her following him with her eyes, for a while, but Kenta kept her busy and it wasn't long before she lost focus, just for a second. That allowed Bryn to tackle her from behind, swooping in low and quickly knocking her off her feet. She lay on the ground facing him. He aimed his blades at her neck but hesitated for a moment. Kyra's face softened. For a second he forgot she was synthetic, which was enough time for her to roll out from under him, get back on her feet, and run away.

CHAPTER 83

Bryn was disgusted with himself, and he could see that outrage reflected on Kenta's face. Not wasting time, he chased after the clone. He knew the risk of facing her alone. He may not make it back, but what option did he have? She had disappeared from view, but he saw which direction she was heading, and that was enough for him. It was better to keep to high ground. It would be easier to spot her from there. He ran. He leapt, covering several miles in less than a minute. It wasn't long before he stood on the tip of the hill, where they stood before, where Kyra commented on how romantic the scene was. He looked out onto the landscape below, falsely replicated to appear natural.

She couldn't have gotten far going this direction. It led to nowhere, circling in on itself, making it far smaller than it appeared to be. He watched for movement below, checking every direction. There was nothing to see. She simply wasn't there. Maybe she had changed course or was hiding out somewhere? There was no way of knowing.

He needed to keep moving. Kyra needed to be eliminated and time was of the essence. But as he was considering his descent, a sudden urge led him to turn, where he suddenly saw her charging at him as if she had appeared from nowhere. He managed to defend the attack from her poleaxe by bracing his arm against the wooden handle. He dropped his weapon. Pain shot to his shoulder. He figured that it was better than to have been hit by the blade. With his left arm now limp, he held on to his other weapon tightly in his right hand.

'This could have ended so differently, Bryn,' she said. 'You and I could have been together and you would never have known that I was a fraud, an imposter. Instead, you had to spoil it all.'

She was becoming angry and came at him again with the axe. Bryn, prepared this time, dodged her aim quickly. He didn't like being left alone with her. If he couldn't defeat the real Kyra with Frasier in the training field, how was he supposed to defeat this manufactured one on his own? He needed to put the thoughts of self-doubt out of his mind. It was going to affect his concentration, and if was going to defeat her, he needed to focus.

Shaking off the numbness in his left arm, he quickly picked up the blade he dropped. She waited for him as though she thought it mannerly. Her eyes shone with confidence. There was no hint of concern that she may lose against Bryn. It was as though she was playing a game and wanted to toy with him.

'Without your friends, there is no hope that you can defeat me. Give up now and I will promise a quick kill,' she offered.

Bryn had enough. It was time for him to attack instead of defending himself. He was getting irked by her sly comments, goading remarks. With both blades raised, he charged at her with full force. His weapons clashed with her axe and her shield. Kyra stood her ground. They fought with speed and strength. Bryn had mastered his father's weapon and felt he had finally earned the right to hold it. He pushed forward so that Kyra had to take a few steps backwards. Realising his strength, she upped her efforts and pushed back.

Bryn concentrated on every swing of the poleaxe, so he wasn't expecting a sudden clout to the temple from Kyra's shield. He stumbled sideways from the force. As he regained his balance, he became aware of how close they had travelled toward the edge of the peak. She was coming at him, discarding her shield, reaching behind for her spear. Just as she lunged, he rolled out of her aim. She hit the ground so hard that the spearhead sank beneath the terrain. Twisting her head and seeing him scamper away seemed to fill her with glee, which Bryn found unnerving. He took that moment as an opportunity to fasten the bases of the wooden handles together, so he too had a spear-type weapon, though his was double long-bladed.

With both hands centred between the blades, he fought on. What ensued was faster than before. Metal on metal, metal on wood; it seemed to go on and on. Bryn tried hard to push Kyra over the hilltop, but she kept her footing on the edge, trying to fight her way forward. What she wasn't expecting was the ground beneath her to loosen. Her footwork was causing it to crumble and her smug look suddenly disappeared as she did. Bryn followed her to the edge and watched as she rolled and tumbled downward.

CHAPTER 84

Bryn went down after her, careful where his feet rested with every jump. She was still rolling and all he could do was follow. He hoped that this would be the end of it, that he didn't have to battle on. A very small part of him wished that she would be okay, but he quickly vanquished the idea of it. She needed to be eliminated, he was told. There was no question. He needed her to die.

Kenta had given up on the idea of pursuing Kyra and Bryn. He understood that there was no way he could catch up. It was best to help the others defeat Lars and then concentrate on finding her with the rest of the team. Hopefully, Bryn would be able to hold her off until then. He needed to be hasty. They couldn't afford any delay.

Kenta saw that Lars had Moses and Alisi pinned behind a rock. They had nowhere to go. Every movement was met with an arrow. His one chance was to disarm Lars, to rid him of the crossbow. Standing behind a tree, he checked his arsenal. He was always careful to pick up any thrown daggers and blades, but the fight with the Borks lost him a few. He'd just have to manage with what he had. With a few glances from behind his hiding space, he had the target in sight. He leaned his back up against the tree, and after several long breaths, he stepped out, launched a volley of small weaponry, and ran straight for Lars. Moses spotted Kenta's approach and came out from behind the rock to join his teammate. Alisi followed suit.

Lars, whose shooting finger had been dislodged by one of Kenta's daggers, stood for a moment, examining his other inflicted injuries. His body must have been stabbed over ten times, blood pouring from each wound. When he raised his head, he had only enough time to see Moses launch his sword before it was embedded into his chest.

Alisi felt like celebrating. Not only did she get her precious shotgun back, but the person who had taken it was now slumped over on the ground, eliminated. She asked Kenta where Bryn was. When Kenta indicated that he was chasing Kyra, without hesitating, they grabbed their remaining artillery and went to find them. Moses was disappointed that Kenta had left Bryn to fight her alone but could see that there was no other option.

Moses watched the higher ground as they searched. He had a feeling they might be up there. Kyra was probably thinking there would be less chance that they would follow suit. Considering the scene was manufactured, there were limitations to how far they could travel. His only concern was if they had doubled-back to the flatland or that Kyra let herself be found so she could get to Bryn first.

Moses' eye was caught by movement. He couldn't quite make out what he was seeing, as the sun was in his eyes, but there was definitely something moving, rolling or running down the hill close by. He led Alisi and Kenta towards the scene, watching as he went. There seemed to be something, or someone, following. He feared the casualty could be Bryn. That fall could do a lot of damage, may even be fatal. As they closed in, they could see the figure slowly getting back on their feet. The figure behind was closing in. They weren't going to make it before they met. This could be the end for Bryn. He feared the worst but their target was Kyra so whatever happened, they couldn't let her escape.

When Bryn caught up with Kyra, he was surprised she was able to get up. Her right arm had gone limp. She supported it with her left. She hobbled as she walked, one leg unable to carry itself. There was a cut on her forehead and one on the base of her neck. The confidence and smugness had evaporated. She looked pitiful, beaten.

'You cannot kill me,' she said. 'It's just not in your nature. You are not cold and callous, like some of the others.'

Bryn knew she was playing him but still couldn't help feeling a little compassionate. Without saying a word, he continued to move forward. She had dropped her weapons in the fall, he noticed. She had nothing to defend herself with. It made the process more difficult than he realised. Another step forward. She countered every step he took with one of her own. Without looking, the back of her foot hit a large stone and she stumbled, almost falling. The tough exterior had now diminished. Tears started to form at the corners of her eyes. Bryn started to feel he was the villain. In any other scenario, he would never have pictured himself in this situation. It was cruel. The Goyteks were cruel to use this form of attack. It was too personal, too brutal.

'Bryn, please!!! What would your mother say? She would be ashamed if she saw you now,' she said, tears streaming down her cheeks. Bryn was only a few feet away. He was trying to figure out the most humane way to finish this off. It was becoming so difficult and he knew he wasn't doing himself any favours by drawing it out like this. He just couldn't bring himself closer…

Within that thought, a shot rang out. His eyes never left Kyra when the cartridge hit her chest. Her whole body tensed. Blood spattered from the exit wound. Her eyes died first and then her body collapsed to the ground.

He stood there, momentarily, in shock. Then, turning to his left, he saw Alisi in the distance. She had her shotgun in hand and was making her way over with Kenta and Moses. He turned to look at Kyra one more time before something strange happened, something so unusual that if he wasn't there he would have never believed.

CHAPTER 85

The landscape around them started to disintegrate, bit by bit, starting with the sky. Moses, Kenta and Alisi stopped in their tracks to observe the scene unfolding. Behind the bright sky was darkness, and as the transformation enlarged, they could see a red hue resting on top of a darkened mountain. As the unveiling grew, the silence around them was broken by the sounds of battle. Explosions, laser fire, the clashing of swords. It resonated throughout the valley, which was quickly disappearing.

Bryn could see several warriors flying on large birds in the distance: ground forces battling beneath. They were fighting high-grade technology, the type only the Goyteks could produce; bulky metal robots, stationary outposts. The scene was chaotic. It only took a minute or so before they had emerged alongside it. Darkness surrounded them. For a moment, neither Bryn nor the others moved. It was difficult to know what was real.

Looking around, there must have been about twenty fighters, human, Hazuru and Shiakana. Moses spotted Gima, Hazuru team leader, running to him. She seemed panicked and out of breath. He put his earpiece on.

'Where have you been?' it translated.

'What the hell is going on, Gima?' Moses asked.

'Did you not get the message, that the Goyteks have sabotaged the games and are in the process of destroying our world?'

This line of questioning could go on for hours, so Moses decided to end it.

'Gima, have we a battle plan and which direction are we heading?'

Gima told him that they needed to get to the opening at the base of the mountain, the one that was being protected by the Goytek artillery.

'Where is the rest of your team?' Moses asked.

'We lost two,' Gima told him. Her eyes were filled with sadness as though she hadn't the time to grieve. 'The Shiakana team are close by. They are down to three but are fighting strong.'

There must have been about fifteen other warriors in the area. It didn't seem enough to inflict the damage needed to advance.

Explosive arrows hailed from above and hit a giant, robust-looking robot. It exploded, causing the base of the mountain to light up, exposing the entrance to where they needed to be.

Moses now addressed the team.

'Check your weapons. Watch out for any others that may have been discarded. We are going to need them. We are going to need them all.'

CHAPTER 86

Laser shots were fired at them as they neared the mountain. They took shelter where they could. Gima stayed, guiding them forward.

Bryn saw two Hazurus leap from high ground and land on one of the robots. Their spears drove into the mechanics and the robot began to flail, throwing one of the fighters off. The other hung on, repeatedly driving his spear through the metal until it fell to the ground. Luckily the fighter who fell appeared uninjured. This was chaos. Bryn had no idea how they were going to get through the Goyteks' defence. His weapon seemed useless as they were so far away. Alisi managed to damage one of the outpost's guns but they were limited in what they could achieve at this distance.

They needed to get close but with those lasers shooting indiscriminately, it felt like an impossible feat.

'Is there another entrance?' he asked Gima, through his earpiece.

'Only the one, and this is it,' she said.

'There are too many of them,' Alisi said.

Another barrage of explosive arrows hit one of the robots. This model was bigger than the other, so although it inflicted damage, it wasn't enough to take it down. No robot was the same. They were different shapes and design.

'You have to watch for the smaller ones,' Gima said, as though she intuitively knew they were studying the enemy.

Bryn saw what she meant. He could see robots, no bigger than a small dog, being dispatched through the base of the larger ones. They would seek out a difficult target, whether behind a rock or in the distance, speed towards it and simply explode. He just saw two lucky survivors jump out of the way of one of them, but he was sure it must have inflicted some degree of injury.

As they closed in, the ground beside them erupted with laser fire.

They needed a plan, Moses thought. They needed to assemble. If they didn't, none of them will survive. The Goyteks' defence was just too strong.

'Fall back,' he shouted. 'Fall back.'

Gima was not impressed with his reaction. 'What are you doing?' she asked.

'We will all be dead in minutes if we continue like this,' he explained. 'We need a strategy, a plan of attack.'

Fighters, one by one, turned to see Moses calling for them to retreat. It particularly enraged the Shiakanas, but seeing that it was Moses shouting the orders, it didn't take long for them to comply. The retreat gave the impression to the Goytek artillery that their enemy had simply given up. They immediately stopped shooting.

When they were far enough away that the base of the mountain was no longer in sight, Moses stopped and gathered everyone around him. Bryn counted twenty-two. More than he had initially thought.

Marchek, the Shiakana team leader, approached Moses. He was incredibly large, substantially bigger than even his team members. 'What is the meaning of this?' he shouted, the magnitude of his voice booming through the earpiece.

'Marchek, it's good to see you. I understand we are under time pressure, but if we continue like this, we will be all dead within the hour.'

'So, what do you suggest we do? What options do we have?'

As Marchek spoke, five large birds that carried warriors landed nearby; the riders disembarked and gathered round.

'The smaller exploding robots dislodge from the larger ones, but I guess the area they dispatch from could be vulnerable. That is a hell of a lot of explosive material stored inside each of them,' said Moses.

'How are we going to get that close? It's suicide,' commented one of the fighters.

'I'll do it,' suggested Bryn. The group looked at him, with surprise.

'We need speed,' said Gima. 'Good for you to offer, but I think us Hazurus would have a better chance.'

'I am Panak.' It was the first time Bryn admitted to it. 'I am coming with you.'

'I count eight of those explosive dispersing contraptions. Four volunteers, two each. The rest of us will offer diversion and focus our efforts on the two remaining outposts,' said Moses.

There now was a plan. The birds took back to the sky, each rider carrying an arsenal of bows and an assortment of arrows. Gima gathered Bryn and two other Hazurus to formulate an attack. Moses had the rest of the fighters spread out so they could charge from all angles.

The remaining Hazurus would attack from above the entrance, the rest from below. The Shiakanas, because of their strength, were charged with throwing missiles, whether explosives or rocks. Everyone there gave them any weapon they deemed suitable for this task.

Waiting for Moses' call to battle, all ground fighters formed a line. They were still far enough away from the entrance not to provoke an attack.

Bryn was given two explosives from Marchek. The Shiakanas were not the bumbling oafs he had expected from what little experience he had with them. Now that he had a translator, he was surprised at how eloquently they spoke. He had noticed a softness and wisdom in their eyes. Marchek reassured him that he had his back. Run like the wind, he had told him. When he could see that all explosives were in place, he would set off the charges.

'On my count,' Moses ordered. 'Three, two, one… Move out!'

CHAPTER 87

Bryn ran as fast as his legs could carry him. Gima and the other two Hazurus were faster, but not by much. As they approached the mountain base, he had his eyes on the target. He was instructed, by Gima, to take the two robots on the far right. The robots were barely mobile. Bryn hadn't seen them wander too far away from the opening they were protecting. He supposed they couldn't move very far off for fear of being knocked out, one by one. The Goyteks possibly thought it would be safer for them to stay together.

He watched as his two targets paced side by side as if they were dormant. He could see three Hazurus launch themselves onto the mountainside, gaining considerable height with every leap. They had their task to fulfil also. Now that Moses had organised the attack, all of them did.

Suddenly, the robots stirred. They must have been spotted or else there could have been a sensor that was set off by their motion. Just as they were noticed, Bryn could hear a commotion from Moses and the others behind. Even though they were still a distance away, they had created enough noise to attract spotlights from both outposts. Gima had advised Bryn they needed to avoid these lights for as long as it would take to get as close to the robots as was feasible. The area around the target was lit up brightly so they could only avail of the darkness for so long.

With their eyes on the direction of the lights, they swerved around them. The robots must have seen something moving, as they started up shooting lasers again, as did the outposts. It felt when they had re-entered the battle scene, chaos kicked off; this time the battle cries from their side outweighed the laser fire.

The robots released their explosive mini bots. They were at the point of no return. One was heading in Bryn's direction. He managed to dodge it before it set itself off. Another came at him. A huge boulder was thrown in its path causing it to explode before it got close. That must have been Marchek, Bryn thought. Targets in sight, he entered the lit-up area and skidded under the first. The hatch was still open, so he threw the device inside. He quickly came around and scrambled under his second target, attaching the other device to its closed hatch door. He had been instructed to vacate the vicinity as fast as he could after the mission was complete. He could see Gima running off and one other Hazuru, but with horror, Bryn realised that the fourth Hazuru didn't make it to their target. He had been hit with a laser as soon as his foot hit the lit-up area.

Gutted, Bryn ran back into the darkness. Within ten seconds the explosions were set off and six of the robots blew up in a ball of flames. The second part of the overall mission was for the three Hazurus, who had clambered up the rocky mountainside, to attack the outposts one by one from above, with the rest of the force coming in from below.

Bryn joined Moses, who was heading for the gate with Kenta and Alisi. Alisi shot at any oncoming mini bots. The Hazurus took down one of the outposts. One left and only two remaining robots. They could do this. It had now become achievable. Another hail of arrows came from the skies and took down another robot. Two left.

Just then, as their confidence had lifted, a rumbling could be heard from the top of the mountain. It stopped everyone in their tracks. Bryn wondered what could possibly be happening now. Was this a natural phenomenon or a consequence of the Goyteks drilling for the source? Whatever it was, it was bad.

CHAPTER 88

Bryn stood with Moses, Kenta and Alisi as they watched rocks split away and roll from the mountain top. Black smoke spewed from the tip and filled the air with an acrid odour. The rumbling from within felt so strong, it sent ripples through the ground where they stood. At this point, it was easy to lose focus. The Shiakanas hadn't, and while everyone else's gaze was focused on what was happening above, they managed to take down another robot.

The riders landed their birds, dismounted, and waved them away. It was more dangerous for them to be in flight during these conditions. The birds became nervous, the air above toxic.

As the rest of the warriors focused on the last remaining outpost, Moses and his team watched the commotion above.

'Do you want me up there?' Bryn offered.

'Too dangerous. The entire mountain structure could collapse from under you,' Moses said.

A large chunk of rock dislodged from the peak and rolled off to the west of them. Moses was thinking that it was some kind of volcanic reaction but now he wasn't so sure.

Something was emerging from within.

The outpost fell and the last robot was being attacked by enough fighters that Gima and Marchek joined Moses to watch the commotion above.

Whatever was in the mountain started to wail and scream so loudly that, on impulse, everyone raised their hands to their ears. Another lump of rock broke away and out of it flames blasted through. Then a head followed.

Bryn couldn't believe what he was seeing. From one side a wing, a head from the other. It was beyond question. What was manifesting was a dragon. It appeared like a shadow against the dark, red sky. Ominous and foreboding. Nothing like the holographic imagery used at the training camp. It was immense and appeared furious that it was woken from its slumber.

'Take your team and get to the source,' Gima instructed Moses.

'I can't just leave you... with that,' Moses said.

'She is right. These things are sent to distract us. Go!' Marchek added. 'We will wrap this up and follow.'

Gima and Marchek left Moses' side. Without wasting time, he called his team together. 'We're going in. Ignore the beast. We have a mission to complete,' he said.

They ran for the cave opening. A burst of flame lit up the spot where they had stood but no one turned their heads, afraid to witness the casualties left behind.

With no obstacles to block the entrance, they made it to the opening in just moments. The passage ahead was dark, lit with only the burning embers of a scattering of torches hung on the walls. There was no end in sight and it certainly didn't make them stop to pause. The farther they travelled, the quieter their surroundings became, until all they could hear was each other's breaths and footfalls.

'There's no one here,' Alisi noticed. 'Isn't that odd? You'd almost expect an army of soldiers protecting the gateway.'

Moses found this to be suspicious also. It felt like an ominous sign. There was no indication of any large machinery to extract the source, or the people needed to use it.

'On your guard. Alisi is right. It's too quiet and I don't like it,' Moses added.

They slowed their pace, carefully listening out for any sound that would hint they were closing in. The passage bent and twisted around corners – they were careful as they approached, not sure what was ahead.

The heat inside the mountain was intense. Sweat soaked their garments and trickled down their faces. Bryn wondered if the dragon was defeated and if there were any casualties from its assault. There was no way of knowing for sure.

Finally, they reached a large aperture, which led to a cavernous, hollowed space. It was difficult to estimate its size due to the absence of light, but it was large enough to cause an echo when they spoke.

'Does anyone see anything that can tell us which direction we are supposed to be going?' Moses asked.

Bryn could hear the trickling of water and caught sight of a few stalactites hanging from above. It felt like they had stumbled upon a cave.

Kenta wrapped a piece of a garment he found in his satchel around one of the outed torches and lit it from the embers of another. The light it produced wasn't significant, but it was enough to give them a better scope of the room. All four of them moved to its centre and followed the guiding light from the torch. When they reached the wall opposite, Kenta noticed a small wooden door. They would never have seen it if not for the torch. It seemed to be old, not recently used and had a large, black, metal ring for a handle. Moses pulled on it. It budged a little with some effort. Cool air hit them as the door came ajar.

Through the door was another passage, as dark as the one before. This time it led straight in front of them, to another wooden door. This door was massive by comparison, and through the gaps shone a white light that outlined its entirety. It must have stood twelve feet tall. It had the same black, circular handle as the one before, but it must have been about six times the size.

Curious. Moses called for weapons to be readied. This must be where the Goyteks were congregated, drilling for the source. They needed to prepare themselves for any eventuality. The Goyteks proved themselves to be unpredictable and determined. There was no telling what or who may greet them on the other side.

It took the four teammates, and all of their strength to pull the door from its frame. The light emanated from the other side was blindingly white. The starkness was exaggerated by the complete lack of sound.

The four brave warriors stepped into the illumination and were staggered by its brilliance.

However, within moments, muffled sounds began to form, colours bled into the white, desperately trying to create a picture. All Bryn and his teammates could do was stand and watch the sequence unfold.

CHAPTER 89

Within the colours, figures began to form. Cries and voices could be heard in the muffled resonance. Moses held his hand up to protect his eyes from the light, but also to see if he could decipher the images that were now beginning to form.

A hint of familiarity began to materialise; whether it was from sight or sound, Bryn couldn't be sure. It caused him to lower his weapons as he felt confident that there was little threat here.

The sounds became voices, and those voices were calling their names. Looking down, they noticed the ground became grainy, sandy. It expanded as they watched, spreading out before them, as though it had always been there. In the distance, people stood, though they could not make out their faces. They appeared to be jumping, hands waving, as if they were vying for their attention.

Another image opened to their right. More people, more cheers, more movement. The imagery of the people expanded. The sky opened up to form a night-time scene, one full of stars and a warm glow from the ground below and the lights above.

Someone was walking to them. With the light behind, they appeared as a shadow first. The closer they got, the more imagery came into view.

The realisation hit them all at once. The scene was the arena, and the person approaching them was Gregor, and in his hands was the Zhavia Shield.

CHAPTER 90

Gregor looked both concerned and relieved as he came to greet his team. Moses stepped closer, unsure if what they were seeing was real, but still willing to put himself forward as team leader – in case of unforeseen jeopardy – before his teammates.

Bryn, Kenta and Alisi stood their ground, without moving a muscle, or uttering a word to each other. They couldn't make any sense of what they were seeing and were not about to make any assumptions.

Gregor knew to be cautious. Moses must be wary, and he certainly couldn't blame him.

'I am supposed to offer my congratulations,' he said when they met.

'I don't understand. Is this another ruse? Are we supposed to battle now? What the hell's going on?' Moses asked, unable to maintain eye contact with Gregor. How was he to know what was real anymore?

'Moses, it's over. We won.' Gregor was trying to sound energetic but knew that it may come across as insincere.

'Gregor,' Moses looked at him now. 'Is that really you?'

'Moses, we've had some trouble with this year's simulation. I can assure you that this is me. What I need you to do is accept this Shield, get your team moving, throw a few waves to the crowd and follow me.'

Moses turned to the team, who had been listening to the exchange. Alisi responded to him with a shrug. Kenta and Bryn had nothing to add.

'Moses, you won the tournament. Your team are the victors. Put a smile on your face, greet the crowds and once you're done, I'll explain everything,' Gregor said. He was becoming impatient.

Moses instructed his team to do what they were told. 'Let's get this over with,' he said.

Their smiles were hesitant to start. The entire scenario had an essence of surrealism, a rapturous reception for four champions who thought the world as they knew it was about to end. Four champions who saw comrades die, saw deceit at the highest level, who put their lives at risk. For what? Entertainment? Was there a more sinister goal?

The crowds were going wild. The team had to complete a circle of the arena, thank their supporters, accept flowers and gifts thrown at their feet. It was tedious, at first. Alisi, after a time, was the first to be enthralled by the reception. She seemed, to Bryn, to be enjoying the experience. Moses and Kenta feigned their excited behaviour but from a distance, the crowd would never have known.

Bryn, on the other hand, was finding it difficult to get involved. He managed to strain a smile, carry a wave, but it all seemed incredibly insincere. What just happened? They were made to feel that they could have died at any moment. There was a constant fear the world would end. He just could not comprehend the sheer deception portrayed throughout the event. His father. Kyra. What could possibly have gone wrong? And, to find out, as he did, he was part Hazuru, was simply inexcusable. The entire idea of the games was a sham. He was becoming angry. It must have been written on his face because Moses couldn't help but notice.

'Bryn, there must be an explanation for this. You saw Gregor. Keep yourself together. Give the people what they want to see. We will get this resolved. Trust me,' Moses said, though not with the utmost confidence.

Bryn wanted to respond. He needed answers, but he didn't even know what to ask. Even if he did, he knew Moses wasn't in the position to tell him what he needed to hear. So, he kept moving, wishing for the celebrations to end. He needed to see his parents. He had to talk to his mother. There were so many questions.

As Moses and his team were received in the arena, the large screens around the stadium displayed the three other teams' effort on the field. Bryn noticed that each scene depicted a different setting and none of them seemed familiar. It dawned on him that Gima and Marchek were never with them before they entered the mountain. They were just programs created to intensify the situation. Another deception, another reason to feel betrayed and let down.

On completion of their victory walk they were ushered in through a door, under where the council sat, and instead of leading to a tunnel down to the travel pods as Bryn expected, this door led to a small banquet hall. A feast was laid out for the teams, on a large wooden table, in the centre of the room. But they were not interested in eating. They had nothing on their minds apart from wanting to hear answers. When Moses spotted Gregor, who was the only person there, he didn't wait to meet him before he asked, he bellowed it across the room.

'What the hell was that?' he exclaimed, taking long, deliberate strides as he approached Gregor. He stood so close to him their faces were inches apart. Moses was furious. Bryn thought he had hidden it well.

'Back off!' Gregor responded, unmoved.

The two men maintained their positions until Moses finally relented. He took a step back but did so in silence.

'The Games were sabotaged,' Gregor told them. 'Not all of the teams, just ours.'

'I don't understand,' Alisi said.

Kenta took a seat, looking deflated, though he couldn't imagine that could be the case.

Gregor turned to Bryn. 'When the decision was made to let you compete, not everyone was happy in the council.'

Bryn presumed he was referring to his Hazuru genes, understanding now that this factor wasn't created but was true.

'As you know,' he continued, 'Panaks are not permitted to take part, but because your bloodline is generations old, it was decided that you could. Your father insisted you at least had the opportunity.'

Bryn didn't know what to say so he let Gregor press on.

'A small number within the council were not happy with the decision, so decided to take matters into their own hands. They created a simulation that would almost guarantee your failure. You would be exposed and shamed, so they thought. It backfired. You won and everyone loves you.'

Gregor was trying to offer consolation, but it provided no solace.

'If members of the council had issues with Bryn competing, didn't they have ample opportunity to air their concerns at the meetings leading up to the event?' Moses asked.

'That would be true, except there wasn't a great concern; at least not until one particular member made it one. He single-handedly turned the views of anyone who would listen to him.'

'Who are you talking about, Gregor?' Bryn asked.

'The person who is responsible for this entire debacle is Samuel.'

CHAPTER 91

There was a knock on the door from the arena. *Not now,* Bryn thought.

Not waiting for a reply, in came Bryn's mother. She seemed weary, unsure of what to do or say, holding onto anger about the situation but also pride; the pride she felt for her triumphant son and what he had just achieved. The big family secret was out, and they were not the ones who broke it.

'Sanne, do you want to take Bryn to the annex room? It'll give you two a chance to talk,' Gregor offered.

Bryn was torn. He wanted to hear more from Gregor, more about Samuel's deceit. He also needed to talk to his mother.

'Your mother can fill you in, Bryn. She knows as much as I do. Go!' Gregor insisted.

Away from the others, Sanne embraced her son. He wasn't angry with his parents. If he had known he was part Hazuru before the tournament, he probably would never have been able to properly concentrate on qualifying. He was sure they would have explained everything once the competition was over. At least, he hoped they would. If it wasn't for Samuel and his meddling, this would have been a glorious reunion. They would have been celebrating the victory and he would have been none the wiser.

'Bryn, we should have told you. But, it wasn't the time,' his mother told him, echoing his own thoughts. 'I never wanted you to compete. I thought it would all have been too much for you,' she added. 'I now know it wasn't. You are strong and smart… and you really do belong in this competition.'

'But you and I are part Hazuru. How could you have hidden it for so long?' Bryn asked.

'Bryn, it's a long story. One I couldn't have told you until now. Unfortunately, Samuel got there before me.'

'Where's Dad?' Bryn realised he was missing.

'He's gone looking for Samuel. They have a score to settle. Samuel needs to take responsibility for his actions. He went too far.'

Sanne and Bryn sat and spoke for what seemed like an eternity. His mother told him of how she was born and raised in Zhivrah, not Norway. Lars was but met her at a competition, the one she tried to compete in but was later disqualified from for being of mixed blood. She had entered through the bloodline of her father's family. Her mother was third generation Hazuru. She was an only child and spent her life training for the chance to compete in the tournament. The council seemed ambivalent to her circumstances, not knowing she was Panak until she confided in Samuel, who was a competitor at the time. He became jealous when she qualified, and he didn't. He used this information for his gain, spreading lies and propaganda. The Panak rule had been enforced many generations before and the council never had a situation where someone had breached the directive.

Sanne was banned from competing and told the same was to be said for any generation that came after. Lars was the one that insisted that Bryn should be able to enter. Yes, he was stronger than most, but that came from both sides of the family. There was no indication, growing up, that he would be faster or display any of the attributes of the Hazuru gene pool. She explained that if any of those traits emerged during the competition, the challenge would become more difficult for the entire team. Moses knew about the circumstances and had agreed to these conditions – though reluctant at first – after speaking to Gregor, before the selection of the team was complete.

It was never supposed to be played out the way it did. There was no reason to play such mind games and create a storyline full of betrayal and deception. Samuel was responsible, and for that, he would be held accountable.

Suddenly, from outside they could hear the sound of rapturous applause and immense cheering. Another team must have made it back. When Bryn, joined by his mother, made it back to Gregor and his teammates, he spotted Alisi peering out through the door. The atmosphere in the room was less tense, Kenta even finding an appetite to snack on some of the food, which was enticingly displayed on the table.

'It's the Shiakanas. They've made it back, though I think they are missing one,' Alisi informed them.

'Where is Samuel now?' Sanne asked Gregor, paying no notice to Alisi's findings.

'Apparently, he left the council stall once he realised Bryn's abilities were playing to the crowd. No one has seen him since,' Gregor said. 'A team has been sent with Lars, to look for him, while another is investigating how he managed to upload software into the game program.'

The Shiakanas entered the room. They were loud and lively, breaking the stillness of the atmosphere. Bryn was curious. He installed his earpiece and went to Marchek, who was filling a plate with as much food as he could get on it.

'Marchek, congratulations. Your team did really well,' he said.

Marchek pointed at his ear to indicate that he wasn't wearing his earpiece and dismissed Bryn, preferring to join his teammates instead. Bryn was disappointed but promised himself he was going to make more of an effort getting to know the other species living in Zhivrah, once this was all over.

The door to the arena opened once again, this time two council members approached Gregor. He took them to one side; Sanne joined them. Bryn, for the first time, realised how ravenous he was and started to pick at the banquet. Moses and Alisi, deciding there was not much more they could do, joined Bryn. Kenta had already eaten his fill.

When the council members left, Gregor instructed that they all sit. They huddled in so they could hear his soft tone.

'What I am about to say must strictly be kept amongst ourselves,' he began. 'The council has informed us that Samuel ordered Tolk to take him to the portal so that he could get back home. He took some Goytek technology and software with him, stole it from their station.'

'I don't believe it,' Alisi responded.

'What happens now?' Moses asked.

'Lars is leading a team. They're tracking him. He will be brought back. They will decide what will be done with him,' Sanne told them.

'Trouble is, it will take time to figure out what he took exactly, and what repercussions it may have,' Moses said.

'There is nothing more we can do now. I suggest we stick around for the other teams to complete and wait for updates,' Gregor said.

CHAPTER 92

The Hazurus finished third, with three players left. Same as the Shiakanas. Bryn asked what happened to the competitors who were unfortunate not to make it. Moses told him that once they went unconscious, they were left behind and collected later by couriers. They were taken back to the dorms to sleep. The formula could sometimes take up to a day to fully wear off.

Bryn was suddenly aware of a key member's absence. Where was Kyra? He asked Gregor.

'She found her portrayal in the games difficult. She ran off. My guess is she went home.'

Bryn felt an instant need to see her. They needed to talk. He understood now, the resentment she felt for him being allowed to compete. He knew she should be allowed the same opportunity. It was unfair and he needed to tell her.

'I'd like to go see her,' he said.

Gregor exchanged glances with Sanne.

'Go after her, Bryn, but you need to get back. There will be presentations once the Goyteks return. You cannot, under any circumstances, miss it,' Gregor said. 'There is a small community dwelling about ten minutes due southwest. Be back in under an hour.'

Bryn didn't waste any time. He disappeared out of a back door that led to a tunnel with a large exit on the left. Outside the arena, spectators were wandering about, taking in a bit of exercise before the estimated time they were given before the last team were due in.

His mind was busy with how the tournament played out, part of him even doubting their return, slightly suspicious they might be still playing. He was so angry at Samuel. If only he had been honest with him from the start, instead of building his resentment to the point that he would sabotage the sport. He needed to talk to his father. For the first time, he felt a connection with him. He fought for Bryn to take part in the tournament in spite of the risks and believed he was worthy. Deep in his thoughts, he didn't see Frasier approach.

'Congratulations, Bryn, you certainly can put on a show.'

Bryn sensed a hint of sarcasm in his voice. He was surprised to hear such a tone from his friend.

'Frasier, there was more involved than you know. I don't think anyone expected it to play out as it did,' Bryn said.

'I heard. It's all the trainees are talking about. Samuel was cruel to do what he did, but he did have a point.'

Bryn was surprised at Frasier's remark but didn't have time to argue it. He started to walk away, thinking that he could talk to Frasier later, but he had more to say.

'It is unfair for us normal Earthians to be up against someone with mixed blood and expect to be picked. You provided so much entertainment, how can we compete?' Frasier's voice was softer now, as if he wanted to explain his feelings so that Bryn might understand.

Bryn couldn't think of a response so didn't say anything. He just kept moving, without turning to acknowledge what Frasier had said.

When Bryn was sure he was going in the right direction, and when he was sure he was out of sight, he started to run. Part of him thought the speed he reached in the tournament was somehow manufactured, not real. He was under time constraints, not that he needed an excuse. It was a moment to try this for himself, a moment to lose himself in an ability he never knew he had. As his pace quickened, he could feel a breeze lift a few stray hairs from his face. It felt liberating, as though he had been let loose from a cage. He leapt into the air and landed about fifty metres away.

Up ahead, he could see a little group of dwellings. Smoke spilt out over a few thatched rooftops. As he closed in, he estimated that there were about a dozen clay-built houses of various sizes. Gardens with brightly coloured floral rockeries met vegetable patches and fruit trees. He slowed down, taking in the sights of children playing, chickens running freely and the sound of a cockerel crowing in the distance. A mother was holding an infant, chatting to another woman as she hung her laundry out to dry. Everyone he saw looked different, not human or Hazuru, Shiakana or Goytek, but had traits of at least two. This was a Panak community, he realised. A home for those who were different from the rest. He could understand that not everyone was interested in the games. The Panaks couldn't compete so it was not surprising that some had decided not to attend.

As he wandered about, he caught sight of Kyra tending to some vegetable plants. She was alone and behaving as though it was just another ordinary day. She wasn't expecting to see him. That was obvious when she glanced at him approaching her. Instead of greeting him, she went back to pulling weeds.

'I know it wasn't you, Kyra. It didn't take long to figure it out,' Bryn said, attempting to break the ice.

'You couldn't have known that, Bryn. You don't know me. You would have never known how I'd react if I were competing in a tournament with you.'

She sounded apathetic, but Bryn knew she cared more than she was letting on. Kyra probably cared more about competing in the tournament than anyone else. He could only assume that her being portrayed as fighting alongside the team she always wanted to be a part of, must have hurt more than she would ever admit.

'Kyra, I don't have much time. You need to come back to the arena. You deserve this Shield as much as the rest of us. Don't let Samuel win. He sabotaged the game because a Panak took part. We need to show them that it's not a bad thing. If you don't come back for the ceremony, he has gained a little victory. He doesn't deserve that right,' Bryn said.

'What about you? Do you think you have the right to take part when I can't? We are just a couple of generations apart. Do you think that's fair?

'I don't know what's fair and what isn't. I just found out. I haven't had time to digest it all.' Bryn understood his participation in the games changed everything, but he wasn't sure he wanted to give it all up. Now that he knew Samuel was the reason the Games were manipulated, he realised that although he felt his life was in danger at every turn, he'd never felt so alive.

'Bryn, go. I don't feel like celebrating and I don't think there is anything you can say that would change my mind.'

Bryn turned to leave. After taking a few steps, he had a notion.

'Kyra, what if we started our own team, one for just Panaks?'

CHAPTER 93

Gregor was surprised Bryn was able to get Kyra to return. He knew she had been hurt badly, probably more than everyone else. He smiled broadly at her when he caught her eye.

Kyra was reluctant to go to the arena at first. She had explained to Bryn that many years before, the council had tried to get a team of Panaks together. There just didn't seem to be enough interest and the council were not the most enthusiastic about advertising. They just couldn't imagine seeing anything that hadn't been a factor featured on another team. Bryn convinced her that it could change. The reception he had gotten from the crowd was incredible. There was no reason they wouldn't react like that if there was a team of them.

He could tell that Kyra would need more convincing but at least she came back with him. Hercule must have joined the team after he left. He was standing with Moses and when the door opened, he went straight to Bryn to shake his hand and hugged Kyra, though she wasn't expecting it.

'This is very exciting, eh?' he said.

'Still can't quite believe it, Hercule,' Bryn responded.

Bryn needed to broach the subject of introducing a Panak team, deciding it would be best to talk to his mother and Gregor about it. But just as he thought he had the timing right, just as the two of them were standing together, the crowd outside erupted again. The Goyteks had finally made it back. The conversation would have to wait. He could see that Kyra was watching him, knowing what he planned to do, and was a little disappointed he hadn't a chance to say anything. She appreciated his intentions though. He told her that if the council refused to grant them the opportunity, or if they couldn't manage to put a team together, he would drop out of the competition. She had to admire him for that. If she was in his position, she couldn't be sure she could make that sacrifice.

The two remaining members of the Goytek team were furious when they entered through the door. They were arguing amongst themselves, oblivious to the presence of anyone else in the room. A council member entered after them, explaining that there would be a break for an hour as they needed more time to revive the other team players, the ones who were sleeping it off in their dorms. It was compulsory for all participants to be present for the awards ceremony.

This was the moment Bryn was waiting for. He wasted no time pulling his mother and Gregor together to talk to them.

'I am so grateful for the opportunity you have given me.' He addressed them both. 'I understand why you couldn't explain everything before I entered the tournament, and I guess you probably think that there was no way I'd ever qualify if it was explained to me when I arrived. I could easily have become preoccupied. All three of you, including Dad, took a risk and in parts, it paid off. But I have to consider future competitions and how it makes the qualifying aspect a little complicated for me and others.'

'Bryn, you have every right to compete. I cannot accept that you would not want to take your father's legacy to the next generation,' his mother remarked.

'Mum, I understand the lengths you and Dad went to, to ensure that I could have the chance to compete. I also understand that Moses and the rest of the team were put under considerable pressure so I could. Samuel will not be the only person to resent me participating, but I think we need to go about this differently. We need a new team, one made up of Panaks, like me.'

'We have tried that, Bryn. It didn't work,' said Sanne.

'Well, we need to try again, Mum. This time, there is Kyra,' he pointed towards her, 'and me. There must be many more out there. It's worth trying again.'

'And, what if it doesn't work?' Gregor asked.

'Then, I won't compete,' Bryn said.

'I don't know, Bryn. If you think this could work, then we can put it to the council. There are no guarantees, but I can ask. Kyra, I need you to join us for a moment.' He gestured for her to come closer. 'If what I'm hearing is correct, I'm thinking you would support the idea of a Panak team? Do you think you could help Bryn to get a team together?' Gregor asked her.

Kyra did something that Bryn rarely, if ever, saw. She smiled.

'Gregor, you know I would.' Kyra was ecstatic.

'Well, I guess we better approach the council once this is all over. You two have a lot of work ahead of you. But today, let's concentrate on what we have achieved. You too, Kyra.'

CHAPTER 94

The awards ceremony took place in the centre of the arena and was truly a magical affair. Any spectators who had taken a break, to go home or just to have a walk, came back refreshed, ready for the celebrations. Banners were straightened, new flags distributed. The band was back in their position, belting out various tunes. All four teams were gathered and ready to make their entrance.

Bryn developed a sense of excitement. It was the first time he had felt this way since they made their way onto the arena at the opening of the Games. He could tell that his teammates had also come round. They had won the tournament, and for that, they should feel proud. Sanne had gone back to the stands and she was joined by Gregor, Kyra and Hercule. While they were waiting, members of the other teams came to congratulate them. All but a few were supportive of their win, in spite of the circumstances. They all condemned Samuel's interference, mainly because it undermined the integrity of the spirit of the Games.

Walking out, the crowd erupted in applause and cheers. There were no hard feelings amongst them, whether their team lost or the discovery of Bryn's extra skill set, it didn't seem to matter. The most important factor was that they were entertained, with all the competitors giving the best of their abilities.

A member of the council, one Bryn didn't recognise, was charged with master of ceremony, including the presentation of the Shield. The teams stood and lined up, facing the council and dignitary stand. Each team was praised for individual efforts and team achievements. Trainers were thanked and gratitude was given to the crowd, for making the Games such a successful event. This was greeted with a loud roar from the stands.

Finally, Moses and his team were called upon. Highlights of their endeavours were depicted on the large screen above. Bryn found it strange watching himself in battle, discovering his ability to leap to the clouds. It all felt like a dream, now that they were back. It hardly felt real anymore.

Each of them was presented with a medal and then re-presented with the large, intricately designed golden plated shield, which had been taken away for safekeeping, earlier.

'It has been our honour to participate in the Zhavia Shield. We are truly grateful for all of your support. We would like to thank Gregor, Kyra and Hercule for their training and guidance,' announced Moses on receipt. 'And of course, you watching. It was such an honour. Thank you very much.'

All four competitors stood on the podium provided and raised the Shield to their victory. The crowd went wild. Bryn had never experienced anything like it. He was almost overwhelmed by the feeling of pride, not necessarily in himself, but them as a team. In a moment of doubt, he became dubious about his decision to quit. It would mean that he would never have the chance to compete with Moses, Alisi or Kenta again. He would never have Gregor as a guide or Tilly to make him tea. But then, he looked at Kyra, her smile. She was happy, hopeful. She seemed confident, and that was enough for Bryn.

The party provided for the teams and spectators went on well into the night. The band played on. The firework display was a sight to behold. There were dragons, depictions of the Games, symbols of peace and prosperity captured by sparkles in the night sky. Bryn was in awe of the festivities. Members of the public wanted to be near him, asking questions and wanting photographs signed. Alisi was lapping up the attention and the local brew, to the point where Bryn wondered whether she was drunk on fame or the alcohol.

Kenta and Moses were deep in light-hearted conversation, Kenta even showing signs of happiness and contentment, something Bryn hadn't previously witnessed. His mother was dancing with a member of the council. Bryn guessed he was an old friend. As he watched, he didn't notice Kyra approach.

'That was a very brave thing you did today,' she said.

Bryn wasn't sure what she was implying.

'You gave up your chance to compete with this team, the people you know and have grown to respect. Your father went to great efforts to ensure you had the opportunity to do it. And here you are throwing it all in, for the notion that we might get a team of our own, together, knowing that our chances of succeeding are slim.'

Bryn appreciated that Kyra had taken his feelings into consideration. He hadn't expected it. He thought it might have been near impossible for her to display such empathy, considering their previous exchanges.

'I appreciate you telling me this, Kyra. To be honest, I don't think I could face the trials again, knowing what I do now. It feels a little like cheating. It's hard to explain,' he said.

'You don't need to explain. Just so you know, I would seriously doubt I'd have this opportunity without you. This is my only chance. I need to thank you for giving it to me. We will achieve great things, Bryn. I have a good feeling about it.'

Bryn was lost for words, but he didn't need to say anything. Kyra had left as quickly as she joined him moments before. He couldn't help but smile to himself.

Still watching the crowd, his attention was drawn to Gregor. He had been talking to one of the other team trainers when a member of the council approached. He was pulled from his conversation so that they could talk privately. The exchange was brief and sobering. As the council member walked away, Gregor craned his head in every direction as if he was searching for someone. He headed straight for Bryn's mother. After a few brusque words, Sanne's demeanour became serious, and as Gregor walked away, she followed at his heels. Gregor whistled in the direction of Moses and

Kenta, signalling for them to come with them. In a moment, the celebrations took a sinister twist and Bryn was curious to find out what caused it.

'I will join the search,' suggested Gregor. 'I have connections, people who may help me locate him. I will take Kenta and Alisi, and we will follow Lars. It may take a bit of time. Samuel is a clever man and with the help of his allies, he could be hiding anywhere.'

'Where are Lars and the team now?' someone asked.

'They have followed Samuel through the portal. They will keep in touch,' Sanne said.

'That settles it. Gregor, you should leave tomorrow morning. Before you go, come with me to the tech room. We will have some useful, discreet gadgets for you, to help in your quest,' said a Goytek council member, through a translator.

'Until Samuel is captured, we have to be prepared to handle any possible intrusion, or strike, that may come our way. I have never witnessed anything like it in our lifetime. Send messages to all warriors, all who have battled before, trainees, confidants. Our way of life is precious. We need to prepare ourselves for anything. The council will reconvene first thing tomorrow. Nobody leaves Zhivrah without prior authorisation,' said the master of ceremonies.

Bryn had heard enough. He had to leave before someone caught him lurking in the passageway. He supposed he wasn't invited to the talks because he was so young, so new to this world, not yet familiar with their ways. It was understandable. But he couldn't help feeling a little left out.

He was sure he could help. He just wasn't sure how. Could he ask Gregor if he could go with them, talk to his mother, join his father? Anything to help find Samuel.

He suddenly realised it was late. The events of the day had worn him down. He needed to rest. It would help him gain perspective. His priority was to find Tolk. He would take him back to the dorms. Then he could sleep. Decisions could be made tomorrow, which couldn't come soon enough.

THE END

ABOUT THE AUTHOR

Gwen Lanigan-O'Keeffe has an active imagination. At the age of eight, she produced an illustrated children's book, *The Mouse in Her House*. Followed at the age of eleven with a thriller, *Barbie Goes to the Jungle*. At fourteen, *Thou Shall Not Write With a Red Pen*, won her critical acclaim for poetry, by her secondary school English teacher. She went on to trying her hand at screenplays and short stories. With a busy career in customer service, none have gotten to the publishing stage, until now. Her debut novel, *Bryan Jahr: Leap of Fate*, showcases what true daydreamers can potentially achieve. Born, raised and living near the sea in Cork with her husband and teenage son, she loves spending time writing, drinking coffee and absorbed in an unputdownable book.

Printed in Great Britain
by Amazon

b188f387-3b5a-4370-a012-2f19a69b2630R01